"I guess I expect you to understand why I have a hard time watching you make yourself bait for a cold-blooded killer," he said.

"I told you that would only be as a last resort, and with proper backup from…"

"Save it for someone who buys that line of bull."

"I can handle myself," Mary said. "Clint, I have to get into that rodeo." A touch of desperation colored her voice. "I can't stop now. I can't give up."

"Do you ever?" he snapped.

"No."

He stared at Mary, remembering last night, remembering all the reasons why this wouldn't work. He should kick her out of his truck, toss her bags on the ground and go to Birmingham without her. And then her eyes went wide and she whispered, "Please," and he was a goner.

Dear Reader,

This month we have something really special in store for you. We open with *Letters to Kelly* by award-winning author Suzanne Brockmann. In it, a couple of young lovers, separated for years, are suddenly reunited. But she has no idea that he's spent many of their years apart in a Central American prison. And now that he's home again, he's determined to win back the girl whose memory kept him going all this time. What a wonderful treat from this bestselling author!

And the excitement doesn't stop there. In *The Impossible Alliance* by Candace Irvin, the last of our three FAMILY SECRETS prequels, the search for missing agent Dr. Alex Morrow is finally over. And coming next month in the FAMILY SECRETS series: *Broken Silence,* our anthology, which will lead directly to a 12-book stand-alone FAMILY SECRETS continuity, beginning in June. In Virginia Kantra's *All a Man Can Be,* TROUBLE IN EDEN continues as a rough-around-the-edges ex-military man inherits a surprise son—and seeks help in the daddy department from his beautiful boss. Ingrid Weaver continues her military miniseries, EAGLE SQUADRON, in *Seven Days to Forever*, in which an innocent schoolteacher seeks protection—for starters— from a handsome soldier when she mistakenly picks up a ransom on a school trip. In *Clint's Wild Ride* by Linda Winstead Jones, a female FBI agent going undercover in the rodeo relies on a sinfully sexy cowboy as her teacher. And in *The Quiet Storm* by RaeAnne Thayne, a beautiful speech-disabled heiress has to force herself to speak up to seek help from a devastatingly attractive detective in order to solve a murder.

So enjoy, and of course we hope to see you next month, when Silhouette Intimate Moments once again brings you six of the best and most exciting romance novels around.

Leslie J. Wainger
Executive Senior Editor

Please address questions and book requests to:
Silhouette Reader Service
U.S.: 3010 Walden Ave., P.O. Box 1325, Buffalo, NY 14269
Canadian: P.O. Box 609, Fort Erie, Ont. L2A 5X3

Clint's Wild Ride
LINDA WINSTEAD JONES

Silhouette®

INTIMATE MOMENTS™

Published by Silhouette Books

America's Publisher of Contemporary Romance

SILHOUETTE BOOKS

ISBN 0-373-27287-1

CLINT'S WILD RIDE

Visit Silhouette at www.eHarlequin.com

Printed in U.S.A.

LINDA WINSTEAD JONES

would rather write than do anything else. Since she cannot cook, gave up ironing many years ago and finds cleaning the house a complete waste of time, she has plenty of time to devote to her obsession for writing. Occasionally she's tried to expand her horizons by taking classes. In the past she's taken instruction on yoga, French (a dismal failure), Chinese cooking, cake decorating (food-related classes are always a good choice, even for someone who can't cook), belly dancing (trust me, this was a long time ago) and, of course, creative writing.

She lives in Huntsville, Alabama, with her husband of more years than she's willing to admit and the youngest of their three sons.

She can be reached via www.eHarlequin.com or her own Web site www.lindawinsteadjones.com.

A very special thanks to Linda H.,
for letting me "borrow" Sweetness.

Chapter 1

The hairs on the back of Clint's neck stood up. Every nerve in his body went on alert. Something was wrong here. He was about to be ambushed.

Shea had plied him with steak and potatoes, his favorite meal, forgoing her usual attempt at some evil casserole that often included the dreaded lima bean. His sister had stocked up on his preferred brand of beer, and after dinner had offered him a cold bottle *and* Nick's most comfortable recliner. She was all smiles tonight, and hadn't even mentioned the fact that he didn't have a woman in his life. Not once. Something was definitely fishy here.

Their brother Boone, a private investigator, and his obviously pregnant wife, Jayne, were in attendance, having made the trip from Birmingham for the weekend. Dean, eldest brother and a deputy with the U.S. Marshals Service, was also present.

And they were all looking at him. Staring. Waiting, just as he did, for the other shoe to drop. Even Justin, Shea and Nick's one-year-old son, knew something was up. He banged a big plastic car on the floor, but his eyes were on Uncle Clint.

Shea glanced at her watch for the tenth time since they'd retired to the family room five minutes or so ago. Nick cracked his knuckles and glanced at the ceiling. Justin cooed and giggled.

"Okay," Clint said, unable to stand the suspense any longer. "Somebody tell me what's going on."

Shea glanced pleadingly at Dean, who sat on the far end of the couch he shared with Boone and Jayne.

Dean slowly shook his head. "This is your party, Shea," he said. "I'm just here for..." He glanced up at his little sister. "Why am I here?"

"Moral support," Shea said softly, before turning her eyes and her smile on Clint.

Shea had always been naturally curious, a trait which had led her to her current career as an investigative reporter for CNN. She could be fearless, unrelenting. Clint was usually proud of his little sister—until she turned those curious and relentless eyes his way.

"Are you going to participate in the Brisco Rodeo this summer?" she asked, deceptively innocent and seemingly sweet.

"Sure," Clint said warily. "Just like I have for the past three years."

He didn't need to rodeo anymore. He had won a few big competitions before he'd given up bull riding four years ago, and he'd invested his earnings well. The horse ranch in north Alabama was finally making a profit. He occasionally worked as a rodeo clown because he liked it. The job was fun, exciting, dirty and dangerous. Just like him.

The Brisco Rodeo was a six-week summer tour across

the Southeast, and he had several friends who regularly worked that tour. Six cities, six weeks. Three or four days in each arena, and then they were off to the next show. His foreman, Wes, had no trouble running the ranch on his own when Clint took off for a few days or a few weeks at a time.

"I have this friend...." Shea began.

A woman friend, Clint knew immediately. For some reason his little sister was forever trying to fix him up. He was close to thirty, but he wasn't there yet. He had plenty of time to settle down. And no inclination to do so. Why was Shea so damned determined to see him married and reproducing?

"Not interested," he said, silencing a stammering Shea before she went any further. He glanced at the close-mouthed occupants of the room, one after another. "And why does it now take the entire family to fix me up with a woman? Is the situation really that desperate? Dean's the oldest and he's not hitched. I don't see you trying to marry him off."

"She does," Dean said sourly. "Just not in front of a crowd. Usually."

"I'm not trying to fix up anyone today," Shea said, her voice too bright and quick. "This is strictly business." Her eyes sparkled with a new, sudden thought. She bit her lower lip. That meant trouble, every time. "Though, Mary is very nice, and she's pretty. And Dean, she's just your type. She's with the FBI, you're with the Marshals Service, you both carry guns. It's just..."

Dean held up a silencing hand. "I was going to let you hang yourself, Shea, but this is just too painful." He glanced at Clint and sighed. "There's been a series of particularly ugly murders over the past four years. Eight women in six different cities, in Alabama, Georgia, Mis-

sissippi and Tennessee. The victims were between the
ages of twenty-four and thirty-six, all blond and attractive,
all raped and then murdered. Three were killed by stran-
gulation, the others were…'' He glanced at Shea and then
at Jayne. ''They were cut,'' he said in a lowered voice.
''The bodies of all eight victims were dumped in isolated
areas and not discovered for some time, which is why the
connection to the rodeo wasn't made until recently.''

A chill ran down Clint's spine. He'd rather go on a
hundred blind dates than process what this bit of information meant. ''What kind of connection to the rodeo?''

''Apparently there's a possibility that all the murders
took place while the Brisco Rodeo was in town.''

''A possibility?''

Shea shrugged and glanced away. ''Some of the bodies
weren't discovered for months, so it's impossible to have
an exact date of death. But a couple of the dates of dis-
appearance are definite, and the others are in the right time
range.''

Clint shook his head. He had been set up, and in the
worst possible way. ''All through dinner,'' he said, ''y'all
knew what Shea wanted and you didn't say a word.''

''She made us promise,'' Boone explained.

''Still…''

Dean interrupted. ''We tried to tell her this was a lousy
way to spring the idea on you, but she wouldn't listen.''

''She never does,'' Boone muttered.

Clint turned his eyes to a silent Nick.

''Don't look at me,'' Nick said, hands up in surrender.
''I thought a simple phone call would work just fine.''

No one could reason with Shea when she didn't want
to be reasoned with, not her brothers, not her husband.

Clint was unhappy with them all at the moment. ''You
want me to spy on my friends. You want me to play

private investigator and sneak around trying to find this guy for you. Nope. Not gonna happen. No way. I like the people I work with. There's not a serial killer in the bunch.''

"You don't know that," Boone interrupted. "You see them once a year for a few weeks. Someone there might be responsible for these murders."

Clint shook his head. "No." Mentally, he ran down a list of the people he knew who traveled with the Brisco Rodeo. They were honest, fun-loving, hardworking people, each and every one of them. They were like family. "If the murders really are connected to the rodeo, maybe it's someone who follows the tour."

"Maybe so," Dean agreed.

Clint placed the flat of one hand on his chest. "I'm not a cop. I'm not a P.I. like Boone or a federal marshal like Dean. I want absolutely nothing to do with law enforcement, especially not the FBI. I am a retired bull rider, a rancher and a rodeo clown. None of those pursuits have prepared me for hunting down a serial killer."

Shea shook her head quickly. "Oh, we don't want you to hunt down the serial killer. We just want you to teach Mary to be a rodeo clown and get her a job with Brisco."

He laid disbelieving eyes on his sister. Hard to believe that what his little sister wanted was more impossible than what he'd thought she wanted. "The tour starts up in less than three weeks."

She smiled at him, calm and completely unruffled. She showed no signs of backing down from this one.

"And besides, I can't see Oliver Brisco hiring a girl rodeo clown."

Shea pursed her lips. "I think you'll find Mary's able to do anything you can do."

Clint grinned. "Oh, really?"

The doorbell rang. Nick, who had probably been dying to get out of this room since the conversation had begun, offered to answer. He left the room and Justin crawled quickly and nimbly after him.

"This is a bad idea," Clint said softly.

"I told 'em that," Boone said. "A girl rodeo clown? Ridiculous. It'll never work."

Jayne patted him on the knee. "Don't be patronizing, honey." She laid her free hand over her rounded stomach. "What if our daughter wants to be a clown?"

"Heaven forbid." Boone, soon-to-be father, looked truly horrified by the very idea.

"We've always been there for one another," Shea said. "I know it's wrong of me to assume so much, to just expect you to do as I ask, but to be honest it never occurred to me that you might refuse."

They heard Nick returning, footsteps soft but certain on the carpeted hallway, and the conversation ceased. Shea's husband walked into the room with Justin in his arms and a woman trailing right behind them.

The disastrous night got a little more interesting when the woman walked into the room. Clint's attention was focused entirely on the newcomer, until everything else in the room faded. Surely this was not Mary.

She was taller than Shea, probably five seven, and she was built like a brick outhouse. The luscious curves just went on and on. Her pale blond hair, sleek and golden, was cut chin-length. She wore a gray suit, which should have been plain, but thanks to her figure was not, and a pair of matching high-heeled shoes that emphasized her long, shapely legs.

FBI Mary was absolutely gorgeous. Clint's mouth went dry. His body reacted the way any man's might when confronted with a woman like this one.

Maybe this wasn't such a terrible idea, after all.

All the Sinclair men stood and Shea greeted her friend with a quick hug. Shea didn't waste any time with niceties. She took the blonde's arm and led her to Clint.

"Clint, this is my good friend, Special Agent Mary Paris. Mary, this is my brother, Clint Sinclair."

The FBI agent laid the bluest eyes Clint had ever seen on him in a calculating way. She didn't smile, she didn't offer her hand. Gorgeous or not, she looked at him as if she were quite capable of chewing up any man—including him—and spitting him out.

Tough as nails, pretty as a picture...and she wanted to be a rodeo clown.

Mary stared at the man before her, Shea's youngest brother, Clint Sinclair. He was tall and lean, with dark brown hair and moss-green eyes. In his jeans and checkered shirt and cowboy boots, he looked very much as she had expected he would. His hair was cut conservatively, but a misbehaving lock and a cowlick in the middle of his forehead kept that conventional cut from looking ordinary.

If she wasn't absolutely desperate, she would immediately dismiss this plan as ludicrous. This pretty-boy *clown* could not possibly be the answer to all her problems. He looked like the kind of man who came with more problems than he could possibly solve. But then, wasn't that true of all men?

No need to waste time by prolonging the introductions. Mary always preferred to get right to business. "I assume Shea has told you why I'm here."

"You want to be a bullfighter."

"A bullfighter?"

"Rodeo clown," he clarified.

It was a ridiculous idea, convoluted and risky and desperate. It was also the only viable plan she had at the moment. "Yes."

He grinned and shook his head. "Darlin', it'll never work."

"Excuse me?" she said coldly.

"It just won't—"

She raised a censuring finger. "Before that."

The man looked truly confused. She imagined that was a semipermanent state for him.

"Don't call me darlin'," she said tersely. "It's insulting."

He was not at all taken aback. "All right, Special Agent Paris." He took his eyes from her and stared down at Shea. "This isn't going to work."

Mary pursed her lips. She should have let the darlin' thing slide, for now. She might've ruined everything by annoying the pretty-boy clown. "Why won't it work?" she asked.

Clint turned his green eyes on her as if he expected them to work some kind of magic. Oh, yeah, he was definitely one of those condescending, annoying types who thought women were second-class citizens. She saw it in his eyes, and in that boyish half smile.

"First of all," he drawled, "you're a girl."

Mary took a deep breath and bit her tongue. A girl! She'd worked with too many men who were firmly entrenched in the good-old-boy network to let that one slide. She was a damn good agent, but she'd had to work twice as hard as any man to get where she was today. Still, she'd been a bit hasty with the "darlin'" admonition. Perhaps it would be best if she saved the argument that she was a woman, not a *girl,* for another time.

"Second," Clint continued when she didn't argue,

"you don't just decide to become a bullfighter and jump into the arena on a whim. That's a good way to get yourself killed. It's an extremely dangerous job."

"I'm sure that's true," she said calmly. "That's why I've come to you for advice on training."

Sinclair shook his head as if she just didn't get it. "You have less than three weeks."

Mary was undaunted. "I can learn anything I need to know as quickly as necessary."

She didn't care for his calculating smile. "Oh, really?"

She had avoided men like this one all her life. Clint Sinclair was charming, condescending, pretty and laid-back. Yes, he was lean, but he was also hard. Muscled from his neck to his calves. But it was his smile that probably got him anything he wanted. *Girls* probably followed him around like besotted puppies and fell at his feet in adoration and ached to play with that annoying little lock of hair on his forehead.

Women did not. If he thought he could charm her with that smile, he had another think coming.

His grin faded, his green eyes lost their hint of teasing and a muscle in his jaw twitched. "How old are you?" he asked softly.

Mary bristled. "I don't see how that bit of information is any of your business."

"Tell me right now, or we're done talking."

Mary didn't like demands, especially not from men she'd just met, but in this case she didn't have many options. "Twenty-eight."

Clint nodded his head slowly. "Fits the profile, doesn't she, Dean? Twenty-eight, blond, pretty." He never took his eyes from her. "You're not just looking to spy on the people who work the rodeo, you're setting yourself up as bait."

She could deny the accusation, but she didn't think Sinclair would buy it. Pretty boy or not, there was something calculating in his eyes. Something intelligent. She couldn't afford to insult or annoy him. And if he knew the truth, he'd toss her out on her ear. Like it or not, she needed him.

"Only as a last resort," she said calmly. "And if it comes to that, I will call in sufficient backup. None of the other victims worked for the rodeo, so in reality I am not setting myself up by following a pattern."

He did not look convinced. "Sounds awfully dangerous anyway. Well, it's dangerous if you're right about the serial killer being affiliated with the rodeo. Which you're not."

"Your opinion doesn't concern me. All I want from you are a few pointers on working the rodeo and an introduction to the man who runs the tour." Oliver Brisco, her prime suspect.

Sinclair was going to refuse. She saw it, in the firm set of his mouth, in the quickly fading spark of fury in his eyes. He was her last chance, her best idea. Her only idea. She'd stood here and held her temper in check—for the most part—and now he was going to turn her down flat and she'd be back to zero.

"Shea," the man before her said softly, in that Southern drawl that sounded like molasses, dark and sweet. "How bad do you want this?"

"Pretty bad," Shea admitted. "One of the stories I've been working on for the past year is about a man who was found guilty of the second murder almost four years ago. He was convicted long before anyone made the connection with the other murders, and all the evidence against him is circumstantial. Mary came to me a few months ago to ask some questions about the case, that's how we hooked up." Shea's entire face softened. "Clint, this guy is sitting in prison for a murder he didn't commit. Until we have more, no one's willing to do anything about getting him out."

"Who made that connection to the rodeo?" he asked.

"I did," Mary said. After hours and hours of studying every detail of those murders, after more sleepless nights than she could count, she'd finally discovered that at the approximate time of each and every murder, the Brisco Rodeo had been in town.

It was the *approximate* that was killing her. The bodies of the victims had been disposed of in remote areas, and not discovered until days or weeks after the fact. The longer the bodies went undiscovered, the harder it was to pinpoint the exact date of death. Until she had more, some people in the bureau wouldn't validate her theory.

"If this is such a great lead," Sinclair said softly, "why isn't the rodeo crawling with feds? Why isn't there an army of agents going in?"

An unexpected chill danced down Mary's spine and down her arms. He was getting too close, asking too many questions. "It's a theory not everyone in the bureau is buying at this point," she said honestly. "There are a few discrepancies in the killer's MO, from murder to murder, some inconsistencies on a couple of the victims." Inconsistencies she had tried and tried to explain away.

"So, this charade of yours might be a waste of time."

She suspected Sinclair was concerned about his time, not hers. "I don't believe it is a waste of time," she said calmly.

"But—" he began.

"This butcher, he doesn't kill his victims right away," Mary said. She couldn't allow herself to be annoyed, to hold a grudge against this man she'd just met because he was her best hope. It was a luxury she could not afford. "He keeps them alive for anywhere from two to four days, from what we've been able to tell. He tortures them. He plays with them." Her heart rate increased, and deep down…deep down something she tried to ignore constricted. "The man I'm looking for is a predator of the worst kind, Mr. Sinclair. If he isn't found and stopped, he will kill again. And again." And again…

Clint Sinclair sighed. He mumbled a foul word. The strawberry-blonde sitting on the couch said, "Hey, I heard that. Watch your language around the babies."

The cowboy leaned slightly to the side and smiled, not so wide as before. "*Babies?* I'll apologize to Justin, but I don't think yours can hear me just yet, Jayne."

"You can't know that for sure."

He gave up easily, humoring the pregnant woman. "Sorry."

After a moment he ran one hand over his face. Hiding? Probably. Considering taking her on? Definitely. Everyone waited for him to make a decision. Finally, Clint jammed his hands into the pockets of his jeans and laid his eyes on Mary.

"My ranch. Be there Monday morning, bright and early and ready to work. We'll have two weeks and a couple of days to get you ready."

"I'm sure I won't need that much time…."

"Take it or leave it, Special Agent Paris."

Two weeks plus. She didn't have that kind of time to waste. She needed to learn what she could from Sinclair and then do more investigation on the men who worked for the rodeo before she joined them. Oliver Brisco, the owner of the rodeo, was her number one suspect, but it would be foolish to dismiss the other men until she had more concrete evidence. But Clint Sinclair didn't look as if there was any room for negotiation, and Mary was desperate.

"I'll be there," she said.

Clint nodded, but he looked every bit as skeptical as Mary felt.

Shea offered coffee and dessert, and while Mary was tempted to decline and get out of there while she could, she decided to accept and keep an eye on the rodeo clown for a while longer. They hadn't exactly hit it off. In fact, Clint Sinclair got on her last nerve. Still, Mary was a firm believer that it made sense to know one's enemies as well or better than one knew their friends. It was too early to know if the clown would be either.

If he'd been with the rodeo four years instead of three, Clint Sinclair himself would be one of her suspects. He had an airtight alibi for that first summer, though. According to her research, he'd been riding bulls at the time and had been laid up in the hospital for several weeks. When the second murder had taken place, he'd been out of commission.

There were a handful of men with the Brisco Rodeo who had been with the tour all four summers. Her money was on Brisco, but every one of those men was a suspect. One of them had killed Elaine.

And she was going to make that man pay.

Chapter 2

Mary had driven by the Sinclair ranch last night after she'd checked into a room in Scottsboro, Alabama, the closest town that actually had a hotel. She was a city girl at heart, at home under bright lights and in the shadows of tall buildings. Her sleekly furnished apartment was located right outside Washington, D.C. The home where she'd grown up, where her father still lived, was in the Chicago area. This place…it was way too much like Mayberry for her tastes.

Down the road from the Sinclair ranch she'd passed a small grouping of buildings. A post office, a barber shop, a café. There had even been a business that looked suspiciously like a general store. Did those even exist anymore? It wasn't a town, not really. It was much too small to be called anything more than a pit stop. But there had been a freshly painted sign there. Welcome to Tandy's Corner.

By morning's light, the house she studied looked different. Last night there had been too many deep shadows. Lit only by the light of the moon, the Sinclair house had been a long, distant building with many warm lights burning in the windows.

This morning, as she drove up the winding drive from the highway, she could see details she had missed the night before. The single-story redbrick structure was huge, sprawling and majestic but not at all cold, the way some big houses were. The barn and a large fenced-in area sat well behind the house, and to the left, parked before a separate two-car garage, sat a white pickup truck that had seen better days. Thick groves of old trees lined the property, and the backdrop to this picturesque scene was the foothills of the Appalachian mountains, blue-gray in the distance.

Clint Sinclair sat on the front porch—in a rocking chair, of all things—sipping at a large cup of coffee and rocking in a slow, easy rhythm. A big yellow dog slept on the porch at his side. It was like a picture out of a magazine; the picturesque background, the house, the dog. The man. Clint rose to his feet as Mary pulled up close to the porch and brought her sedan to a lurching stop. The dog awoke and stood, too, tail wagging.

"Special Agent Mary Paris," Sinclair said as she stepped from the car. "Good morning."

"Sinclair," she said simply.

"How about some breakfast before we get started." He looked her up and down, as if judging her attire for suitability. She wore lightweight, loose-fitting pants, sturdy running shoes and a baggy white T-shirt. He wore well-worn jeans, a blue-and-green-checkered shirt and cowboy boots.

Oh, God. The truth hit Mary smack-dab between the

eyes. Before this was all over with, she was going to have to buy herself a pair of cowboy boots.

"I don't eat breakfast," she said as she contemplated the possibilities. Pointy-toed snakeskin boots? No way. Red chip-kickers with fringe that swayed when she walked? Not her style. She was suddenly struck with the thought that her hair was not nearly big enough for this assignment.

"You really should eat something before we get started," Sinclair said. "Katie makes great biscuits, and if you want some eggs, she can whip up just about any style right quick."

"Katie?"

"My housekeeper."

Mary tried to push down her suspicions. Of course Sinclair had a housekeeper. She couldn't see him cooking and cleaning for himself. Men like him never did. "She gets an early start. What time does she arrive?"

"She lives here."

Mary walked toward the porch. As usual, her original impressions had been correct. "I'll just bet she does," she muttered. Guys like Clint Sinclair didn't live alone. There was always a bevy of adoring women hanging around practically begging to do whatever he wanted. Women like that made her embarrassed for her gender.

Sinclair smiled. "Come on in and meet her. Since you'll be around for a couple of weeks, you should get acquainted. I'm sure you two will get along just fine."

Mary bit back the urge to demand that they get to work. The sooner she got started, the sooner this nightmare would be over. Besides, she had no desire to get acquainted with Clint Sinclair's *housekeeper*.

The dog, who was bigger than she'd realized from her position in the car, came up to take a good, long sniff.

"Down, boy," she said beneath her breath.

"Don't mind Mutt," Sinclair said with a smile. "His bark is worse than his bite."

"Mutt? Your dog's name is Mutt?"

"It's what he answers to." Sinclair held the front door open for her, and she stepped inside. Mutt followed. As she'd suspected it would be, this was a man's house, decorated in leather and dark wood and plain off-white walls. Katie hadn't managed to add that woman's touch, at least not here in the front of the house. An overall masculine feel suited Clint, and yet felt comfortable.

The large den to Mary's left was rugged, with a fat leather sofa and two matching chairs, a long coffee table and a lighted case that housed a number of trophies and gigantic silver belt buckles. To her right was a doorway that opened onto what looked like a home office. Again, leather and dark wood dominated. There were no flowers, no decorative pictures on the white walls, though as they walked down the hallway toward the kitchen at the back of the house, they passed a number of framed family photographs. Shea and Nick. Justin, with his parents and then alone. Snapshots obviously taken at some long-ago Christmas, when there were no spouses or little ones to be included in the photo.

The kitchen was where she saw a woman's touch. The curtains were lacy and parted to let the sunshine in, there were hastily arranged wildflowers in a vase on the table, and instead of dark walnut the cabinets and table were made of a warm oak. The walls were painted yellow. She suspected Clint Sinclair was not a yellow person.

A woman stood at the sink, her back to them as she washed dishes. She had long dark hair pulled up in a ponytail and hummed a semicheerful tune as she worked. Her hips twitched in time to the off-key rendition.

"Katie darlin'," Sinclair said with a smile. "This is Shea's friend Mary."

Katie darlin' turned around slowly, a wide smile blooming on her attractive face. She was scrubbed and natural, with no makeup at all, a button nose and eyes that positively twinkled. And she appeared to be about six months pregnant.

There were obviously things Shea didn't know about her brother.

"Let me fix you something to eat," Katie insisted, drying her hands on a towel.

"I don't eat breakfast," Mary said.

That pert nose wrinkled. "Well, that's too bad." If anything, Katie's Southern accent was more pronounced than Clint's. "Are you sure I can't fix you something?"

"Positive."

"Eggs? Biscuits? Maybe some pancakes. I make really great pancakes. From scratch!"

"No," Mary said again, more forcefully this time.

Katie nodded, her smile fading. She was obviously disappointed. Mary realized she was about to begin the longest two weeks of her life.

The back door opened, and a grinning man who'd obviously already been hard at work walked in. His jeans were well worn, his cotton shirt and light brown hair were touched with sweat. He didn't look to be much older than Clint, and he walked with a pronounced limp.

He headed straight for Katie. "I told you to go back to bed and lie down," he said.

"I will," she promised, her face lighting up as she watched the man approach. "As soon as I finish these dishes."

"Why are you washing by hand when there's a perfectly good dishwasher right here?"

"I just have a few dishes to get out of the way," Katie argued sweetly. "There's not enough to fill the dishwasher, and I don't want to let dirty plates and a greasy frying pan sit here all morning."

The sweating man shook his head, then he leaned down to give Katie a quick kiss.

Mary felt a small twinge of disappointment. Here she was all ready to discover that one of Shea's supposedly perfect brothers had a flaw—and a pregnant live-in housekeeper was a *big* flaw—and then Katie turns out to be someone else's darlin'.

"Mary, this is my ranch foreman, Wes. Katie's his better half."

"Pleased to meet you," Wes said, stepping forward with a wide smile and an outstretched hand. "You must be Shea's friend who wants to have a go at the rodeo."

"Yes," Mary said simply.

When she'd found out that Clint's foreman had also once been on the rodeo circuit, she'd insisted that Wes not know the real purpose of her visit. All she needed was for the wrong person to find out what she was up to, that she was a federal agent, and the gig would be over. Finished.

And if that happened she might never have another chance to find Elaine's killer.

Special Agent Mary Paris had a bug up her butt about something. About *everything,* Clint imagined.

Shortly after her arrival he'd changed into suitable running shoes, shorts and a T-shirt, and now he and his clown wanna-be ran side by side down the trail that wound just inside the perimeter of his property. Mutt ran with him, as usual. Every now and then they passed through welcome shade, but most of the run was made in bright sunlight.

Special Agent Mary stayed right beside him, matching him stride for stride. She'd kept up really well at first, but she was beginning to lag. She didn't much like lagging, he could tell. Apparently she was one of those women who thought she ought to be able to do anything and everything as well as any man.

Her baggy clothes were covered with sweat, she was red in the face and had her hair pulled back and up in one of those short ponytails that looked like a little straw broom sticking out of the back of her head. She shouldn't be sexy as hell.

But she was.

Clint slowed down, coming to a stop in the shade of an ancient oak tree. "Time for a break," he said, reaching for the water bottle that hung from the loose belt he wore.

"I'm fine," Mary said breathlessly. "Really."

"I'm sure you are. It's just time for a break."

She didn't argue with him, but reached for her own water bottle and took a long swig.

Clint dropped down and gave Mutt a drink from his water bottle, patting the dog's head as he lapped up the cool liquid. When Mutt had had all he wanted, the dog found a grassy spot and plopped down to rest.

This was such a mistake, Clint thought as he watched Mary regain her breath and her composure. It was wrong in so many ways, for so many reasons.

"I have an idea," he said.

"What kind of idea?" Mary asked suspiciously.

"I can get you into the rodeo without making you go through all this."

"I'm fine," she argued. "It's just that the humidity here is higher than I'm accustomed to."

"Don't you even want to hear my idea?"

She sighed. No, she obviously did not want to hear his idea. There was annoyance in the way she looked at him, in the way she stood. "Fine," she said unenthusiastically. "Let's hear it."

It was a good idea, much better and much safer than her cockeyed plan. "The first stop on the tour is a four-day show, Thursday through Sunday. We're starting in Birmingham this year. During the first show we always present a Rodeo Queen, and she travels with—"

"No," Mary said insistently. "I will not wear big hair and a cowboy hat and fringe and parade around with a fake smile on my face while I give the crowd my royal wave." She demonstrated, fingers together, palm cupped as she gently rocked the hand.

Clint nodded his head. "You'd rather wear orange hair, greasepaint, a funny hat and a painted-on smile."

She might have blushed. It was hard to tell, since she was already red in the face. "Yes."

"All right. This is your party, darlin'." She didn't like being called darlin'. It rankled her, for some reason, made her lips thin and her blue eyes go flinty. "I mean, it's your party, Special Agent Paris."

She pursed her lips, for a moment. "Maybe you should just call me Mary."

"Pretty name."

Mary hooked her water bottle to her own belt and started to run, almost as if she were escaping. She didn't much like chitchat.

Clint took off after her, and Mutt leapt off the ground to follow.

"What's next?" Mary asked when Clint pulled up alongside her.

"When we're finished with the run, we'll get you settled in."

She glanced at him. "What?"

"We'll get your things out of the car and take a little break, have some lunch and then this afternoon we'll work on a few basic maneuvers."

"My *things?*"

"You know, suitcases, bags of makeup, trunks full of shoes…"

She stared straight ahead. "My bags are at the hotel in Scottsboro, where I'll be staying."

Clint grinned. "For better than two weeks? Goodness, darlin', you don't have to make that trip every morning and every night. I have a couple of guest rooms right here in the house."

Mary turned her head and laid her eyes on his face; a lesser man would have flinched, he was certain.

"No, thank you," she said coolly. "I prefer to stay in a hotel."

"Fine by me," he muttered. He wasn't disappointed. Not really. He didn't care what made a woman like Mary Paris tick. Man, she was definitely…different.

"You know," he said as they made a turn and ran into blessed shade once again, "you really should consider the Rodeo Queen idea. It would be much easier, big hair and all."

"Won't work," she said simply.

"Why not?"

Mary stared straight ahead as she continued to run at a steady pace. For a while, he thought she wasn't going to answer. Finally, she did.

"All I plan to do is gather information. Talk to people, try to connect the dots and put faces to names and eliminate suspects." She glanced at him suspiciously, perhaps wondering how much she should share. Mary Paris didn't look like a woman who gave her trust easily.

He saw the unspoken *but* in her eyes, in the tense set of her mouth. "I knew you wanted to make yourself bait!" he snapped, angry that any woman would consider anything so dangerous. Danger was a part of Mary Paris's job, but in his world women were gentle creatures who were meant to be protected. Sheltered. Mary and his world clashed, big time.

"I certainly wouldn't do anything so foolish." She turned her eyes front again. She'd settled into an easy, steady pace and looked as if she could run all day, high humidity or no high humidity. "Not on my own."

"But," Clint prodded.

Mary's eyes remained set on the horizon. "The women who were killed by this guy, they were all…" She paused, as if she were carefully considering her next word. "Quiet," she finally said. "Six out of eight of them weren't missed for days, which is one of the reasons no one ever linked the cases together or to the Brisco Rodeo."

"You did."

"I had an advantage."

"What's that?"

She shook her head gently. "Before I started looking into the case, what you had was six different jurisdictions all going at the cases from a different perspective. The killings were not identical, just similar in an eerie kind of way. If anyone bothered to look." She shook her head slightly. "In the two instances where there was more than one murder in a jurisdiction, the investigators for each victim were different! People retire, they go into other departments…and when a murder sits for a while and the victim doesn't have someone pushing at the police to find her killer..." She paused and took a few steady breaths.

"They get shoved aside," Clint said.

"Yeah," Mary said in a lower voice. "While I don't plan to bait the killer at this time, it might become an option later on. With the proper backup, of course," she added. "A Rodeo Queen would be missed right away, I imagine."

"So will a rodeo clown," Clint assured her.

"I need to blend in. Disappear. I need to be invisible, Sinclair."

He knew she had her reasons for doing things this way. That didn't mean he had to like it. "Why not just be in the crowd every day?"

"Three or four shows per town, six cities. You don't think that might raise a few questions?"

He shrugged. "Groupies."

Mary rolled her eyes in disgust. No, she'd never pass for an adoring groupie. "Groupies?"

"Rodeo hos," Clint said with a wicked grin.

Special Agent Mary gave him a quick, censuring glance. "Wouldn't work," she said. "I need to get close to the people in the rodeo."

"Some of the fellas get *real* close to the groupies."

"Fellas like you?" she snapped.

"No way."

She huffed once, as if she didn't believe him for a minute.

Clint shook his head. "I can't tell you how bad I think this idea of yours is."

"I didn't ask for your opinion, Bozo." She sped up and Clint stayed close behind her.

Bozo? Yeah, she definitely had a bug up her butt.

* * *

"You want me to do *what?*" Mary asked, shading her eyes with one hand. The sun shone bright overhead. It was just past noon and she was starving. Absolutely, positively, would-kill-for-an-Oreo starving.

Telling Sinclair that she was so hungry she felt hollow would be admitting that she should have taken him up on his offer of breakfast, and she wouldn't admit that she'd made a mistake. She never did.

They stood in the center of a corral that was empty but for the two of them, and Sinclair pointed to a rustic section of fence. "Over the fence," he said again. "As quickly as you can."

With a shake of her head, she ran to the fence and climbed over. Seemed pretty quick to her, but Sinclair was not satisfied.

"Again," he said.

Mary walked toward him, never hinting that she ached all over, never letting on that she was so hungry she'd snatch a cookie from a small child if she had the chance. "I thought that particular move was more than sufficient."

"Sufficient? Honey, when a bull is chasing you, sufficient doesn't cut it. Try again."

"Honey" now, as well as the occasional darlin'. The man was getting on her nerves in the worst way.

"Sure thing, Giggles." She turned and began to run again, toward the fence.

Clint flew past her when she was halfway to her target, and with no more than one hand on the top of the fence he vaulted over. The move was so quick, so damned graceful, she felt like an elephant in comparison, plodding toward the obstacle.

She made it over the fence but needed a boost from her foot on the bottom rung to accomplish the task.

That chore done again, Clint sat on the fence in question and shook his head. "I don't think two weeks is enough time to get you ready."

Mary was tired, hungry and forced to admit that this irritating man could do something she could not. "It'll do." It would have to.

Clint Sinclair was incredibly easygoing. It wasn't natural. After all, Shea was anything but laid-back, and the other two brothers…they both looked like they spent most of their lives wound pretty tight. But so far Clint was Mr. Agreeable. He hadn't said a word about her calling him Bozo and Giggles. In fact, he seemed to find her somehow amusing.

She didn't like it.

Sitting on the fence, pondering the situation, he didn't look quite as easygoing as he had earlier in the day. At least he had the good grace to sweat, almost as much as she did. He had great legs, muscled and lean, and for the first time today his neck was corded. Strained. He ignored the dog who danced at his feet.

"You want to know why Wes limps the way he does?" Sinclair asked in a tight voice. "The reason he will always limp when he walks? The reason why he's lucky to be walking at all?"

"No, but I imagine you're going to tell me anyway." Mary climbed onto the fence to perch beside Sinclair, taking care not to sit too close.

"He was too slow getting over the fence."

She glanced toward the house, which seemed so far away. She'd bet her life there were cookies there. A sandwich, maybe. Hell, a crumb! What about those pancakes Katie had offered to make? "Maybe you should just teach me a few jokes and let that be it."

Clint shook his head. "That's not what a rodeo clown does, dar...Mary."

Ah, maybe the Giggles bit had gotten to him, after all. "I know."

"We are in the arena to protect the cowboys, to draw the bull away from them after they're thrown. Yes, we entertain the crowd, too, but that's not why we're there."

She looked at him. Why couldn't Shea have had an ugly rodeo-clown brother? Clint Sinclair was too good-looking, too charming, too...too. Two weeks! Two weeks of getting into better shape, learning the tricks of the trade, keeping him at a distance. And after the two weeks were up, they'd be together every day until she found Elaine's killer. Maybe she could convince him to allow her to take his place, not join in as an extra.

There was no time or place in her life for a man, not anymore. She hadn't even thought about getting close to anyone since she'd lost Rick. It was too damned hard, to fall in love and think you had forever, and then find out, from a voice on the phone, that "forever" was a lie.

"Special Agent Paris," Sinclair said, his voice low, his expression darkly serious. "I've played along with you up to this point, for Shea's sake, mostly."

"I know that."

"At the end of your two weeks, if I don't think you're ready, if I think that there's even a remote possibility that by stepping into the arena you're putting your life or the life of a cowboy at risk, you won't have my cooperation. No introduction to Brisco. No more pretending. This is not fun and games. If you can't do the job as well or better than any other bullfighter, then you're going to have to find another way to get in."

"I'll be ready," she assured him.

"You'd better be."

* * *

Two weeks, and the rodeo would be under way. He could hardly wait.

But he would wait, no matter how anxious he became in the next few days. His fingers itched, and deep inside he felt a knot of pure excitement. The anticipation was always exhilarating, and with each passing year that anticipation grew more delicious.

He sat on a bench in the crowded shopping mall, watching women walk past. Some of them glanced his way, most did not. He was invisible here, one of the crowd.

His eyes were drawn to a woman walking his way. A blonde. Pretty, but not gorgeous. Nice full breasts. Gold earrings dangled from her delicate ears. As he watched her walk toward him, he felt his excitement grow.

But he knew this woman would be all wrong for him. She was too confident, her walk too sure. She came closer, and he saw the wedding ring on her left hand. No, she would never do.

Not that he would actually take a woman from the mall, he just liked to pretend. To plan. To imagine. And since this was just pretend, he might as well choose the woman who appealed to him most.

The woman walked past him, never so much as glancing his way. She had a nice back view, too.

He stood, checked his watch so anyone paying attention would think he had somewhere to be, someone to meet…and then he followed the woman, keeping her in his sight while maintaining a safe distance.

She was leaving the mall. Perfect. She walked through the main doors, shifted her shopping bags and walked quickly into the parking lot.

It was dark, the parking lot lit by bright streetlamps. There were people around, but no one close.

He could take her if he wanted to. He could walk up behind her, surprise her and before she knew what was happening he'd be in her car.

No. He stopped in the middle of the parking lot and watched her go. It wasn't time, and she wasn't right. And no matter how tempting the woman was, he couldn't afford to kill in the town where he lived. He was too smart to make such a blunder.

He smiled as the woman got into her car. Two weeks wasn't such a long time to wait.

Chapter 3

Clint watched Mary vault over the fence with much greater ease than she had on Monday. Six days of running, lifting some light weights, jumping rope and practicing the pivot, and she was…better. Not there yet, but certainly well on her way. She was even getting pretty good with a lasso.

He'd pushed Mary hard, asking more of her than he'd thought any woman would go for. They ran. They raced across his homemade obstacle course. They spent their days sweaty and dirty, and when it was done they were both exhausted.

And then they ran a little more.

Any other woman would have quit by now, but Mary Paris wasn't a quitter.

Too bad. He'd been so sure that first day, that by the end of the week she'd decide his rodeo-queen ploy might work just as well as her ridiculous idea. No way. He had a feeling Mary wouldn't ever admit she was wrong, not even if that meant she was headed for serious trouble.

It was all a waste of time. None of the men he worked with were capable of the kind of crimes she suspected them of. Yes, someone out there had committed these murders, but it wasn't a man he knew and worked with. You could look at a person who would do something like that and just…know. Couldn't you? A shudder rippled down his spine. That wasn't true and he knew it. Monsters like the one Mary was hunting didn't come with a neon sign that identified them as evil, they didn't have a look about them that might warn a potential victim or the police. He probably appeared and behaved perfectly normal…right up until the moment he grabbed some poor woman.

Dean and Boone had both been sending him frequent e-mails about the case, making sure he had the pertinent information about the crimes and generally giving him brotherly grief for getting into the middle of one of Shea's schemes. The information they provided gave him both sides of the story. He could see why no one had ever tied the crimes together; the method of death and jurisdictions were different. But Mary was right about there being something eerily similar about the victims and the murders. All blond. All attractive. And those missing earrings in at least four cases was creepy.

As for the other, he let the guys get away with ribbing him, because he knew if they'd been the ones singled out by their baby sister, they would have gone along with whatever cockeyed plan she cooked up, too. They had always been such pushovers for Shea.

"Again?" Mary asked as she walked toward him. She was covered with sweat, her hair had seen better days and her clothes were so baggy they disguised her killer figure.

But there was something about the way she walked that made him feel her approach deep down. Something about her lips, perfectly shaped and full and rosy, even though she wore no makeup, that said, "Come and get it."

So, why did he know that if he tried to move in and get *anything,* he'd end up flat on his back with a gun pointed at his forehead? And why did that make him want her even more?

Her firearms were usually pretty well disguised, but Special Agent Mary was always armed. Always. Her baggy shirts often hid a revolver housed in a holster at her waist. There was an ankle holster, too, usually—but not always—hidden by her loose-fitting trousers.

What on earth was she afraid of?

"No," he said as she reached him. "We're done for the day."

She glanced up at the afternoon sun. "So soon?"

"It's Saturday."

"What difference does that make?"

He smiled at her. She was always so serious, but on occasion there was something almost endearingly childlike about her sober intensity. And she would clobber him if he dared to suggest that right now she was bordering on downright *cute.* "It's Saturday night. Time for a little dancing, a couple of beers, a few laughs…"

She rolled her eyes.

"Don't you ever go out and have a little fun? Or is that against FBI regulations?"

"Of course I…have fun," she said defensively. "But not usually when I'm working."

He had a feeling Mary Paris didn't take many days off, that every day was a workday. "All work and no play makes Mary a dull girl."

"Woman," she corrected.

"Sorry," he said. "Dull *woman*." He looked her up and down. Yep, Mary was fine, no matter what shape she might be in at the moment. "You're welcome to join us. Katie and Wes will be there. I know Katie would enjoy having another woman along."

"No, thanks," she said, her eyes on the house as they walked in that direction. "I really should stay in and work on my juggling."

"You're pretty good at that."

"I could be better."

With the sun on her face Mary looked golden warm and for a moment, just a moment, she looked not at all fearsome. He wouldn't tell her so, though. A man had to tread carefully around a woman like this one.

"We'll be at Dexler's Roadhouse, and we should get there about eight or so. In case you change your mind," he added quickly. He could offer to pick her up at her hotel, but that would sound too much like he was asking her for a date. No, she'd never go for that.

She didn't ask for directions to Dexler's Roadhouse, in case she really did change her mind. Clint suddenly had a heartbreaking picture of Mary Paris alone on a Saturday night once again. She'd practice her juggling, reaching for perfection as always, and maybe she'd spend a little time online. Not chatting with friends or playing games, but researching her case and filing flawless reports.

And when that was done she'd crawl into bed and try to sleep, but sleep wouldn't come. Not easily, at least, and not quickly. She'd toss and turn, trying to get comfortable, wondering why she couldn't sleep when her body was so tired.

There were better ways to spend Saturday night. A beer or two, a slow dance or two, a few laughs. Did Mary laugh? Maybe. He really would like to see her laugh.

Beers, dancing and laughing behind her, when Mary went to bed she still might not get any sleep…but what a night it could be.

Clint shook off the thought. Mary was Shea's friend, and an FBI agent searching for a serial killer. As far as he could tell she didn't like him at all. Again, he had that mental picture of making a move and finding himself flat on his back with a gun to his head.

Mary practiced her juggling for a while, after grabbing a quick bite at the hotel restaurant. Katie had tried to convince her to stay for dinner at the ranch and then go out with them tonight, but Mary had passed. Graciously, she hoped. Katie had really made an effort to be welcoming. In spite of Mary's initial resolve not to like Sinclair's housekeeper and friend—she did.

There were a million reasons why she should not socialize with Clint Sinclair. He was Shea's brother, for one thing. She had heard too many stories about the Sinclair men to be completely comfortable dancing with one. More important, he was a part of this case, and nothing and no one could be more important than finding the man who had killed Elaine and seven other women.

Mary had always been driven. Well, almost always. For a brief time with Rick she'd been happy. But after hearing that Elaine had been murdered she'd gone into overdrive. The self-recriminations had been agonizing, almost as painful as the grief. Why hadn't she gotten in touch with Elaine more often? Taken vacations to visit her old college friend? Made sure Elaine was safe and protected and…dammit, the man who had done this had to be caught, before he killed anyone else.

Shea didn't know that one of the victims had been Mary's friend. There hadn't been a reason to tell the reporter, who would probably be unable to pass up the chance to use the interesting tidbit on her show, now or later. Josh, her superior at the bureau, knew that Elaine was an old college friend, but he had no idea how close they'd been. And telling him she hadn't seen Elaine in seven years had not been a lie. They hadn't *seen* each other in that many years. But they had written, talked on the phone, e-mailed now and then. Mary was afraid Josh wouldn't let her anywhere near the case—officially or on her own time—if he knew how personal this case was.

Which was why she hadn't told him that the reason she'd pursued this case so doggedly was more than ambition.

Bored with juggling, Mary went to her computer. She had a few e-mails waiting for her; two from her sister, Janice, who lived in Colorado with her husband and little girl; one from her sometime-partner Lewis, who was on family leave since his wife had recently delivered baby boy number three; a quick note from Josh; and a long, rambling e-mail letter from her father.

There was no news to speak of from any front. Nothing enlightening from Lewis or Josh, no family emergencies. Lots of "how are you" and "don't work too hard" and one dig from Lewis about getting too chummy with the rodeo clown.

She'd had nothing unprofessional to say about Sinclair in her unofficial reports to Josh or the occasional e-mails to Lewis. And of course Lewis had no way of knowing that Clint was sexy and sweet and annoyingly…perfect. So how did he know that dig about getting too chummy with the clown would hit too close to home? Lewis. He always knew!

Why didn't these messages cheer her up? Why did she

now feel lonelier than she had before she'd checked her e-mail?

Mary glanced at the clock. Eight-fifteen. Right about now Clint and his friends were getting their evening started. A beer, he'd said. A little dancing. Some laughs. She shook her head. No, the last thing she needed was to get too friendly with Sinclair. This association was strictly business.

Since Rick had gone, there hadn't been any dancing. There had been no nights out, unless you counted the occasional quick beer with the guys after a successful job. Her job was her life now, the men she worked with were her family.

Mary loved her sister, but they had very little in common. They had taken different paths. Their father couldn't understand why his youngest daughter had dedicated her life to her job, instead of settling down with a nice man.

Settling down. Ha. That wasn't for her and never would be. It hadn't been for her mother either. When Mary had been twelve and her sister, Janice, fourteen, their mother had walked out. Though their father had tried to shield them from the truth, they'd heard things. There had been another man. Money taken from the checking account. Mary and Janice had gotten the occasional motherly Christmas card from various parts of the country, and in the beginning there had been belated birthday cards, as well.

These days, nothing. Mary couldn't remember when she'd last heard from her mother. When Rick had mentioned having kids, Mary had panicked. She wasn't ready, might never be ready! What if she was like her own mom? It had taken months, but her husband had convinced her, slowly and surely, that she would make a wonderful mother.

And then he'd gone and let a drunk driver run him down on the street.

Mary covered her face with her hands. "Stop it," she muttered against her palm. She wouldn't feel sorry for herself, wouldn't sit here and daydream about what might have been. There was no *might have been,* only reality. And in reality, she was a woman who had nothing but her job and liked it that way.

She shut down her laptop and went to the closet. Maybe she needed to get out of this depressing hotel room! If she did seek out Dexler's Roadhouse, what would she wear? Her jeans didn't leave room for her ankle holster. They were too tight. Though if she wore a baggy shirt, she could wear her revolver at her waist. One weapon would probably be enough, if she did decide to go anywhere. Probably. The clothes she wore every day for training with Clint were much too casual even for a roadhouse. The conservative suits she wore so often wouldn't do. She'd stick out like a sore thumb.

It didn't matter. She wouldn't actually go. An early evening, that's what she needed. She'd never complain to Sinclair, but she ached all over. She had been in good physical shape when she got here, but she had never been pushed so hard. Sinclair was a tough coach.

She'd had a shower earlier, but a good hot soak would surely do her good. A soak, her pajamas and then to bed.

It was a normal Saturday night at Dexler's. People came from all around to dance, drink and visit. Clint recognized almost every face.

Strangers rarely wandered into this particular roadhouse. From the highway it looked like a ramshackle, weathered barn decorated with a couple of neon beer signs. Only the bravest of souls would dare to walk in not knowing what they might find.

But in truth Dexler's was pretty tame, as roadhouses went. It was the same crowd most weekends, neighbors and friends. Tim Dexler had hired himself a bruiser of a bouncer a couple years back, and Joe could handle any kind of trouble that came this way. There was rarely trouble.

Clint glanced at the door on occasion, sometimes when it opened for a new customer, sometimes while it was solidly closed. Had he really expected that Special Agent Mary would lower herself to come to such a place? That a beer and a few laughs might appeal to her?

Yeah, he had.

There was a lull at the moment. The band was taking a break and the only noise came from the roar of laughter and conversation that stretched across the long room. Katie laid her hand on his arm and leaned close.

"When the band starts up again, you should ask Tracy to dance." She nodded at her friend, who sat at the bar on the opposite side of the room bracketed by two girlfriends. "She likes you," Katie added in a lowered voice.

"Maybe later." He didn't want to hurt Katie's feelings, but her friend gave him the willies. Of course Tracy liked him; she was a groupie. A rodeo ho. There were lots of people who followed the rodeo with genuine interest. They appreciated the sport, they loved the thrill of it the same way Clint did. But there were a few, just a few, who looked at the whole thing in a cockeyed way. When he was cornered by Tracy, the rodeo was all she wanted to talk about. Bright-eyed and tongue-tied when she looked at him, all she really saw was a few silver buckles. Been there, done that…and he had no desire to go back.

Just as the band began to take the stage, the front door

opened. Out of habit—even though he had given up on watching Mary walk through that door—Clint turned his head to see who had arrived.

And grinned when she walked into the room, letting the heavy door swing closed behind her.

Mary hadn't seen them yet, but she was searching, her eyes scanning the room. Clint didn't stand and wave her over. Not yet. For a moment he just watched.

Her hair was down tonight, as it had been when he'd met her at Shea's house. Pale, sleek and soft, it touched her chin and swung gently when she turned her head. Her jeans were too new for ranch work and fit like a glove, showing off the shapely legs her normal baggy trousers disguised. The jacket she wore couldn't hide the fact that she had an hourglass figure that might make any man's mouth water. His weren't the only eyes on Mary at the moment, he was quite sure.

Her gaze finally scanned this section of the room and Clint lifted his hand to wave her over. Was that a half smile on her face? A touch of relief? If so, those telling signs came and went quickly.

She crossed the room, weaving around tables. A goodly number of eyes followed her progress, the eyes of men who liked what they saw. Mary ignored them. She didn't even seem to be aware of the men who watched her. No one spoke to her. She had an air about her, a regal bearing that very clearly said, "Don't touch."

"You made it," he said when she neared the table. He and Wes both stood and Clint grabbed a chair and held it out for Mary. She looked at it for a moment before sitting down. Did she find it offensive that he occasionally acted like a gentleman? Was she so damned tough she didn't want a man to open the door for her, hold out her chair?

After a very short hesitation, Mary sat without comment. When she was seated, Clint and Wes sat, too.

"I hope it's okay if I join you," she said. "I changed my mind."

"A woman's privilege, or so I hear," Clint said. He was afraid if he asked too many questions, if he teased Mary about her change of heart, she'd bolt.

"I'm so glad you decided to come!" Katie said enthusiastically.

"Yeah," Wes said with a wide grin of his own. "You worked hard this week. You deserve a night off."

Clint signaled the waitress and asked Mary what she wanted to drink. After a moment's hesitation she passed on the beer and ordered a diet soda. Because she was on duty twenty-four hours a day? Or because she was deathly afraid of losing control?

Mary studied the long room and the people in it. "This place is not exactly like I thought it would be," she said. "I expected more smoke and misbehaving cowboys."

"We have a few misbehaving cowboys now and then," Clint said.

"You're sitting next to one," Katie teased.

"And we would never take Katie anywhere where she'd have to breathe secondhand smoke," Wes added. "It's not good for her or the baby."

"Nobody smokes anymore anyway," Clint added. "And if they do, there's a smoking area out back."

"It's a great place," she said, sounding almost surprised.

Over Mary's shoulder, Clint saw that Tracy was headed this way, her too-curious eyes on Mary's back.

"Dance," he said, standing and offering Mary his hand as the country-western band on the stage began to play a slow number.

"Maybe la—"

Clint interrupted Mary's polite refusal by taking her hand and pulling her to her feet. She was not a woman accustomed to taking orders, not like this. His eyes met hers, he begged her silently…and apparently she saw something there that made her hang on to his hand and say okay, because that's just what she did.

He nodded to Tracy as they passed her, he and Mary arm in arm on their way to the dance floor. Tracy's smile faded a little, but she continued on. She and Katie could visit for a few minutes, and then, with any luck, Tracy would return to her friends at the bar.

"Okay," Mary said as he took her in his arms to begin the dance. He didn't hold her too close. He didn't dare. "What's up?"

"Nothing," he said.

She smiled. "You are such a bad liar, Sinclair."

Mary Paris was not an accomplished dancer. Her movements weren't exactly awkward, but it was clear that she didn't dance like this often. Of course she didn't. Dancing meant getting close. He had a gut-deep feeling Mary Paris was very cautious about *close*.

"You're wearing a gun," he said. "A shoulder holster." His fingers traced the gentle curve of leather beneath her jacket. Beneath that jacket she was warm. Warm and soft and curved in all the right places. He ignored his initial reaction to the woman in his arms, shook his head and tsked. "Don't you ever go out unarmed?"

"No," she answered seriously. "Who's the woman?"

"What woman?"

"The one you ran onto the dance floor to escape. The pretty lady with the big brown hair and too much makeup who's sitting in your chair talking to Katie at the moment."

"You don't miss much, do you?"

She shook her head, sending those soft, golden strands dancing.

"Tracy is a friend of Katie's. They went to high school together, stayed in touch over the years."

"She spooks you, Sinclair. It this Tracy an old girl-friend of yours?" she asked.

"No," Clint said succinctly.

"You don't like her."

"She's…not my type."

The dance floor was crowded, their motion was re-stricted, but as the song continued Mary's movements gradually seemed a little more confident. Maybe she was getting comfortable here. Maybe he was just getting used to the way she felt and moved in his arms.

"What is your type?" she asked.

It was a personal question, too personal for their current situation. But he had a feeling if he backed off she'd never dare to ask him a personal question again. "I guess when the time comes I'll settle down with a sweet country girl. Somebody who's a good cook and wants a bunch of kids and enjoys simple things, like I do."

She didn't make fun of him, like he'd thought she might. "What kinds of simple things?"

"This is coming dangerously close to a meaningful conversation, Special Agent Paris," he teased. "Are you certain we should continue?"

"Why not? I do live dangerously, on occasion."

Yes, this was definitely living dangerously.

"Simple things," he said. "Riding a horse so fast you feel like you're flying. Watching the sunrise. Taking off on a moment's notice to see something new, to do some-thing new. White-water rafting. Hearing a child laugh. Coming home."

She watched him, her eyes unflinching, her mouth inviting. "Sounds like a roller coaster."

"Life is a roller coaster."

She gave him a soft smile. "So, your life is just one wild ride."

"Yeah." Something in her eyes, a spark of interest, a lively fire, gave him the courage to continue. "Life is full of simple pleasures, like dancing with an armed woman or making love under the stars."

Mary wrinkled her nose and her smile faded. "Satellite technology," she said softly.

"What?"

"Where have you been, Sinclair? Under the *stars?* Have you never heard of our advanced satellite technology?"

He grinned. "Why would any government be interested in focusing in on my little horse ranch?"

"It's not that they would," she said. "But that they could."

"You worry too much."

"You don't worry at all."

As he spun Mary around, she looked at the table where Katie leaned close to Tracy so they could talk, and Wes watched his wife with loving eyes.

"Will they continue to live with you after the baby is born?"

Was she neatly changing the subject? Probably. Talking about making love under the stars made him itch. Did Mary itch? Ever?

"Just for a while. In the fall I'm building them a house up on that hill at the north end of the property."

"It's pretty there," she said.

"Katie likes it. She picked the spot and the house plans just a few weeks ago."

She probably didn't mean to, but Mary was beginning to relax. Her breathing was slower and deeper. The body against his yielded, slightly. Clint was aware that Mary fit in his arms very nicely, at ease and drifting closer into him with every step.

"Won't it be expensive to build Wes and Katie their own house?" she asked. "Is your horse ranch really all that successful?"

"It's just money," he said with a shrug.

She smiled. "Just money."

Yes, she did have a nice smile. "I can always make more if I need to." He'd probably never need to, unless the ranch really started sucking in the cash. He'd won enough money bull riding to get himself started, and a few good investments had made him financially secure, if not rich.

Again, Mary looked at Wes and Katie. "They're such a lovely couple," she said. "He adores her, she loves him. I don't think I've ever met two sweeter people. They're so ideal together."

"You have no idea," Clint said softly.

She listened too closely. Something in his voice made her push for more. "What does that mean?"

"Nothing."

"Something. Tell, Sinclair." She wasn't giving up. He had a feeling she never did.

He glanced at his ranch foreman and friend, and at Wes's pregnant wife. "When Wes was hurt a couple of years ago, Katie was right there. We thought he would die that night, and for days after they said he might lose his leg." His heart thudded. "She never left his side. His rodeo days were over, his life was in danger. He was, at best, maimed for life."

"She loves him. Of course she never left his side."

Memories from four years ago—flashbacks to his own accident—shouldn't hurt still, but they did.

"Katie never cried," he said. "She's not a strong person, but she found strength for Wes because he needed it. She sat there in his hospital room, day and night, and demanded that he live. And he did."

"And since he couldn't rodeo anymore, you asked him to be foreman at your ranch?"

"The ranch was just in the planning stages at that time," he said. "But as soon as I had things up and running, Wes and Katie were there. They were married at the house a little more than a year ago."

For a moment Mary said nothing, and then she glanced sharply up at him, blue eyes piercing and searching. Something about that glance grabbed him down deep, made him forget that she was a fed, that she was Shea's friend. She was relaxed, but he was not. He fought the urge to pull her head to his shoulder.

"Sinclair," she whispered, "did you build that ranch so Wes and Katie would have a place to go?"

"Don't be silly," he said quickly. "I've been dreaming about my own horse ranch all my life."

"But you didn't build it until Wes was hurt."

"Coincidence."

"I don't believe in coincidence."

The music came to an end, and a quick glance showed him that Tracy was leaving the table on the arm of a friend who'd asked her to dance. Good. He really didn't want to have to deal with making chitchat with her tonight. And she was sure to ask questions about Mary. She probably already had, but since Wes and Katie didn't know much, they couldn't tell much.

"You're hiding something," Mary said softly as they walked back to their table.

"Me? You're the one with the gun under your jacket," he said in a low voice.

"You know what I mean, Sinclair. There's a skeleton in your closet somewhere. No one is as *nice* as you appear to be."

"You make that sound like such a bad thing."

"Not bad," she said as they reached the table. "Unlikely."

"Most people are nice."

She snorted as she took her seat. "No," she said, her smile fading. "They're not."

Life in general, being in the FBI and seeing too much, some heartbreak in her past…something had made Mary bitter. She searched for the worst in everyone; she was always on the lookout for those skeletons.

Cynical, distant and complicated, Special Agent Mary Paris was about as far removed from his *type* as any woman could be.

And Clint wanted her so bad he could practically taste her.

Chapter 4

Mary felt almost guilty showing up on Clint's front porch with bag in hand. There had been a mix-up at the hotel, and when it came right down to it, the horde of bass fishermen who had taken over the place were much more important to the hotel than a woman who had already been there more than a week. She could have made a scene, she supposed, planted her feet firmly and kept her room, but the truth of the matter was she had never expected that she'd actually be here the entire two weeks Clint had insisted on. She'd been so sure she would learn everything necessary quickly.

She'd reserved her room for a week and had been lucky to keep her bed the past couple of days. It was her own fault she'd lost her room.

When she'd explained the situation to Clint and asked for a recommendation for a hotel that wasn't an hour's drive from his ranch, he had insisted that she stay here. And she hadn't argued. Not once. That was so unlike her.

Clint opened the door, looking unnaturally wide awake, considering that it wasn't yet eight o'clock on a Tuesday morning. "Come on in," he said, stepping back and opening the door wide. "Are your other bags in the car?" he asked, glancing down at her single piece of luggage.

"I have a few things in the trunk," she said. A couple of suits, high-heeled shoes, one nice black dress. "But everything I need is here." She hefted the bag and Clint closed the door on a too-warm morning.

Mutt, who no longer treated Mary like a stranger, padded up to say hello and Mary stroked the dog's head with her free hand. "Such a good boy," she murmured.

Clint took her bag and headed down the hallway. Mary started to protest that she was perfectly capable of handling her own luggage, but the protest died on her lips. She simply followed Clint—walking cautiously down the main hallway, then taking a turn that led to a wing she had steered clear of since her arrival.

The bedrooms, four of them, were along this long hallway. Katie and Wes shared one of the bedrooms and would be here until their house was completed. Clint no doubt had the largest room. A master suite, she imagined, but nothing fancy. He simply wasn't a fancy kind of guy. Everything about him was solid and down to earth. And still, there was definitely more to Clint than met the eye.

"Here you go," he said, throwing open the door of a room situated in the middle of the hallway. "Bathroom's across the hall. Towels are in the linen closet." He pointed to the hallway closet before heading into the bedroom. "If you need anything you can't find, just ask Katie. She knows where everything is."

"Wow," she said as Clint tossed her bag onto the bed.

"I hope this will suit you," he replied.

The room was unexpectedly pretty, with a pastel quilt

on the queen-size bed, a vase of flowers on the antique dresser and lace curtains in the wide window. The view beyond that window was breathtaking. "It's beautiful."

"I would say thank you, but to be honest, Katie did most of the decorating. I can't take credit for anything but the den and my office. The rest of the house has Katie's touch."

It didn't matter that her relationship with Clint Sinclair was strictly professional, that she was here on official business and that in the beginning she hadn't even liked him. There was something charged about having a good-looking man in the room where you slept, standing by the bed, rocking back on his heels as if he could take a tumble and land on the mattress at any moment. That charge was decidedly electric, as if lightning coursed through the room and her body.

In the past week, she had seen firsthand that Clint had more stamina and grace than any other man she'd ever known. He was incredibly strong, unexpectedly agile, and limber. She couldn't help but wonder, as any red-blooded woman might, what kind of lover he would be.

For the past two years, she hadn't so much as thought of a man in that way. There would be no more love for her, there would be no more passion. It hurt too much when that love was taken away.

But since coming here, she felt as if she were slowly waking up from a long sleep. She liked being lost in her safe slumber, but Clint had been shaking her shoulder and telling her it was time to get up. Like it or not, she was aware of him in a way she had not expected.

Janice had told her this would happen one day. That she would stop feeling numb. That she would realize that life went on no matter what we wanted or expected.

"Need any help getting settled in?" Clint asked.

That perfectly innocent question made Mary tingle. It was that lightning again. Oh, this was turning into an absolute disaster! She never let a man, any man, affect her this way. She wasn't a *girl,* she was a fully grown woman who knew better. "No, thanks. We can get to work and I'll unpack later."

"Whatever you say." He turned and walked out of the room, and Mary followed.

Okay, the man did have a nice set of buns. Any woman might realize that fact if she happened to be walking right behind him. And damned if he wasn't graceful! In a completely masculine way, of course. This man had surely never tripped over his own two feet or made an awkward move of any kind. A man like this, when he turned his full attentions to a woman…Mary shook off the unexpected thought. She'd been in Mayberry too long if she was actually thinking about…

No, she was not *thinking about.* She absolutely, positively could not afford that. "What are we working on today?" Juggling, jogging, jumping fences or jumping rope, pivoting, leaping over hurdles, running Clint's homemade obstacle course. They usually worked on a combination of those things.

"I think we'll do a little riding," he said. "You're due for an easy day."

"Riding what?" she asked.

Back in the main hallway, not far from the kitchen, Clint stopped and turned to face her. "Horses," he said softly. One eye narrowed slightly. "You *do* ride."

"I watched some films," she said with a shrug. "It doesn't look particularly hard."

Clint closed his eyes, muttered something completely obscene that took her by surprise and then shook his head.

"What kind of a woman tries to worm her way into a rodeo when she's never even been on horseback?"

Any momentary sexual attraction she might have felt vanished. "I watched several rodeo films. The clowns don't ride."

"But you're going to be around horses and bulls all day long. You need to be comfortable with the animals. A skittish woman sticking her nose in where it doesn't belong can turn everything upside down."

"I suppose I'm the skittish woman where I don't belong."

"Yes!"

Mary smiled at him. She could handle confrontation much better than feelings that came out of nowhere and ambushed her. "If *you* can ride a horse, *I* can ride a horse. Slappy," she added with just a touch of disdain.

Clint took a long, deep breath. "Fine," he said. "You want to ride? We ride."

Special Agent Mary was an FBI agent, she was here of her own volition and she knew exactly what she was getting into. Maybe. It wasn't his job to protect her, to watch over her, to make sure she didn't do anything foolish.

She couldn't ride a horse, it had taken her four days to be truly comfortable around *Mutt*—putting this woman in the rodeo was going to be a disaster.

Apparently Mary was finally comfortable around him as well as Mutt. She was no longer armed at all times. Right now she wore snug jeans, a pale yellow button-up shirt and her hair was in one of those little ponytails. No gun. At least, not that he could see.

They walked back toward the house, after a nice, long ride. Mary tried not to hobble, and she was almost successful. There was a little hitch in her getalong, though, a funny kind of limp that gave her away. He'd kept the horses at a job trot during the entire ride. It was the best pace for the animals...but brutal on the rider's backside.

"So, how do you like riding?" he asked.

"It was fine," she said noncommittally.

If she was sore now, by tomorrow morning she wouldn't be able to get out of bed. He wondered how she would react if he called the whole deal off here and now. She wasn't ready. She would never be ready. Mary was going to make as good a rodeo clown as he'd make an FBI agent, on two weeks' training.

"How about we go to the roadhouse tonight?" he asked, smiling at her back. "A little dancing might be a nice way to unwind."

She groaned, then caught herself and became quiet. "I think I might have to pass. I have some paperwork to catch up on."

"Can't you do your paperwork tomorrow?"

"I'd rather get it done and out of the way."

Clint imagined she'd spend the evening in bed with a hot pack and a bottle of aspirin. They'd ridden pretty hard this afternoon, going faster and longer than they had this morning.

He hadn't pushed Mary because he'd wanted to hurt her. Like it or not, he needed to know how far she would go before saying uncle. Apparently Mary never gave up. No surrender. Take no prisoners.

"All right," he said, not wanting to push her any more than he already had.

Wes met them as they entered through the back door and stepped into the kitchen. Mary didn't stop but lifted her hand in a quick greeting as she kept on moving through to the hallway. When she was almost out of hearing, Clint heard her mutter something and groan.

"What's her problem?" Wes asked as he poured two cups of coffee.

"She's never ridden a horse before today," Clint said.

Wes turned around with a huge grin on his face and handed Clint a heavy mug filled with strong, black coffee. "You're kidding, right? Y'all will be heading to Birmingham in a week. What are you going to do?"

Clint shook his head. "I think I'm going to have to put her in the barrel."

"Oliver's got a barrel man, or did last time I heard."

"I know." Clint sipped at the coffee. He hated lying to Wes about Mary's reason for being here, but by telling the truth he'd put his friend and foreman into the same boat he was in. Wes would be forced to lie to his friends. "I might have to pull a few strings."

Wes gave Clint a suspicious smile. "You sure are going to a lot of trouble for this girl."

"She's Shea's friend. What am I supposed to do?"

Wes nodded his head in that way he had, as if he were trying to appear wise. "You like her."

"I do not!" Mary Paris was everything Clint didn't want in a woman. She was out to save the world, didn't trust anyone, carried her guns as if this were the Old West and she was the town marshal. She would never find any satisfaction in the things he wanted from life. If she hadn't been searching for her serial killer, being on the ranch for more than a week probably would have driven her bonkers.

"You like her a little bit," Wes added in a lowered voice.

Clint shrugged. "Maybe a little," he admitted.

"Otherwise you would've told her a week ago that this is never going to work."

"She's not so bad."

"So I've noticed. Still…"

"I'm not going to let anyone get hurt," Clint promised.

"You're going to do her job and your own?"

Clint set down a half-empty coffee cup. "If I have to."

Katie and Wes had plans. Dinner with Katie's family; someone was having a birthday. It sounded as if Clint was going with them, which suited Mary just fine. As soon as everyone was gone, she was going to climb into bed and go to sleep. She didn't care that it wasn't even seven o'clock yet. She hurt all over and she needed a good night's sleep. Something like twelve hours. Maybe twenty-four.

But when dinner was over and it was time to go, Clint shooed Wes and Katie on their way and promised to finish the dishes himself.

"You're not going?" Mary asked as the back door closed on Wes and his pregnant wife.

"Nah," Clint said, rinsing the last of the dishes and placing them in the dishwasher. "Katie's family gets a little wild at these birthday shindigs."

"Too wild for a rodeo clown?" she asked with raised eyebrows.

He grinned and shifted his body slightly. It was very charming, very attractive. Her heart did a strange and unexpected flip. So did her stomach.

"Besides," he said, "I didn't like the idea of leaving you here all alone."

"I don't need a baby-sitter."

"I know." He closed the dishwasher and started it running, before turning to lean against the counter and face her dead-on. "You go right ahead and do your paperwork. I'll just watch a little TV and get to bed early."

He flashed her another one of those charming smiles.

Surely the man had a weakness. A flaw. A chink in his armor. Surely he did…but she hadn't found it.

Well, she could count the fact that she ached all over and he didn't as a flaw. He must've known that riding all day would leave her in pain. So, he had a small spiteful edge that he tried to hide from the world.

She wouldn't give him the satisfaction of knowing how much she hurt. That was her flaw. Pride. She turned her back on Clint and headed for the hallway.

"How about a glass of Miz Agatha's muscadine wine before you get to work?" he asked before she'd gotten far.

She wasn't a drinker, to be honest. She didn't have much tolerance for alcohol of any kind. But oh, a glass of wine might be as good as any painkiller. She could have a glass and then retire to her room. She might even pretend to work while she crawled under the quilt and slept and dreamed wine-induced dreams.

"Maybe one glass."

Clint reached into the cabinet. What he grabbed was nothing fancy, just little juice glasses that had once contained jelly. She smiled as he handed her the glasses and then reached into a high cabinet for a bottle. One of three, she saw as he snagged a bottle and swung it down.

She might be suspicious of his offer and wonder if he hadn't felt a moment of that inappropriate attraction this morning when he'd shown her to her bedroom, but jelly glasses with cartoon ducks on them and homemade wine hardly made for a well-planned seduction.

"You want to take this to the den?" he asked. "We might be able to find something on TV."

"Sure."

He followed her into the den, and she was very careful not to walk as if she hurt all over. Somehow letting Clint know that she couldn't do everything he could rankled her. She didn't want to let him know that she ached.

She placed the jelly glasses on the coffee table, and Clint snagged the remote and turned on the television. While he poured the dark red wine into the glasses, Mary channel surfed, looking for an interesting show to kill some time. A movie, maybe, or something funny. She could use something funny right about now. No clowns, though. She really wasn't in the mood for clowns.

They sat at opposite ends of the couch and watched a few minutes of a really bad movie. Since Mary didn't handle her alcohol well, she steered clear of drinks with lunch or dinner, especially when the meeting concerned business. One beer was her limit. Goodness knows she didn't want to end up acting goofy around Clint Sinclair! Fortunately, the wine was sweet and didn't seem to be going to her head. And it did help her aches and pains.

Clint seemed to be paying attention to the movie, so his sudden statement caught her by surprise. "I really think you should reconsider the Rodeo Queen bit."

Mary didn't even glance his way. "No."

"You're gonna get hurt," he added in a kind voice.

"I hope not, but if I do I can handle it."

He sighed and poured more wine into his jelly glass. When he hefted the bottle in her direction she held out her own glass. "I think we're going to have to try something new," he said.

Something new. She could barely handle the old stuff! "Like what?"

"I'm going to put you in the barrel."

She didn't know what that meant, but she didn't like the sound of it. "You can try," she said in a voice colored with warning.

Clint smiled. "You said you'd watched rodeo films."

"Yep."

"The clown in the big white thing in the center of the arena? That's the barrel man."

"Oh," she said, taking a long swig of the sweet wine. It didn't taste at all like alcohol. "So I've trained for the past week for nothing."

"No. It's still a dangerous job, and you need to know everything I taught you. But when things get hairy and the bull charges the barrel, you duck down and you're protected. You might get knocked around a bit, but it's better than being out in the open."

"Barrel woman," she said, testing the sound of it on her tongue.

"The problem is, Oliver's had the same barrel man for the past five years. He's not going to like the idea of replacing Eugene."

"How are you going to convince him to do that?"

Clint drained his glass before answering. "I don't know." He placed his heels on the coffee table and Mary did the same. Somehow her white tennis shoes looked tiny next to Clint's scuffed cowboy boots.

Her aches didn't seem so bad at the moment, though the soreness in her butt was still there to remind her of the day on horseback. She squirmed on the couch, trying to get more comfortable.

"Will we be riding tomorrow?" she asked.

"Maybe in the afternoon, if you want to," he said. She glanced at him and caught a glimpse of his telling expression. How could a smile be innocent and wicked at the same time? Clint Sinclair managed.

"We can go riding first thing in the morning," she said, already dreading getting into the saddle again. "Today's ride was quite invigorating."

Clint shook his head. "Don't you ever say uncle?"

"Nope," she said. "Never." Somewhere along the way he'd refilled her glass. It was full again.

"I can't go in the morning," he said. "Too bad."

"Why not?" she asked as she took another sip.

"I promised Miz Emily I'd be in church next Sunday. There's this hymn she wants the choir to sing, and she wanted to make sure all the men would be there. Apparently it just doesn't sound right otherwise. She's dragging us all in for choir practice tomorrow. She wants to meet early, before Bob and Marty have to be at work."

Mary rotated her head slowly to look squarely at Sinclair. "You *sing*," she said.

"Not very well," he admitted. "And not often. But it's a small church and…"

"And Miz Emily coerced you," she interrupted, trying to imitate Clint's Southern drawl. "What did she do? Bat her lashes and promise you a dance or two at the roadhouse so you'd sing in her choir?"

"Actually, she promised me peach cobbler."

"I'll bet she's just your type." Apparently the wine had loosened her tongue a bit. "What was it you said you wanted? Some simple country woman who likes simple things. I'm sure being able to cook a peach cobbler is high on your list of requirements."

Clint grinned widely. "I never thought of that, but yeah…she's just my type. Sweet and sunny. Loves to cook. On a nice day you can find her outside tending her garden and taking great pleasure in it. She's not the type who would be interested in taking off with me on a moment's notice, though. She's more of a homebody. Still…what man wouldn't consider himself lucky to have a woman like Miz Emily to come home to?"

Mary snorted.

"Unfortunately, she's eighty-two years old and stands about four foot seven. She's too short for me."

Mary took a deep breath as she processed this information. She'd done it again. She'd made a fool out of herself by assuming the worst about Clint Sinclair. "All right," she said skeptically. "What is it?"

"What's what?"

"You have to have a flaw," she said, snapping at him. "I've been here for more than a week, and in all that time you've been sweet and helpful and you haven't made one crude, sexist remark." She stopped. "Except the girl and darlin' stuff, and damned if I haven't started to get used to that. You take care of your friends, you sing for old ladies, you're helping me because your sister asked you to and you'd do anything for your family." Her mind spun as she shook her head. "No one is perfect, Sinclair. No one. Not even you. So, why don't you just tell me straight out what your flaw is." Maybe then she wouldn't lie awake at night trying to imagine what it was.

"My flaw," he said.

"The blemish on your apparently impeccable character. What the hell is it?" Every man had one...no, every man had several. Some more than others.

She'd practically told him she thought he was perfect. Any other man would have thrown that in her face with a smarmy grin. Not Sinclair. He was so unexpectedly real. There was no artifice in him, no massive ego she had to fight past to see who he really was.

"I have plenty of flaws. I'm only human."

"Prove it," she said in a challenging voice.

He moved toward her, slowly sliding across the couch so that they were almost thigh to thigh. Mary's heart kicked. She'd been close to Clint before, she'd been close to him all week. Why did *this* closeness make her bones quiver? He placed his jelly glass on the coffee table and took hers from her hand to set it beside his.

Surely he wasn't going to…he wouldn't even think of being so foolish…

But he was so foolish. Clint Sinclair shifted his long body, tilted his head. He gazed at her face, his lips parted slightly. Mary could actually feel the sexual energy that danced between them. Like it or not, that energy was not all Clint's; it was hers and his, mingling, charging the air they breathed. She didn't want this, she didn't need it…all she had to do was tell Clint to back off, and he would.

A man didn't look at a woman like this unless he meant business. Mary said nothing. She didn't move, she barely breathed.

He leaned down and kissed her, laying his soft lips over hers. She could've backed away from the gentle caress, but she didn't. For a moment Mary held her breath, shocked at the sensations that rippled through her body, surprised by the power in something so simple as a kiss. It had been such a long time…

Clint was a wonderful kisser, of course. His lips were firm, but not hard. Soft, but not *too* soft. He moved those lips just enough; not holding anything back, but not pushing too hard. It was a perfect kiss.

Then again, maybe it was the wine that made her body grow warm and her mind spin. Mary searched for an explanation for her response to the kiss. Maybe it was the wine that made the ache in her body shift.

Clint didn't push and shove, he didn't lean over her possessively and lay wandering hands on her body. There was no grabbing, no testing of her boundaries. Their lips touched; nothing more. His mouth moved, and after a moment so did hers. It seemed like forever since she'd had a proper kiss. She hadn't realized how hungry she'd been for this touch. The kiss grabbed her down deep, took hold, made her desire more in an unexpected way.

Yes, she was waking up. Feeling. Wanting. A part of her wanted to draw away and reach for the numbness that had protected her for the past two years. But something stronger craved more. More warmth. More thrilling contact. Her lips searched and tasted, and she gratefully closed her eyes and allowed herself to simply feel.

Mary felt as if she'd been starving, and this kiss fed her. She was the one to reach out and touch the man who kissed her, to grasp the front of his shirt in one fist so she'd have something solid to hold on to. Solid and real, that was Clint.

When he took his mouth from hers it was with obvious reluctance. Maybe the kiss had grabbed him, too.

"I can't believe I'm kissing a clown," she said, her voice a surprisingly husky whisper.

"Neither can I," Clint said, his voice as raspy as hers. He came back toward her but stopped when his lips were almost on hers. He hesitated.

"My flaw," he whispered. His hand came to her face, his thumb traced her jaw. "I always fall for the wrong woman."

Chapter 5

Clint threw himself into the menial task that sometimes relaxed him: cleaning the barn. Most people hated cleaning out a barn. He not only didn't mind, there was something soothing about the chore.

He had Wes showing Mary how to apply the grease-paint she'd have to wear. When he'd left the house they'd been situated in the dining room, tools and face paint spread across the long table while they laughed at Mary's initial attempts.

It had been two days since he'd made the mistake of kissing her, and even though he knew nothing could come of this churning in his gut, he couldn't get what he wanted off his mind.

He hadn't been teasing when he'd told Mary he always fell for the wrong woman.

In his younger days he'd made his share of mistakes, being drawn to the flash and finding out too late there wasn't much else *but* flash. He'd been too quick to fall for a pretty face, as young men were. He'd only had to fall once to learn his lesson.

Tonya had been the last. She'd been the perfect girl-friend for a while. As beautiful as they come, apparently devoted, supportive and loving and attentive. She wanted everything he did. Or at least she said she did.

He'd asked her to marry him that night before his last bull ride, and she'd said yes with a squeal and a kiss and a promise of something more to come after the rodeo was over. But they'd never had that night. He'd been thrown and the bull had turned on him. One of the bullfighters and Clint had ended up in the hospital.

Clint couldn't remember exactly what had happened after the chute had opened and the bull had bucked. Those few seconds were lost to him, and they always would be. He imagined it was just as well. Besides, enough people had described the accident to him. The way he'd been thrown, the way the bull had turned, the unexpected and potentially lethal attack of an angry animal.

The injury had been so serious he'd ended up lying in that hospital bed thinking about retirement. Why not? He had Tonya, enough money to start the horse farm he wanted and he was alive. He was determined never to sit on a bull's back again. At the time, he'd had more than his fill of the rodeo.

When he'd told Tonya he was going to give the rodeo up and settle down, she'd tried to talk him out of it. At first anyway. When he'd finally made her understand that he was done with the rodeo, finished, ready to move on to another part of his life, she'd returned his ring and left him lying there physically unable to chase after her. With a few direct words she'd made it clear she didn't want a horse farmer as a husband. She wanted a bull rider, a rodeo star.

All his plans, and the woman of his dreams had turned out to be nothing more than a buckle bunny.

In her own way Mary was as wrong for him as Tonya had been. She was here because her job demanded it, and if she had her choice she would stay far away from the kind of life he wanted. She tolerated him, she even kissed as if she wanted him. But she wasn't the kind of woman who would stay.

The last thing he needed was to fall for a woman who wouldn't stay.

If he went to his family for advice—which he wouldn't—he knew what they'd say. Shea would advise him to marry the woman who had gotten under his skin, ASAP. Boone would tell him to sleep with Mary and get her out of his system. Until he'd met his wife, Boone was of the mind that all women were basically alike, and any one would do on a given night.

Dean's advice would be more complicated, and might even make sense. There would probably be a list of pros and cons presented, as well as a few scary scenarios. In the end, big brother would insist that since Clint knew he and Mary were wrong for each other, he needed to keep his distance. Dean was big on responsibility and thinking things through and planning ahead. Yeah, Dean always made more sense.

But Dean's life, from everything Clint could see, was dull as ditch water. At least Boone managed to have a little fun along the way.

"Ta-da!"

Clint turned around, shovel in hand, to see Mary standing in the open doorway of the barn. Wes was right behind her, a wide smile on his face.

Mary's face was painted in white and red, with touches

of black here and there. She wore a red wig, complete with long, braided pigtails, and a smile as wide as Wes's.

He couldn't help but smile back. "Cute."

"Thank you."

"Now all we need is a name."

"I have a name," Mary protested. "Just in case someone decides to poke around, I'll use my mother's maiden…"

"Mary Mary Quite Contrary," Clint interrupted.

"Well, that's kind of insulting," she said, not acting at all insulted. "What's your clown name? Giggles? Slappy? Smiley?"

"Clint Sinclair," he answered.

Sensing trouble, Wes slunk away as Mary stepped into the barn. "Why do you get to have a normal name, while I have to be Mary Mary Quite Contrary?"

"Because I'm a bullfighter and you're a barrel man."

"I thought you said Brisco had a barrel man."

"I'm taking care of that."

She shook her head and those red pigtails went dancing. How could he want her even now? She looked ridiculous. Silly. Not at all the gorgeous woman he knew her to be.

"I don't want to cost anyone their place," she said.

"You won't."

"You can find the old barrel man another job?"

"Yep."

She cocked her head and smiled. "Mary Mary? It doesn't seem fair."

"Life isn't fair," he said as she came closer. "And besides, you are contrary."

She opened her mouth.

"Don't try to deny it."

Mary closed her mouth and smiled again. Hadn't there been a time when he'd thought he'd give anything to see her grin like this? He hadn't known that smile would grab him, deep and hard.

Knowing what his family would advise him to do, Clint decided that Boone probably made more sense than the others. That was a first.

"You're almost ready," he said.

"Almost? What's left?"

Mary stopped when she stood a few feet away from him. Neither of them had mentioned the kiss. They'd continued on as if it hadn't happened, trying to pretend that nothing had changed, trying to pretend that this was still a purely professional relationship. Was she even half as wary as he was? She didn't seem like the kind of woman who would flirt and tease. No, she was all business, all the time.

That kiss had been very unbusinesslike.

"A friend of mine has a bull," he said calmly. "Not a rodeo bull, but you do need to get up close and personal before we head to Birmingham."

Did Mary realize that she drew up her chin and stiffened her spine? She gave herself away. Like it or not, she was scared. "When?"

"This afternoon."

She nodded, but something in the air had changed. The physical attraction between them was still there, crackling and alive and almost tangible, but Mary's fear made everything feel different.

"There's still time to back out of this," he said.

"No," she snapped. "I can't do that."

"Surely there's another way—"

"No!"

He wasn't surprised by her reaction. "Mary Mary Quite Contrary." He reached out to touch her face, to run his thumb through the white greasepaint on her jaw.

"It's important to me," she said softly, not stepping away from his touch or slapping his hand away, as she would have a week ago.

He wiped a trace of the greasepaint from her face, trailing his finger to her chin. "I know, but that doesn't mean I have to like it."

"I'm a grown woman, Clint. I can take care of myself."

Clint was definitely a step up from a coldly delivered Sinclair or a sassy Giggles. And yet, nothing had changed. Mary was in charge and she didn't want any man to protect her. She was as stubborn as any bull.

"I just have a bad feeling about this."

He had a bad feeling about everything. Mary's insistence on going to the rodeo as a clown; his growing need to protect her in spite of her objections; his urge to kiss her, right now.

His hand drifted upward and his thumb wiped away the white greasepaint that covered Mary's lips. They were fine lips, finer than he had realized when he'd first seen her. Those lips were full and well shaped and soft. Silky. Begging to be kissed.

Surrendering, he leaned down and laid his mouth over hers. Easy, soft, a questioning kiss. She wasn't fuzzy-headed with muscadine wine this time, and she might very well give him a shove and an order to back off.

She didn't. Mary kissed him back, her eyes drifting closed.

Clint tugged off the red wig and placed his arms around Mary, pulling her close. Her body fit nicely against his, the way a woman's might. She was stiff for a moment, her body not as immediately welcoming as her mouth had been. But then she relaxed. He felt it, as though a wave of ease washed through her body. Her arms snaked around his waist, her lips parted and softened.

He flicked the tip of his tongue into her mouth and she moaned, deep in her throat. He wasn't the only one here flirting with surrender.

Yeah, Boone's advice was definitely the way to go.

It was Mary who pulled away first, dropping her arms, turning her head and breaking the contact of mouth to mouth. Her makeup was smeared, her lips au naturel and well kissed. When she looked up at him again, she grinned. "You're wearing almost as much greasepaint as I am."

He raked his thumb across his face, finding traces of makeup here and there.

"Your nose is red," Mary said, pointing at her own red nose.

Clint did his best to wipe away the greasepaint, and Mary even reached out a hand to help him, wiping away a speck of white from his cheek.

"This is not a good idea," she said softly as she found another smear of greasepaint on his chin and wiped it away.

"I know."

"It's just…working together all the time, and living in the same house, and…I'm sure it's perfectly natural." She sounded as if she was reasoning with herself, not him.

"Is it?"

"That has to be it."

Yeah, there had to be a reasonable explanation. Special Agent Mary Paris couldn't possibly fall for a rodeo clown who lived out in the boonies. When he looked into the night sky he saw stars, she saw space-age technology. He couldn't believe anyone he knew could ever do the things her serial killer had done. She saw the possibility of darkness in everyone she met.

In the end, it didn't matter how much he wanted her. There would be no surrender. They didn't have a chance.

The farm they'd driven to was less than half an hour away and in many ways was similar to Clint's place. Rolling fields, old trees, low mountains in the background. But there were cows everywhere here, and the farmhouse was older. It was white and sturdy-looking, very Southern, but not as impressive as Clint's house.

His friend, the owner of this gentle farm, had left them to their own devices. It was just Clint, Mary, a barrel and a bull named Sweetness.

This was her own plan, Mary thought as she watched Clint saunter over to Sweetness. She was not going to have second thoughts at this late date because the bull was bigger than she'd expected, because she didn't like the way he looked at her or because Clint Sinclair was a great kisser. None of that was relevant.

Clint actually reached out and touched the bull, who was not particularly happy to be with them. The animal snorted and kicked one hoof in the dust. Mary jumped. Clint did not.

"Always remember," he said in a soothing voice, "that the bull is an unpredictable animal. They're dangerous. Deadly, even. And they won't think twice about stomping you into the ground and breaking every bone in your body."

"You're not going to scare me into giving up," Mary retorted.

"Whether you give up or not," Clint said without turning to look at her, "you should be scared. Only an idiot would get close to a bull and not be scared."

"You don't look scared," she countered.

"I've been doing this for years," he said with a wink and a half smile. "I might not look scared, but I'm definitely anxious." With his hand on the bull's head, he stared at her. "Get on over here."

She couldn't very well say no! This was her reason for being here, and if she said no now, Clint would blackball her from the rodeo. She'd end up playing Rodeo Queen, big hair, red cowboy boots and all.

Moving cautiously, she headed for Clint and Sweetness. The bull laid its eyes on her suspiciously. Could a bull look suspicious? Of course it could.

"Every now and then you have to punch the bull on the nose to get his attention away from a cowboy," Clint said softly.

"You're kidding."

"Nope."

Mary studied Sweetness with a narrowed, critical eye. Clint said the bull was an unpredictable animal. Of course, he was right. That was especially true of a beast as large and obviously ornery as this one. "Why on earth would you punch a bull on the nose?"

"Your job is to distract the bull so the cowboy can get up off the ground and to safety. A cowboy is much too vulnerable, lying in the dirt after he's been thrown."

"So you make sure the bull is coming at you, not the cowboy."

Clint nodded. "Since you'll be in the barrel, you'll have to get the bull's attention by waving something that will catch its eye and making lots of noise. You try to draw the bull away from the rider, get it to charge you."

Her mouth went dry. Surely there was a smart comeback for that, but at the moment her mind was blank. "No problem," she said, almost choking on the words.

Sweetness snorted and Mary took a quick step back.

Jumping fences and riding horses until her butt went numb was a piece of cake next to this.

Clint looked at her as if he could see right through her, and he wasn't buying her display of bravery. "Sit on the fence," he said. "Or on the other side, if you feel better there."

Mary retreated to the fence and sat on the top. She really would feel safer standing on the other side of the fence, but she didn't want Clint to know that.

Clint turned his back on the bull and headed for the barrel. With an agility she had come to expect from him, he jumped onto the top of the barrel, his feet braced on either side of the rim.

"This is the safest place to be when you're in the arena."

"On top of the barrel?" she asked, trying for a flippant tone.

In a flash, Clint dropped down and disappeared into the tall white barrel, before standing so that he was exposed from the chest up. "Like everything else, you have to be quick. You have to get the bull's attention, and when he charges you drop down. The bull will most likely hit the barrel and you'll roll. You'll get tossed around, bruised, jostled like you can't imagine."

"Sounds like a great job."

"Mary…"

"Sorry."

Clint spent the next half hour goading Sweetness, but the bull was having none of it. Except for a gentle nudge against the barrel, Sweetness lived up to his name.

Finally Clint gave up and walked to the fence. "Your turn," he said, offering a hand and urging Mary from her seat.

"My turn to do what?"

He led her to the barrel. Climbing in was a chore, and she didn't accomplish it without help from Clint. He wasn't happy about that, even when she explained that she only had a problem because she wasn't as tall as he was. When she was in the barrel, getting out was a problem.

Clint was not pleased.

"I'll work on it," she said. "We still have a few days."

A few days. She had been so sure she could learn everything she needed to know in a week or less! Her schooling in the rodeo arts had been more complicated than she'd imagined and more physically demanding than she could have dreamed.

Clint assisted her out of the barrel and onto the ground, where her feet once again met good, solid dirt. "I'll practice getting in and out of the barrel," she said again. "I only have to get in once, right? I don't really have to stand on top like you did. Right?"

"Sure," he said, not sounding at all convinced.

"I'll be fine. I can do—"

"I've heard this before," Clint said sharply. "If I can do it, you can do it."

"That's right." Mary lifted her chin slightly. If he wanted to argue about this, she was ready.

The bull ambled their way, and movement out of the corner of Mary's eyes took her attention away from any potential argument with Clint Sinclair. The bull was *huge!* And it was headed straight for them.

Clint stepped between Mary and the bull. "Go," he said.

"I'm going to have to get used to this." Besides, Sweetness didn't look like he was going to do them any harm. He just wanted to say hello. "There's no reason to run."

Sweetness snorted.

"Okay," Mary said. "I'll wait on the fence." Or perhaps on the other side.

When she was standing safely behind the fence, Clint patted the bull on the neck and headed her way. How could he turn his back on that animal! He kept his eyes on her, not once glancing over his shoulder to see if Sweetness followed.

He vaulted over the fence. "You're not ready," he said as he headed for his truck.

"I am!" Mary said as she followed him. He didn't glance over his shoulder to look at her either. He should have. He should fear her much more than a bull named Sweetness.

When he reached his truck, he turned to face her, shaking his head as if she were a misbehaving child. "Why are you so determined to do this? It doesn't make any sense. There has to be a better way. Why you? Why not send a man in to do this job? Give me a reason, Mary. Make me understand."

The words were on her tongue and she swallowed. No one could know the truth about Elaine. No one. Especially not Clint. He had already seen a weakness in her—she liked him. She liked kissing him. If things were different she'd like more than a kiss. To tell him why she was so determined to do this herself…no, she wouldn't turn into a whining, clinging, weepy female!

When she didn't answer he climbed into the truck. She hurried to the passenger side, certain that he'd leave her stranded here if she didn't.

Katie and Wes had gone to bed early and Mary had been not long behind them. The house was quiet when

Clint made his way to the kitchen phone and dialed Eugene's number.

The barrel man answered with a hearty hello.

"Eugene? This is Clint."

The barrel man laughed. "Want to give me more money to pretend I've got a twisted ankle and hobble around while you fellas do all the work? I tell you, that's the best deal I've ever gotten."

"Actually," Clint said, hoping he didn't sound as sheepish as he felt. "I'm calling to make sure you show up in Birmingham fit as a fiddle and ready to work."

"The deal is off?" Eugene asked too loudly. "What was it, a joke?"

"No, no. And I'll still pay you, just...she's not ready. She'll never be ready."

"She?" Eugene asked, again too loud.

"Yeah," Clint answered.

"It's a good thing you called me back. Oliver woulda had a heart attack if you showed up with a girl clown in tow."

"I know. She's good," he said defensively. "She's better than I thought she'd be when we first got started, but..."

"But what?" Eugene urged.

But I like her too much to worry about her for six weeks. She's quick but she's not quick enough. She's good, but she's not good enough. She's going to kill me when I tell her what I've gotta do. "She's just not there, you know?"

"I know," Eugene said, as if they were commiserating. "Man, she must be some piece if she's got you even thinking about dragging her along for the summer."

"It's not like that," Clint said quickly. "She's a friend of my sister. That's all."

"Definitely not worth all this trouble," Eugene said.

"Nope."

"Well, I'll see you in Birmingham," Eugene said brightly.

If I live that long.

Mary left her bedside lamp off and dialed by the light of the cell phone. Lewis answered on the second ring.

"How are things at the circus?" he answered. Of course, he had seen her number on his caller ID.

"Rodeo," she said. "Not circus. And everything's fine."

"What's up?"

She and Lewis had been e-mailing fairly often. He was, after all, her sometimes-partner and her friend. The call wasn't necessary. How could she tell him that she'd called because she needed to be reminded of who she was? That she was beginning to like it here?

"How's the baby, Papa?" she asked.

"Oh, he's fine. Fat and happy, sleeps and eats and fills his diapers. What a life."

"And Judy?"

"She's doing great."

If there were more guys like Lewis in the world, she might actually consider getting married again one day. He was solid as a rock, loved his wife to distraction and adored his kids. He was honest, dependable and occasionally funny, though never quite as funny as he *thought* he was.

Rick had been that kind of man. Steady. Good. Before she'd met him, she'd had a couple of bad experiences with men...boys, more honestly...who were not so kind. Oh, they could put on a nice face, they knew how to say what a girl wanted to hear. But they weren't good through and through. Not like Rick. Mary blinked away unexpected tears. She didn't think about her husband often. It hurt too much.

It occurred to her that Clint had some of those qualities. Maybe that's why Rick had been so very much on her mind lately. She shook off the memories, old and new, and gave Lewis her full attention.

"You have a couple more weeks of leave, don't you?"

"Yeah," he answered. "The time off has been great, but I'm itching to get back to work. How's the clown treating you?"

"Fine," she whispered. Clint was around, somewhere. After she'd gone to bed, she'd heard him puttering around the house. Right now he was in the kitchen, she thought.

"So," Lewis continued, more relaxed—or so it seemed by the sound of his voice. "What's this clown really like? You haven't said much about him in your e-mails, only that he's been *helpful*." He managed to say that last word with disdain.

"He has been helpful," she said defensively.

"And?" Lewis prodded. He would not be satisfied with anything vague, and he certainly wouldn't allow her to ignore the question. He'd always been like a big brother, and since Rick's death he'd been downright protective. Overly protective at times.

Mary sighed. "Sinclair's a stand-up guy. He's honest, works hard, lives fast. He's actually rather charming, in a good ol' boy kind of way. You'd like him."

"How charming?" Lewis asked, breezing right past the other attributes she'd listed.

She didn't dare tell him, or anyone else, that she had

actually kissed Clint. "Charming enough," she admitted in an offhand way, "but nothing I can't handle."

"I don't doubt that," Lewis said. "Look, Judy's doing great, much better than she did with Donnie. I don't need any more time here at home. To be honest, the boys are driving me a little nuts. I could stand to get out of the house for a bit. I can head out of here in a couple of days, hook up with you in Birmingham, check out this charming clown of yours for myself, back you up—"

"No," she interrupted. "I'm not doing anything more than nosing around. You'd be bored silly."

Lewis sighed into the phone. "Why do I have a hard time believing that?"

He knew her too well…but he didn't know about Elaine. "I'm too smart to get in too deep while I'm on my own." Her heart fluttered. Was that a lie? "Everything's going great. If I find anything when I join the rodeo, I'll call you and then I'll call Josh." She took a deep breath. "Maybe my theory is wrong and there's nothing to find."

"You don't believe that," he muttered. "If you did, you wouldn't be there."

"I'm fine. Enjoy your time with Judy and the baby and forget about me."

Lewis had everything Mary had convinced herself she didn't want. Marriage, babies, the whole nine yards. She never felt jealousy or even a touch of envy when he talked about his family. So why now?

She had made her choice. With Rick gone, she didn't expect to have any of those things. He had been her one chance to have all those things every woman wanted, and her fear of being a terrible mother and a drunk driver had taken all those dreams away. All of them. Gone. Dead. Not for her, not now, not ever.

"I don't like you being there alone," Lewis said in a lowered voice.

"I'm not alone," she said too brightly. "I have Bozo to keep me company."

"Why don't you go to Florida and get a tan. Wait awhile. Do a little more research off site and see if we can come up with something concrete. I'll back you up with this theory, you know I will."

She couldn't wait. Six weeks and the summer tour would be over. If she was right, two more women would be dead. "I'm just going to poke around the rodeo a little. Should be more fun than getting a sunburn and sand in my bathing suit."

"You gather information, and that's it."

"I know, I know. Josh reminds me by e-mail at least twice a week."

"Just be careful," Lewis warned.

"You know me, Lewis. I'm always careful."

When Mary ended the call, she didn't feel any better than she had when she'd crawled into this bed. And when Clint shuffled down the hallway an hour later, she was still wide awake.

Chapter 6

On Saturday night they'd gone to the roadhouse again. Mary had danced with Clint, but not so many times that people might talk. He'd also danced with a couple of other women, but never with Katie's friend Tracy.

On Sunday morning, Mary had put on *tasteful* makeup and one of her conservative suits and gone to church with Clint, Wes and Katie—ignoring Clint's protests. No wonder he'd tried to make her stay home! He might sing in the choir to appease Miz Emily, but he wasn't very good. Since the rest of the choir was no better, he fit in nicely.

They spent the next couple of days working long hours, getting ready for their trip to Birmingham. With each passing day, Mary grew more anxious. The adrenaline was pumping, her mind was spinning. She knew the feeling well; she was preparing to do battle.

She loved her job.

Clint had not been his usual self for the past two or three days. He'd been almost distant, his thoughts defi-

nitely elsewhere. Jokes had been few and far between, and
he neatly ignored their two kisses, as did she. He had
something on his mind. Something he did not want to
share.

Mary helped Katie with the supper dishes. The pregnant
woman had protested that a guest should not be doing
chores, but Mary insisted. When Mary insisted, she got
what she wanted.

"Are you excited?" Katie asked as she rinsed off a
plate.

"Sure," Mary said truthfully. "Tomorrow is the day."
She felt her heart pumping, and it seemed that every color,
every sound, was more intense and precise than it had
been yesterday.

"I never knew a girl who wanted to be a rodeo clown
before."

Mary didn't bother to tell Katie that she was not a girl.
There hadn't been any insult intended, she knew that. "It
should be fun," she said simply.

Katie grinned widely. "You sound just like Clint."

Without pausing in her drying chores, Mary asked, "I
do?"

"Yep. He's always got to have something going on,
you know what I mean? He spends plenty of time here at
the ranch, and I think he loves it. But after a while he's
got to go off somewhere and do something exciting."

Like white-water rafting, or being a rodeo clown. Or
falling for the wrong woman. "He's here at the ranch
most of the time, though, right?"

"I guess," Katie answered, as if she were not quite
sure of her answer. "But after a while he gets antsy, you
know? He starts to fidget."

She could understand that. It was one of the reasons
why she loved being a part of a flying squad. No desk for

her…at least, not for very long. Maybe Clint was a kindred spirit, a like-minded sort, a…what was she thinking?

"When Clint settles down and gets married that will change." Mary nodded her head and made herself imagine the life Clint would someday make for himself here at this ranch. The little woman, a herd of children. Peach cobbler and racing horses. The roller coaster.

"I don't know," Katie said skeptically. "A man is what he is, you know? I can't see Clint ever really settling down."

Again, something they had in common.

Anxious to change the subject, Mary nodded to Katie's rounded belly. "Are you getting anxious?" She knew the answer to that question, from the way Katie talked about her unborn child.

The mother-to-be grinned widely. "I can hardly wait. Just a little over two months, that's the day. Wes is so tickled that it's going to be a boy. He always said he wanted our first child to be a son."

"What about you?"

The girl blushed. "When I found out I was pregnant, I didn't care if it was a boy or a girl. All I ever wanted was a healthy baby. But when the doctor told us the baby was a boy, I got so excited." In a lower voice she added, "We're going to name the baby after my daddy."

"That's nice."

Mary spared no more than a passing glance for Katie's rounded belly. A baby was no longer a part of her plan. It didn't fit in, not anywhere. And still, there was a small twinge of unexpected…disappointment.

They finished cleaning the kitchen in record time, once their conversation was over and they turned their attentions to the simple tasks. Katie went to bed early, these days, and Mary needed to finish packing.

Come tomorrow, she was going to begin her career in the rodeo.

It was a great night for a meteor shower, the sky clear and the city lights so far away they didn't dare intrude upon the spectacle. All was quiet. Even Mutt was asleep. Clint was the only one interested in staying up past midnight to see the best of the display.

He couldn't sleep anyway. Tomorrow morning he and Mary were supposed to head for Birmingham to prepare for the first show of the summer tour. And he hadn't told her yet that she wasn't going to be the barrel man, that he couldn't throw her into the arena and wait for her to get hurt. She was going to be furious when she found out.

Since sleep was impossible, he might as well lie here and enjoy the view.

The pickup-truck bed was hard, but he'd thrown a folded blanket under his head and was comfortable enough. A meteor streaked across the sky, leaving a spectacular trail before fading into nothing. He'd always checked on when the meteor showers would be visible, even when he'd been a kid. Dean and Boone had not been interested, but many nights he and Shea had sneaked out of the house and found a nearby spot where the lights didn't interfere with the view too much. They'd lived in a residential neighborhood, though, so there had always been streetlights and porch lamps to cast light into the night, muting the view.

Nothing muted the view here. The stars were sharp, the sky black, the shooting stars spectacular.

He couldn't keep his mind on the display in the sky. How would he tell Mary that she wasn't going to be a rodeo clown? He should have known from the first day that it wouldn't work. She was in great shape, she'd learned a lot in two weeks and he knew a few bullfighters who were no better than she was. She might even get a job on her own, if she played her cards just right.

But she wasn't good enough. He couldn't spend the next six weeks worried about whether or not she was going to get herself or someone else hurt. Out of the arena, when she was hunting her serial killer—he might not like it, but that was her business. This was his.

She was going to be livid.

A fair head came into view, a voice whispered, "Hi."

"You decided to join me after all," he said, sitting up as Mary approached the truck.

"Couldn't sleep," she said, tilting her head back to look up. "I figured I might as well check it out. I've never seen a meteor shower before." She waited half a minute. "Where is it?"

"Be patient."

A moment later, a shooting star streaked across the sky.

"Wow," Mary whispered.

"Climb in," Clint said, scooting to one side and pushing the blanket he'd been using as a pillow over for Mary.

"I'm fine," she said, almost suspiciously.

Clint lay back with his hands beneath his head. "Whatever you want. You will get a crick in your neck if you stand like that too long, though."

For a few minutes, she stubbornly stood by the side of the truck, oohing when another meteorite left a trail across the night sky, shuffling her feet when she began to get uncomfortable. "Okay," she finally said, climbing up and over the tailgate. She'd taken the time to dress in worn blue jeans and a dark blue T-shirt. "As long as you behave yourself," she teased.

"I always behave myself," he said as she reclined beside him.

"Almost always," she responded in a soft voice.

For a little while they lay there, side by side, commenting only when the meteor shower gave them something to ooh and aah about. The night was warm, but a nice breeze kept it from being hot, the way summer nights in Alabama could be.

Now would be the best time to tell her, Clint imagined. *Nice meteor. Great night. Oh, by the way, you don't have a job with the Brisco Rodeo because I made damn sure the barrel man will be there ready to work.*

"I never did thank you," Mary said, her voice velvety soft to match the mood of the night.

"For what?"

"You didn't have to do any of this." She rolled over and propped herself up on one elbow. "I know it's been a royal pain, to teach someone who doesn't know anything about the rodeo to be a bullfighter. You could have sent me packing any time in the past two weeks. You could have refused to help that night at Shea's house."

"I probably should have," he admitted, dreading telling her the truth.

"Yeah, but you didn't," she whispered.

Mary fell back and stared up at the night sky, waiting for another shooting star. Her breasts rose and fell steadily, her pale cheek and bright hair caught what light there was on this dark night. She was so beautiful. He wanted to kiss her, one more time, before she kicked his ass.

Clint rolled toward her. "Don't thank me."

Mary looked up at him. Two weeks ago, there had been no way she'd lie beside him this way. Suspicious, always on guard, she would have felt the need to rise up herself, to make sure they were nose to nose. Two weeks ago, she would have been wearing at least one weapon.

Tonight she wasn't armed. Somehow, in the past two weeks she had started to trust him. And he was going to blow it, big time.

But first he was going to kiss her. He lowered his head, moving slowly and giving her plenty of time to move away. She didn't. He hadn't thought she would. She was drawn to him the same way he was drawn to her. Strongly, reluctantly. And yeah, it was nice.

While he kissed Mary, her arms circled his neck. She kissed him back.

This time she didn't taste like muscadine wine or greasepaint. She tasted like a woman; she tasted like Mary. Lord, he loved the way she tested his lips with her tongue, the way the tips of her fingers brushed through his hair. Every touch was soft and easy, so gentle and yet tinged with hunger.

He was tumbling, falling like one of the meteors in the sky. And he had just about as much control.

He waited for Mary to remember that there were satellites in the sky, invisible eyes looking down, but she seemed to have forgotten about her space-age technology. She just kissed him, deeper, longer and more demanding.

More than anything, he wanted to make love to Mary here and now. Before he ruined everything with the truth.

Mary tried to convince herself that Clint really wasn't such a great kisser. It had just been so long since she'd let a man hold and kiss her this way she'd forgotten how wonderful it could be. Warm. Tingly. Outrageously sensual. Who was she kidding? He really was a great kisser. She relaxed and let herself enjoy.

He'd kissed her before, but this was more than a kiss.

It touched her in a way she had not expected to be touched, ever again.

His hand slipped under her T-shirt, firm, gentle fingers raking across skin that had been unexplored for so long. He was tentative at first, as if he thought she might push him away. She didn't. She deepened the kiss a little, and his hand delved beneath the shirt to cup her bra-covered breasts, one and then the other. Clint Sinclair had well-shaped, large, warm hands that were tender and not at all clumsy. Was there anything clumsy about this man? Of course not.

Had she come out here hoping for this? Hoping that he would kiss her? Touch her? She didn't want to think about what was happening, what might yet happen. She simply wanted to feel again.

Clint rolled her onto her side, never breaking the kiss, and his free hand reached around and under her shirt. With a single flick of his fingers, he unfastened her bra.

Deft fingers moved the undergarment aside, and then Clint's hand was on her bare breast, cupping, caressing, his thumb flicking over the sensitive nipple that was already hard.

He was moving too fast, but she didn't mind. It was right. Good. She thought about what Katie had said about Clint never being satisfied. That wasn't true. He just wanted more from life than most men. He wanted everything faster, higher, hotter and closer.

So did she.

Mary's insides clenched and unclenched. She wanted Clint. She really shouldn't, it wasn't a good idea…but her body wanted his in a way she had not imagined possible. Oh, if she thought about this too long and hard she would run. She didn't want to run.

Mary untucked Clint's shirt and laid her hand against his flat, bare stomach. She felt him quiver at her touch.

The kiss was interrupted for a moment. Clint pulled her shirt over her head and slipped off the bra. Night air touched her naked skin, her back and her breasts. It was a new sensation, luscious and forbidden. She unbuttoned his shirt, kissing his neck while she worked her way down, parting her lips to suck gently at his flesh, to taste his sweat on this too-warm night.

She removed Clint's shirt and dropped it to the side, and when that was done he kissed her neck. His lips were warm and gentle, his tongue teasing. It was a kiss Mary felt to her bones, and beyond. While he continued to lavish attention on her neck, his hands caressed her breasts. His palm learned the shape of her, his fingers teased the nipples. Heaven help her, she could come apart here and now.

This was *definitely* faster, higher, hotter and closer. And still, not close enough. Mary squirmed as she struggled gently to find a position that brought Clint even closer. Their tongues danced, delighting in the sensations their bodies experienced and wanting more. Touching him was an experience in itself. Everything about Clint was hard and muscled, taut and smooth.

There was nothing but the night and sensation and a burning need. Burning. She was definitely burning. Clint unsnapped her jeans as neatly as he had unfastened her bra—with one flick of his fingers. He lowered the zipper, and in anticipation Mary felt a deep shudder ripple through her body.

In an instant, something in Clint changed. He slowed his once-frantic movements, his mouth came to hers for another long kiss. She could feel him pulling away from her, in a way she could not understand. It was as if they'd been on a speeding train, and for no reason that train was slowing down in the middle of nowhere.

"Mary," he whispered against her mouth. "I want you so much."

All she could manage was a hum of approval before she kissed him again.

"But before we go any further, there's something I have to tell you."

Those words weren't exactly a dash of cold water, but they were definitely not what she'd expected to hear. "Something that can't wait?" she asked.

"I wish it could wait." He brushed a strand of her hair back with one finger. "For a while there I convinced myself it could wait…but it can't."

"What is it?" she kissed him quickly, again.

He took a deep breath, kissed her one more time. "When I go to Birmingham tomorrow, you're not going with me."

That was a dash of cold water. "What?"

He placed his arms around her so they were bare chest to bare chest. "You're not ready. You're good, but you're not good enough."

"I am!" she insisted, pulling her body slightly away from his.

"You're not," he whispered. His head shook slightly. "I couldn't bear to see you hurt."

Mary's chin came up. She still trembled, she still ached. But she was also angry. Two weeks, wasted! "I can do my job."

"As an FBI agent? I'm sure you can. As a bullfighter?" He shook his head. "No."

"You could have told me this days ago and saved me some time." She shoved him away and grabbed her T-shirt, yanking it over her head.

"I just decided the other day," he said.

"You never intended to take me to the rodeo." She rose to her feet. "You've been leading me along, making me think you intended to hold up your end of the bargain, and all along this was just some…some game to you."

"That's not true." Clint stood, too, bare chested and too tall. "Last week I called the barrel man and offered to pay him to fake an injury."

"I never asked you to do that," she said. He'd said he'd get her in. She hadn't expected him to pay off someone to assure her a place.

"A couple of days ago I called him and told him to be ready to go on as usual."

"Why?"

"You're not ready," he said again.

She turned, wanting nothing more than to escape. Had she really been about to make love to him? Here? Outside, under the stars, in a blaze of mindless passion that was so unlike her. She glanced up as two meteorites streaked across the sky. Clint grabbed her shoulder.

"Tell me what to look for," he said in a lowered voice. "I'll find your serial killer for you, if he's really with the rodeo."

"No."

"Why not?"

"You say I can't do your job? Well, you sure as hell can't do mine."

He pulled her against him, and the pickup-truck bed rocked. "I still want you," he said. That was all too evident, with their bodies pressed together from chest to knee. "But I couldn't make love to you without telling you this first."

Most men would have, she knew that. Most men would

have taken what they could get and *then* told her the bad news.

It didn't make this moment any brighter. "You can't yank the rug out from under me and expect...you can't ruin everything and then..."

He let her go. "I was afraid of that."

Mary climbed over the tailgate and onto the bumper. "Thanks," she said as she jumped to the ground.

"Thanks?"

"Your need to be Captain Good Guy, superhero from the sticks, saved me from making a very big mistake." She tried for a tone of voice that was sharp and emotionless.

"Did it really?" he asked flatly.

"Yeah." She turned her back on him. "See you in the morning, Sinclair. Try to leave without me and I'll arrest you."

"On what charge?" he asked from the back of the truck.

"Obstruction of justice, for a start."

He didn't follow her, thank goodness, so there was no one to see her begin to tremble as she walked into the kitchen, no one to see the tears fall down her face.

Captain Good Guy, superhero from the sticks. Clint was still ticked off about that as he threw his bags into the bed of the pickup the morning after Mary had walked out on him and the meteor shower. The way she'd said it was what rankled, still...like she would have preferred it if he'd slept with her and *then* told her he wasn't going to get her a job with Brisco.

Maybe she would have. Maybe she was one of those women who liked guys who treated them like crap.

Funny, but he never would have thought that of her. She liked herself too much for that nonsense.

Then again, maybe not.

Before he could climb into the driver's seat, Mary burst through the front door, a bag in each hand. Clint took a step forward to help her with the bags but stopped before he'd taken a full step and fell back to lean against the door of the pickup.

Special Agent Mary Paris looked the part, he'd give her that. No more chic gray suit and high heels. She wore blue jeans, a buttoned-up blue shirt and a pair of black cowboy boots she'd bought in Scottsboro last week.

She threw her bags into the back of the truck, having no trouble hefting them over the side. Wes and Katie stepped onto the porch to wave goodbye, and Clint stepped back to stand beside Mary.

"You forgot something," he said in a low voice.

"I didn't forget—"

He reached into the bed of the truck and snagged her bra, hooking it on one finger and whipping it up and around to present it to her on the end of that one long finger.

She blushed as she snatched it from him. "Thank you, *so* much," she said, frost in her voice.

"You're welcome, ma'am," he said, bowing to her ever so slightly. "Captain Good Guy to the rescue."

She had the good grace to look contrite. "Sorry about that," she whispered.

"What?"

"I said I'm sorry," she said, a little bit louder. "What do you expect? That I'll just give up on what I've planned for *months?* That I'm willing to write off two weeks of hard work and months of research because you think I'm not ready?"

"Is everything okay?" Wes walked to the end of the porch, limping more than usual this morning.

"Fine," Clint said with an insincere smile. He turned his eyes to Mary, who had hidden the bra behind her back. "Get in the truck."

She ran to the passenger side and jumped in. As he started the engine, Clint turned to look at her again. "I'll tell you what I expect. I expect you to consider the lives of the cowboys and other bullfighters in the arena. Should they have to risk their lives for your assignment? Should they?"

"I can handle my—"

He held up a finger to silence her, and amazingly she obeyed it.

"As long as nothing goes wrong, you could handle yourself just fine. But Special Agent Paris...something always goes wrong."

"Of course I don't want anyone else to get hurt," she said contritely. "That's why I was willing to spend two weeks here getting properly trained."

"Could I become an FBI agent on two weeks' training?"

"Of course not."

"What makes you think this is any easier?"

She pursed her lips. Dammit, would he ever again look at her and not remember how close he'd been? Would he ever be able to look at her and not want to take her, then and there?

Neither of them had planned it, neither of them wanted it, but something had happened. Maybe it had started with that first dance at Dexler's, or with that first muscadine kiss. Maybe it had started the first moment he'd laid eyes on her at Shea's house. He felt something unexpected growing inside him...but he knew nothing could come of it. He and Mary were too different. And in another way, they were too much alike.

"Most of all," he confessed, "I guess I expect you to understand why I have a hard time watching you make yourself bait for a cold-blooded killer."

"I told you that would only be as a last resort, and with proper backup from—"

"Save it for someone who buys that line of bull."

Mary pursed her lips but didn't try to argue with him.

"A butcher, I believe you called him," Clint continued in a lowered voice. "A man who targets women very much like you. Boone and Dean have filled me in on some of the details you didn't share about the crimes you're trying to tie together."

"I can handle myself," she said.

"I don't have to like it."

"Clint, I have to get into that rodeo." A touch of desperation colored her voice. "I can't stop now, I can't give up."

"Do you ever?" he snapped.

"No."

He stared at Mary, remembering last night, remembering all the reasons this wouldn't work. He should kick her out of his truck, toss her bags on the ground and go to Birmingham without her.

And then her eyes went wide and she whispered, "Please," and he was a goner.

Chapter 7

He laid the earrings across his dresser, admiring the way each one caught the morning light. Eight bright, dangling earrings, each one different in its own way, sparkled with memories. He laid a finger against the first one in the row. It was gold, real gold. Even after all these years, it was as brilliant as it had been on the day he'd taken it.

She had screamed most of all.

He was aroused and electrified, as he always was at the beginning of the tour. Such anticipation. Such a thrill. He felt that thrill down to his bones, and as he caressed the earrings before him he remembered each woman, each kill. If he had a smaller degree of discipline, he would go out right now and choose his next victim.

No. That would never do. It wasn't time. Not yet. Part of the exhilaration was in the planning. In the anticipation. In the knowing that he was smarter than everyone else.

And he was smarter. He'd taken great care to make certain no trail led to him. Choosing the right time, the right place…the right woman. That made all the difference. No one even knew he existed. There had been no sensational headlines about a serial killer, no breaking news on the television.

He should be annoyed to be anonymous still, and on some days he was. What he had done was genius…someone should appreciate that. He soothed himself with the knowledge that one day he would be feared and respected by many people. The time to reveal himself would come and a worthy adversary would step forward. Not this year, not the next. But eventually. One day, when the box where he stored his treasures was filled to the brim. When the thrill had gone and he needed something more to make his bones sing.

But for now, his box was practically empty. The eight earrings he had collected barely covered the bottom of the wooden box he had carved himself that first summer. There were many summers ahead of him. He shouldn't be thinking of fame now…it was too soon.

He smiled as he returned the keepsakes to their proper place. The earrings kept him going through the year. They excited and pleased him when he took them out of the box to play and remember. A lesser man, a weaker man, would continue to kill year round. Not him. He had a great deal of discipline, and he would not lead the authorities to his door by committing murder near his home. That would be foolish, and he was not a foolish man.

Some days he was annoyed that he couldn't take his anger out on the woman who had earned it; the woman who had pushed him into discovering the rage he'd kept buried. To do so would turn suspicious eyes his way, so that could not happen. Not now, not ever.

He turned his mind to happier thoughts. Soon he would have new memories and new keepsakes. He could hardly wait.

"No."

Oliver Brisco sat behind the plain metal desk in his trailer office while Mary and Clint stood on the other side of that desk. There were no chairs for visitors.

Brisco was everything Mary had expected. Of course, she'd seen his photograph and studied what she could find about his life. But no photograph or research could've prepared her for the emotionless depth of his dark eyes or the chill in his voice as he rejected Clint's perfectly reasonable proposition.

On the drive to Birmingham, she and Clint had come to an uneasy compromise. She wanted to be in the thick of things, to be in the midst of the action. But in truth she'd take any job she could get here at Brisco Rodeo.

"She won't be in the arena," Clint said. "She'll just work the crowd. Entertain the kids before the rodeo starts, work the stands during the events."

"No," Brisco said again. He was a striking man, with sun-kissed skin and wavy black hair that touched his collar. And he was big, with muscular arms and large hands. He'd have no problem capturing and imprisoning a small, defenseless woman like Elaine.

Mentally, she ran down the list of details about Oliver Brisco. Thirty-seven years old. Divorced. Had a kid, a nine-year-old daughter he hadn't seen since she was four. Mary didn't know why Brisco hadn't seen his daughter in five years, but that didn't speak well of him. Since his bitter divorce there hadn't been any other marriages or even serious relationships that had been uncovered. He was an unpleasant man who fit the profile perfectly.

"I can juggle," Mary said, trying not to sound too desperate.

"Miss," Brisco said, laying those dark eyes on her. "Would you mind waiting outside?" He gestured with one hand to the door of his trailer, which was parked near the civic center arena, where the rodeo would take place.

"Actually, I would mind," she snapped. "I'm not a child. Anything you have to say—"

He shook his head and turned to Clint while Mary was still in midsentence. "I can't believe you'd drag in a girlfriend and try to get her a job. I expect better of my best bullfighter. She must be pretty damn good in the sack to get you to—"

"I'm not his girlfriend!" Mary insisted before he could say any more. She wasn't alone; Clint's protest echoed hers.

"She's a friend of my sister," Clint said in a calmer voice. "And she's always dreamed of working in the rodeo."

Brisco, who continued to sit behind his desk, grunted. "Not a girlfriend, huh?"

"Absolutely not," Mary said.

"No way," Clint added in a lower voice.

"I can make balloon animals," Mary added, rather pathetically.

Brisco shook his head. "I really don't need anyone else. My roster is set."

What would she do if he kicked her out? Follow the rodeo like a groupie? Become a rodeo ho? Ask Clint if she could be his makeup man?

"I'll work for free," Mary said quickly.

Brisco laid those dark eyes on her again and she shivered. He was her prime suspect, and he certainly appeared to be capable of murder.

"Are you one of those chicks who has a thing for bronc riders or bull riders?"

"No," Mary said indignantly. Chick? It was much worse than Clint's easy *darlin'* or even *girl*.

"Because if I catch you screwing any of my athletes you're out of here."

"I don't have a thing for anyone," Mary said coolly. "I simply want to spend the summer being a clown. Is that so difficult for you to believe?"

Brisco almost smiled. It was difficult to tell. "I'll let you work here in Birmingham, and if you do well we'll talk about the rest of the tour."

Mary breathed a sigh of relief. "Thanks. You won't be sorry."

Actually, if he was the man she was looking for he would be sorry. Very sorry. Realizing that this man might be the monster who had raped and murdered Elaine made Mary's heart beat too hard and fast. Her mouth was dry. Her fingers and her knees trembled.

There was a very good reason for keeping agents who were personally involved in cases far away from the investigation. When she looked at Brisco and wondered if he was her man, she didn't think about the other seven victims, she only saw Elaine. And in her mind she saw too much. Her imagination provided pictures more vivid than the crime-scene photos. In her really bad moments, she could hear Elaine scream.

She knew her job, she knew what was expected and required. But when she thought of Elaine she didn't want to arrest the man responsible...she wanted to kill him.

"You think he did it, don't you?" Clint asked as they walked toward his truck.

"Who?" Mary asked too sharply.

She thought she was so cool…and in truth he didn't think anyone else would have picked on the change in her body language the minute they'd walked into Oliver's office.

"Brisco," he said. "You think he's your guy."

"I'm not ruling out anyone at this point," she said with a professional crispness to her voice.

"He's a suspect," Clint said, pushing for a more satisfactory response.

"I can't talk about the details of my case."

"You think he did it," he said, more certain than ever that Mary thought Oliver Brisco was a murderer and a rapist.

"Clint." She cast him a censuring glance.

"You're wrong," he said, opening the passenger door for her.

Mary gave him a "what are you doing?" look before she stepped into the truck. At least she didn't close the door and open it again for herself! Sometimes he expected her to be just that stubborn.

She didn't say anything until they were on the street headed for their hotel. Some of the performers stayed in trailers at the site, but he never did. He helped with the animals when necessary, and he was always happy to lend a hand. But he was only needed during the bull rides, which were split into two sections. One at the beginning of the show, the other at the end.

Besides, he hated sleeping in a trailer. He'd done it for too many years, when he'd first started with the rodeo and had needed to be on call at all hours of the day.

"Any man connected with the Brisco Rodeo is a suspect at this point," Mary said once they were down the road from the site.

"Even me?" Clint asked teasingly.

"Of course not," Mary answered in a low voice.

At least she didn't suspect him. She knew him too well.

"You were in the hospital when the first murder took place," she continued, "and still laid up when the second occurred. You're in the clear."

He gave her a quick glance. Of course, she had only eliminated him from her list of suspects because he hadn't been physically able to commit the first two murders. If he'd been with Brisco four years ago, he'd be a suspect, too. He was certain. If that had been the way of it, Mary never would have come to him for help. She never would have almost made love to him under the stars.

"I still say it could just as easily be someone who follows the rodeo," he argued. "A wanna-be, maybe."

"Maybe," she said softly. "I hope not."

"Why?"

She didn't answer for a moment. "It's not that I maliciously want one of your friends to be a killer, it's just that if he is following the rodeo he'll be harder to catch. He'll blend in, maybe change his appearance slightly from one town to the next. Maybe not even show up at every stop. If I don't find him, and quick, we'll have two more dead women by the end of the summer."

"I can't see Brisco doing the kinds of things your guy's done. Yeah, he's gruff, and not particularly sociable, but—"

"Sinclair," Mary interrupted. "Can you see anyone you know committing a brutal murder?"

"No," he admitted.

"No one can. We can't imagine how anyone could hurt another living being in that horrendous way, and whoever the man is…he can't be a friend, someone you've laughed with or had a drink with or had over to your house for dinner. But he is. He can appear to be perfectly ordinary one minute—'' Mary turned her head and stared at him ''—and turn into a monster the next.''

''Still…''

''These murders are very carefully planned,'' Mary interrupted. ''He doesn't lose control…at least, not in the planning stages.'' She sounded like she'd choked up a little on that last sentence. A deep breath, and her voice was perfectly steady again. ''The victims aren't missed for days, which means he chooses them very carefully. Not a single body has been found in less than a week's time after the victim's death. There's no usable DNA, no footprints, not a single decent clue to go on.'' She relaxed visibly. ''He took one earring from four of the victims. Four of the others weren't wearing earrings, but I think maybe the killer took both from them. He did that on purpose, to throw us off.''

''Earrings. That's not much to go on. One or both might have been lost during a struggle. Maybe the victims who had both missing didn't wear earrings at all on that particular day. In the cases where one is missing, maybe the bodies were mishandled, or…''

''I've heard all this,'' Mary snapped. ''Every argument, every rationalization. No one wants to admit that we have a serial killer on our hands, because right now there are two men sitting in jail who have been convicted of two of the murders. The man in Shea's story and one more, a man who was divorced from the third victim. Admitting these crimes are connected means two innocent men are in prison.''

''Yeah, but *earrings*…''

''That's his weakness,'' Mary insisted. ''That's how we'll catch him.''

''What if he doesn't hang on to them?'' Clint asked.

"He does," she said, not leaving room for the possibility that her one solid clue might lead nowhere.

The hotel where they'd be spending the next several days wasn't exactly four star, but it was nice enough. It was definitely better than the Scottsboro hotel where she'd spent more than a week.

She and Clint rode up on the elevator together. She carried her own bags and had slipped the card key into the breast pocket of her shirt. Clint seemed slightly uncomfortable. He was obviously still having a hard time envisioning one of his buddies as a killer.

Yeah, she still had her money on Oliver Brisco. She knew there were several others who had to be considered as possibilities, but it was Brisco who set her nerves and her instincts on edge. His ex-wife was blond and attractive, and in at least one of the photographs Mary had been able to round up the woman had been wearing dangling earrings. That was hardly evidence, but it did point her toward the outwardly caustic Brisco.

When the elevator stopped on the fourth floor, they both got off. They both turned right. She should have known better than to let Clint make their reservations! He'd probably requested rooms side by side.

Sure enough, when she dropped her bag on the floor before the door to room 416, Clint passed close behind her and stopped at 418.

Best not to comment on the arrangements he'd made, not just yet. This was an issue that had to be addressed, though. She couldn't have Clint at her heels all the time! That would be fine for gathering initial information, but if she did have to put herself out there as bait, no one could believe she and Clint were close in any way. She had to appear to be expendable.

She let herself into the room without comment, allowing the heavy door to close behind her. Her accommodations were decent. Not shabby but not luxurious either. It would do. She'd miss the warmth of Clint's house, though, and Katie's cooking and Wes's lame jokes over dinner.

A knock sounded at the door. It had to be Clint, she thought as she turned on her heel. They definitely had to have a talk! The knock came again as she reached the door, but it didn't come from the hallway door.

It came from the door that adjoined her room to Clint's.

She threw the door open. "You got us connecting rooms?" she asked tersely.

"Yep." He didn't even have the decency to deny his hand in this.

She wished he were shorter. She had to look up to glare into his eyes. "We can't have people thinking we're… we're…"

"Involved?" he said when she faltered.

"I'm your little sister's friend, nothing more. If anyone suspects that we're, umm…"

"Sleeping together," he finished calmly.

Mary felt a blush rise to her cheek. "It'll ruin everything."

He clenched his jaw. His normally bright eyes darkened and his lips, those lips that smiled so easily and often, thinned.

She wondered if he would mention that they almost had slept together. She hoped he would not. In fact, she hoped he had already forgotten about last night! Her training was over and now she had to devote every second of her time to finding Elaine's killer. Clint was a distraction she could not afford.

"No one has to know this door is here, much less that

it was opened,'' Clint said in a lowered voice. "But if you plan to make yourself bait for a sicko, I plan to be close enough to do something about it."

"I repeat, for the umpteenth time, that I am not setting myself up as bait. I am here to investigate, that is all."

"Right," he muttered.

"I don't need you getting underfoot," she said calmly.

"Underfoot?" he asked, an incredulous lift to his eyebrows.

"Underfoot."

"I'm just supposed to sit back and let you offer yourself up to a man who rapes his victims and then cuts them up."

"Clint! I told you, he's never picked anyone who's worked at the rodeo…"

"You're blond, you're definitely pretty and you're here. Deny it all you want, but you fit the profile, and if your theory is right, you've put yourself in the sights of a serial killer."

Mary swallowed hard. "It's not going to come to that."

"But you don't know for sure…."

"I can handle myself."

Frustration colored Clint's face and made him look formidable. No endearing lock of hair or casual stance could make him look like the easygoing Clint she knew and…knew.

"Dammit, Mary, you don't know that you can handle this. You don't know who or what he is. You don't know when or how or *if* he'll come after you."

"For now, I'm simply gathering information. It's a perfectly safe assignment."

And if that didn't work, she had a pair of earrings that were very much like those in the killer's collection. Dangly, ostentatious gold earrings, very unlike the studs she usually wore. She couldn't possibly tell Clint she'd packed those earrings just in case…

Mary started to close the door, giving it a little push. Clint stopped the motion with a booted foot. "The door stays open."

"Not on your life, Giggles."

His jaw tensed. "The door stays open, or I go to Oliver and tell him everything. *Everything,* Special Agent Paris."

Her right eyelid twitched. "I could have you arrested for obstruction of justice."

"Go right ahead."

"Don't tempt me."

They stared each other down. If Clint knew the truth, he really would hit the roof. He'd turn on her in a heartbeat and there would be no safe cover from which to study Brisco and the other rodeo regulars. The killer would go under. He'd hide once he knew she was searching for him. She couldn't afford to lose everything she'd worked for because Clint Sinclair had decided to turn macho on her!

She should thank him, she supposed, for deciding to be so honest last night when they'd both been half naked and he'd been minutes away from being inside her. Something inside her lurched at the memory, and she pushed that reaction deep. Sleeping with him would have been a huge mistake. The hugest. What had she been thinking?

Oh, yeah, she hadn't been thinking. For the first time in so long she could not remember, she'd been swept away. It had been the night, the meteor shower, the way they kissed.

Mary closed the door halfway. As she turned around she said, "Come into my room without an invitation and I'll shoot you."

She expected a smart retort, but Clint said nothing.

Chapter 8

It was clear by the odor in the dirt-packed enclosure that the animals had arrived. Mary wrinkled her nose as she followed Clint through the arena. She didn't want anyone to think that the two of them were anything more than casual friends, but she did need to meet everyone. Clint could make introductions and then back off.

Unfortunately, Clint Sinclair was no better at "backing off" than she was.

It was true that she had allowed herself to be momentarily distracted by the attractive, well-mannered, charming cowboy. But now that she was here all distractions had to be put aside. Nothing in this world was as important as finding Elaine's killer. Nothing. Especially not an annoyingly sexy rodeo clown.

"Clint!" Squeals, in stereo, broke the uneasy silence.

Clint turned toward the noise and smiled widely as two semidressed girls ran toward him.

Mary herself did not care for the term *girl*, when applied to a fully grown woman, but these squealers didn't look to be more than twenty years old.

Clint gave each girl a big hug while Mary hung back and studied them. Identical twins, they were both dressed in tights. Form-hugging, shiny, full-body electric-blue tights. Both girls had long dark brown hair pulled back into ponytails, and equally dark eyes. They were somehow exotic and girl-next-door wholesome at the same time.

"Mary." Clint turned to face her. He was sandwiched between the squealers, and had tossed easy arms over their shoulders. "This is Amber," he said, nodding to the girl on his right. "And this is Tiffany."

How could he tell? She couldn't see any difference at all, not in their faces, their bodies, or in the way they moved.

"Ladies, this is Mary," he continued. "She'll be joining us for the summer."

Tiffany's smile faded. "You've never brought a girlfriend with you before."

At the same time Mary insisted, "I'm not his girlfriend," Clint said, "She's just a friend of my little sister."

Tiffany got the message. Her smile grew wide again.

"The Kirkland twins are trick riders," Clint continued, that awkward moment out of the way.

Each overly pert girl gave Clint a kiss on the cheek before stepping out of his embrace.

"Mary's going to be a clown," Clint said.

The twins stared at her, wide-eyed. They each took their time looking her over. "Not a bullfighter!" one of them said.

"Nope," Clint muttered.

"Where's Eugene? Isn't he coming?" one of the twins asked.

"He'll be here. Mary is just going to work the crowd before the show and during intermission. You know, make balloon animals for the kids. Juggle." His eyes met hers. "Mary Mary Quite Contrary. That's her name."

"Oh," one of the twins said. "Okay. Well, that's different." The simple comment sounded very much like an insult.

Clint glanced down at Amber. Or was it Tiffany? Mary was still confused. "Is Sam here yet?"

Sam. Mary made an effort not to snort. Sam was probably short for Samantha. What was she? Rodeo Queen? Another trick rider?

"I saw him this morning," one of the twins said.

Him. Mary felt almost deflated. Since she'd met Clint Sinclair she'd done her best to paint him as a ladies' man, a charmer, a man who had a string of women he led around like the pied piper. And she was always wrong. Always! Still, it just wasn't possible that he was as perfect as he seemed to be. It was…unnatural.

"If you see Sam around, tell him I'm here and looking for him," Clint said.

"Sure thing." The bubbly, curvaceous twins waved goodbye and Mary managed a tight smile. The smile did not come easily. Good heavens, was she *jealous?* Impossible.

"Sam?" she asked as they walked toward the calf pen.

"He's the other bullfighter. My partner. He's the best. Next to me, of course."

Mary shook her head. According to the information she had, the other rodeo clown was named James Grady. She searched her memory, and saw the name in her mind. James *Samuel* Grady. She was letting her tenuous personal involvement with Clint color her judgment already! She should've made the connection. "Second best, huh?"

She managed to snort under her breath. "*And* he's your friend. You never intended on letting me into the arena, did you?"

"I considered it," Clint said easily. "But you would have been a third, not a replacement for Sam. I thought we were clear about that."

Mary decided she wasn't going to argue with Clint, no matter how much she wanted to. Sweetness was one thing. These pens of bulls, many of them much larger than she'd imagined they would be, were another entirely. At the moment she was quite happy to be Mary Mary Quite Contrary, juggler and maker of balloon animals.

She hadn't actually made balloon animals in years, but she was pretty sure the skill would come back to her quickly.

Now that she was in the midst of the Brisco Rodeo, thanks to Clint, Mary ran down her list of suspects. Oliver Brisco topped the list, he was number one. But until she had more evidence he was not the only possibility. At this point, any man who could be placed at the rodeo on the dates corresponding with the murders was a suspect.

At the present time, none of the athletes—the bull riders, bronc riders and calf ropers—were on her list. She hadn't been able to place any one of them in all six cities at the right times, and besides…they seemed to go directly from one rodeo to another, very often riding in more than one rodeo in a weekend. They also usually traveled in groups of two and three, and the man she was looking for worked alone.

Eliminating the athletes didn't leave her with a shortage of suspects. There were two members of the management staff who had been here for the past four years or more, as well as a lighting director and an announcer. Erwin Connors, who rode a dancing horse, had also been with the Brisco Rodeo for more than four years. At fifty-two years old he didn't top her list, but she wasn't ready to eliminate anyone. Not yet. Eugene Hitt, the barrel clown, was also on her list, though he, too, was older than the profile indicated her killer to be. Still, profiles had been wrong before.

Then there was Sam. Clint had been with the Brisco Rodeo for three years, but James Grady, Sam to his friends, apparently, had started here four years ago. Right before the murders began.

Brisco, his management, the lighting director, the man with the dancing horse, the announcer and the clowns. One of them was a cold-blooded killer.

Three of them were crowded into one room of a trailer that had seen better days. Sam slept in a back room of the trailer, preferring to stay close to the animals when he traveled with the rodeo. He said he hated hotels and would prefer a cardboard box. The trailer was a little better than a box.

One room was devoted to a big mirror, a rack for costumes and a table laden with greasepaint.

Mary was already mingling with the crowd, handing out trick ropes to the kiddies as they arrived. Once the ropes were gone she'd entertain them with balloon animals. Juggling would come later.

She should be perfectly safe…but he didn't like it. Not at all.

If he was smart, he'd walk away. Now. Tonight. He didn't need to get caught up in Mary Paris's problems. His life was simple these days, and if he occasionally wished for more he remembered how easily the simplest of plans could be blown apart.

Until this year, he had never really connected his decision not to ride again to what had happened after. Tonya and the bull that had thrown him had become one. One mess, one step back he didn't dare take.

He suspected turning his back on Mary wouldn't be an easy thing. In fact, he was pretty sure that it would be damn near impossible.

Clint applied a quick smear of white greasepaint on his face, just as Sam did.

"Okay," Sam said as he worked before the mirror. "Who's the girl?"

"I told you—"

"A friend of your sister," Eugene interrupted. "Sorry, Sinclair. I don't buy it."

"Neither do I," Sam said.

Sam was not yet twenty-five years old, but he'd been rodeoing all his life. He was a damn good bullfighter and a decent person. Eugene was a family man, fifty years old, potbellied and constantly smiling. Neither of them were capable of the crimes Mary suspected them of. He was so tempted to tell them why she was really here.

He didn't keep Mary's secret because he was afraid of making her mad or because he thought she might be right. He kept her secret because she trusted him, and to tell anyone of her deception would be a betrayal of that trust.

He liked Mary more than he'd liked a woman in a very long time. Still, they didn't have much of a chance, he knew that. If he blew this investigation for her, they'd have no chance at all.

He sat in a rickety chair and put on his cleats, tying them good and tight. "Sorry, fellas. That's all it is. She's a friend of Shea's, and that's it."

"Eugene tells me you actually thought about putting her in the arena," Sam said with a wide grin. "Have you lost your mind?"

"It's what she wanted," Clint said with a shrug as he stood. "I tried to accommodate her, but I eventually had to tell her that she just wasn't good enough."

Sam whistled. "She doesn't strike me as the type who would take that news well."

Clint grinned. "She didn't."

Forty-five minutes until the rodeo got under way, and he was antsy as hell. Mary was sure her culprit was living and working right here in the rodeo. He was just as sure that her man could be one of the many faces in the crowd.

And she was out there all alone.

"I'm going for a walk," he said, heading for the door.

"You never stroll around the arena before the bull riding gets started!" Sam protested with a smile.

"I think there's a little redheaded freckle-faced clown out there calling Clint's name," Eugene teased.

"Maybe I just need some fresh air."

Sam made some comment about what he thought Clint needed, as the door to the trailer closed.

Cowboys were arriving, paying their fees and getting their back numbers. Clint knew many of them, and he definitely knew most of the bull riders. There were a few new faces, though. Young, expectant faces. Most of them would end up eating dirt tonight. It was his job to make sure that was the worst that happened.

Bull riding was a dangerous sport. Eight seconds might not seem like a long time, but when you're sitting on the back of a bucking bull that can weigh up to two thousand pounds, those seconds can seem like an eternity. Sitting on the back of a bull was like being caught in a tornado. You held on tight and prayed, and for eight seconds, if you were lucky, you had the ride of your life.

He made his way to the front of the arena and positioned himself behind a souvenir stand where he could see Mary but she could not see him.

He couldn't help but smile as he watched her. His own face paint was sparse. White on his cheeks and across the nose, a little on the forehead. The rest of his costume was put together with his job in mind—not entertainment. The cutoff jeans were in shreds, allowing him freedom of movement, and the knee-length pants beneath those jeans were tight but not binding. No matter what, he had to be able to move. The cleats he wore allowed him to make quick turns and twists without slipping. True, the shirt was bright red and was decorated with yellow polka dots, and the suspenders were just as bright. But his hair was his own and his black cowboy hat fit him well. He wasn't just a clown, he was a bullfighter.

Mary, on the other hand, was a clown. Her face was painted, as he had taught her, in white and red. Even her nose was painted red. She sported big, painted-on freckles. The wig was red, with long braided pigtails that went this way and that. Her shirt was rainbow colored and striped, her suspenders red, her pants baggy.

She even wore the big shoes.

To look at her you would never know that underneath that costume was a beautiful, exciting, arousing woman who had crawled under his skin and was currently making him crazy.

Mary wasn't his type. He knew it, she knew it. Nothing could come of this…but it wasn't over between them. There was too much left undone and unsaid. When this was all over with, when she'd caught her serial killer and was off the job, he was going to get her back under the stars again.

She handed out trick ropes and shook hands with the little kids who weren't terrified of her. What was it with some kids? Clowns were fun, right? But there were always a few who were scared, kids who grabbed on to their mama's skirts and held on tight.

When she turned this way, Clint stepped back and into the shadows. Mary needed someone to watch her back, but she would never admit to such a thing. He'd keep an eye on her when he could, keep close tabs on her at all times. But he absolutely, positively could not let her know he was watching.

Bull riding was the first event…and the last. The rodeo opened with one half of the riders and ended with the other half. Mary, who was already dizzy from blowing up those blasted narrow balloons, found a semiquiet place to stand and watch as the event was announced.

The announcer introduced the riders, and each one received hearty applause. Clint and Sam were introduced last, and they walked into the arena waving their cowboy hats. Clint's was black. Sam's had once been white.

It wasn't fair. She looked like an idiot! Clint looked sexy as all get out, face paint and all.

The Brisco Rodeo Queen was announced. Melanie Anne Dunlap. She rode slowly through the arena on a beautiful white horse, making a wide circle. Just as Mary had suspected, she had big hair—red in this case—and was quite familiar with the royal wave. She wore lots of fringe, which went well with the hair. A large number of males in the crowd hooted appreciatively.

That done, Eugene Hitt was introduced, and he walked into the arena and toward the red barrel in the center of the ring, waving at the crowd. He was dressed like Elvis, complete with potbelly, white rhinestone jumpsuit and exaggerated sideburns. For him, the crowd went nuts. As he walked to the barrel he told an old groaner of a joke. Everyone laughed.

Mary held her breath as the first bull and rider came out of gate four. It was all over too fast. The bull bucked, the rider flew off and landed in the dirt, and Clint and Sam safely herded the loping, riderless bull through the exit gate. This was the dangerous work Clint said she couldn't handle? She was insulted all over again.

The second bull and rider, coming out of gate two, were a repeat of the first event. The announcer bellowed, "Bulls two, cowboys zero," as the bull exited the arena.

Blowing up all those skinny balloons was more dangerous than this.

Then the third bull and rider shot out of gate five. The bull bucked, but this rider managed to stay on for eight seconds, until the buzzer sounded. The crowd cheered. The cowboy dismounted.

And the bull turned on him. This animal was not going to exit gracefully. Clint and Sam tried to get the bull's attention, but the huge, angry animal had decided to chase the man who had ridden him, and would not be easily distracted.

Until Clint ran up and popped the bull on the nose.

Again, Mary held her breath. Her heart lurched in her chest. What was he thinking? You didn't hit a bull in the face! He'd said he would do just that when she'd met Sweetness, but the beast in the ring was not Sweetness! The bull did turn his attention to Clint, and Sam helped a limping cowboy to safety while Clint played getaway, cutting this way and that. The crowd loved it. Clint was toying with the bull—or else the bull was toying with Clint. It was difficult to tell.

Finally, Clint led the lumbering animal to the exit gate and it obediently left the arena. The crowd applauded.

Mary found an empty seat and sat down. Hard. She could never again call him Giggles.

"Mary?"

She turned, tilted her head back and saw a familiar face staring down at her; a grinning Boone Sinclair with his very pregnant wife on his arm.

"I told you that was her," Jayne Sinclair said with a smile. "How are you?"

Fine was not a sufficient answer. Her heart pounded too hard. There was a short delay in the arena. Eugene was telling more bad jokes, and the crowd loved it. Finally Mary said, "Did you see what he just did?" She should stand to face Boone Sinclair and his wife, but her knees were shaking too badly to even think about standing.

"This is your first night, right?" Boone asked. "That wasn't anything unusual. Sometimes things get really hairy out there."

That wasn't *really hairy?* What did it take to alarm these people?

"You're his older brother," she said in a lowered voice. "Can't you make him *stop?*"

Boone laughed. "No. Clint loves what he does too much. I wouldn't dare ask him to give it up."

Mary took a deep breath. He loved playing with angry bulls. There it was, revealed at last. She had seen Clint's defect, the flaw she had been so diligently looking for.

The man obviously didn't have a lick of common sense.

Between the rounds of bull riding, Clint usually sat in Sam's trailer. Not tonight. Tonight he wandered the arena until he saw Mary. A few kids gathered around, some of them wanting his autograph in their program. He obliged, keeping a cautious eye on Mary Mary Quite Contrary.

Occasionally his eyes scanned the crowd. Was the man

she hunted out there somewhere? At least when she was in costume she didn't fit the type of victim the killer was targeting. And still…he didn't like it.

He saw Boone coming from two sections over. Jayne, who now officially waddled, was with him. Clint stepped back, into a nook between sections, and waited for his brother to join him. From here, he could still see Mary.

"I didn't figure we'd see you until after this shindig was over," Boone said.

When he was in Birmingham, Boone was usually at every performance. If you asked Boone if he liked the rodeo you'd get a very quick *no*. But he was always here.

"Just stepped out of the trailer for a breath of fresh air," Clint said.

Jayne wrinkled her nose. "*This* is fresh air?"

Clint grinned. "Just wait until Sunday afternoon, after we've been here for four days."

Amber and Tiffany were performing and had everyone's attention. Including Mary's, from what he could see. The twins were amazing. They'd been riding since they could walk, and could do the most amazing acrobatics on the back of a racing horse.

"You're missing it," he said to Jayne, nodding to the arena floor.

She turned her eyes to the performance. "How on earth do they do that?" Again she wrinkled her nose. "I can barely make it up and down the stairs."

"How much longer?" Clint asked.

"Five weeks," Boone said.

"And two days," Jayne added. "Unless I deliver early. I could deliver early." She sounded hopeful.

She leaned against Boone and watched the twins in the arena below.

"I've been instructed to encourage you to quit this dangerous business,'' Boone said to Clint, while Jayne watched the show.

"Shea again?'' Clint asked.

"Nope. Your little FBI agent,'' he said in a lowered voice.

"Mary?''

Boone nodded. "She was quite concerned.'' His eyebrows lifted in silent question.

Clint ignored that question. "If she heard you calling her my little FBI agent, she'd kick your ass.'' He kept his voice as low as Boone's. No one could know that Mary was a fed. Her life would really be in danger then.

"Bring her over for an early dinner, one night while y'all are in town.''

"Yeah,'' Jayne said. "I order Chinese really well these days.''

Clint grinned at his sister-in-law. Talk about a woman not being someone's type! He never in a million years would have imagined Jayne, senator's daughter and real Southern lady, and Boone as a couple. But they were so happy together. Boone even seemed content.

"Maybe,'' Clint said. "I'd love to spend some time with y'all, but I'm not sure I can drag Mary away from the rodeo for even a few hours.'' He found her again, watched her show a kid who couldn't be more than five years old how to use his new trick rope.

"And I won't leave her here alone.''

Boone left Jayne watching the acrobatics on horseback and pulled Clint into the shadows. "Are you sleeping with her?'' he asked without preamble.

"Of course not,'' Clint answered without a change of facial expression or tone of voice. Very cool. Very nonchalant.

"Liar.''

"Not this time," Clint said, again without emotion.

"Well, when you do sleep with her, please be careful." Boone glanced back to Mary, and then looked Clint up and down. He popped one of Clint's striped suspenders. "*Very* careful. If you two reproduce, the poor kid would have very big feet and horrible taste in clothes."

"You're the one who's reproducing, not me," Clint said with a grin. "And speaking of fashion sense…" He looked his older brother up and down as critically as Boone had studied his bullfighter attire. "Do they make black clothes for babies? Or do most people not want their children dressing like undertakers?"

Boone scowled. "Don't change the subject." He glanced at Jayne. "Everything is pink," he whispered. "Everything! Clothes, walls, little shoes." He held his thumb and forefinger about two inches apart. "Tiny pink shoes."

"And you're loving every minute of it." It wasn't a blind guess. Boone's dark eyes positively twinkled when he talked about the baby. It was downright unnatural.

Big brother smiled. "Yeah, I am."

Chapter 9

Mary handed the blue balloon animal to the little boy who had requested it. Instead of saying thank you, the kid sneered.

"This isn't a horse!"

Mary continued to smile. "Of course it is."

"It looks like a wiener dog."

Didn't all balloon animals look like wiener dogs? "You have to use your imagination," Mary said calmly.

The boy snorted, and after a moment's consideration gave the balloon sculpture a squeeze that made it burst with a loud pop.

At least the child found that destruction entertaining. He laughed gleefully.

Annoyed but silently reminding herself it was part of the job, Mary moved on. She listened to bits and pieces of conversations, searched for a face that did not belong with the others. There were so many families here, so many excited teenagers. It should be easy to spot her killer in the throng, but she knew it wouldn't be. If the man she was looking for was one of the crowd, she'd never find him. She sauntered along the concrete mezzanine walkway, her eyes scanning the multitude of faces. She waved at the kids who waved at her and smiled widely as she handed out the already-made balloon animals that hung from her belt.

But her eyes didn't stay on the children; they studied every face of every man she passed. There were more than eight thousand people here. She could easily eliminate a large number of men, those who were too old, too young, a smiling man balancing a toddler on his knee. And still, she had no shortage of suspects. Who would have thought that so many people went to the blasted rodeo?

It was time for the last round of bull riding, and Clint was on the arena floor again. She could fight it all she wanted, but the truth of the matter was she loved the way he moved, so strong and unexpectedly graceful, in his cleats and shredded jeans and suspenders. Foolish man! Playing with bulls. What was he thinking? He could stay on his horse ranch. He didn't need to do this. So why did he continue to come back year after year? What was he trying to prove?

Men.

"Mary, Mary." The soft, dark voice calling her name came from the shadows surrounding an exit.

"Who's there?" She stepped toward the exit.

"Quite contrary." Standing out of the light's glare, she could see that the man calling her name was Oliver Brisco, who wore a strange half smile.

The man gave her the creeps. That wasn't a particularly professional observation, but if she had a single female instinct, Oliver Brisco set it on edge. "Surely you could get a better seat," she said casually.

"I prefer to watch from up here," he answered. "I've seen the rodeo before. All my life, in fact. It's the crowd that interests me."

Was he looking for victim number nine? "It is an interesting group of people," she said.

"The kids really love it," Brisco answered. "And there are always a few people in the crowd who have never seen a cowboy on a bucking horse or a bull, or seen a trick rider. Their eyes light up and they hold their breath…it's a whole new experience for them."

That explanation didn't sound particularly ominous, but Brisco could be covering his real reason for standing up here so high, lost in the shadows while he watched the faces.

Mary's heart thundered. Was she carrying on a conversation with the man who had killed Elaine and seven other women?

"Thanks for letting me do this," she said, taking a single step closer.

"Don't thank me until I decide whether or not you'll go any further than this weekend's performances." He smiled at her. "So far, so good. The kids seem to like you."

It was a good thing she hadn't bopped that one little boy over the head with a balloon wiener dog. Apparently Brisco had been watching.

"What does your family think of your new career?" Brisco asked, shifting his feet.

Her heart thumped. Was he leading her? Pressing to find out more about her personal life? Maybe he was just curious, but she didn't think so. It definitely wasn't friendly conversation. Brisco didn't do friendly.

"I don't have any family," she said softly. As far as Brisco knew, she had to be easily expendable. Just in case nothing else worked, just in case she had to put herself out there as a potential victim.

His smile died. "I'm sorry to hear that. Surely there's someone special who wonders why on earth you decided to become a rodeo clown for the summer."

"No."

He stared at her, openly suspicious.

A bit of truth was called for, maybe, in order to convince him. "I don't have good luck with men. I was married, a few years ago." A tingle worked its way up her spine. "He died. It's easier to just…" Be alone, be safe, keep her heart tucked in close and shielded. "Since then I keep to myself, for the most part."

"You were burned and decided it's better to be alone than to expose yourself to the flames again."

Mary nodded.

"I know how you feel," Brisco said in a low voice. "Though it was a divorce that scorched me, not death."

"I'm sorry," she said.

He shrugged his shoulder, dismissing her concern. "What about Clint? Surely there's more between you two than meets the eye."

Mary shook her head. "No. If his sister hadn't begged him to drag me along, he would have dumped me out on the side of the road miles away from Birmingham. I think I kinda get on his nerves."

There was a shout from the crowd, and Mary turned just in time to see Clint lead the bull on a merry chase. Her heart leapt unpleasantly. The man had no common sense at all!

"I don't think he even likes…" She turned, just in time to see the exit door swinging shut. Oliver Brisco was gone.

* * *

He was distracted, and he didn't like it. He didn't like it at all. The new girl. Mary. At the moment she didn't look at all like the kind of girl he liked to target, but this afternoon…this afternoon he had seen her everywhere he turned. Blond hair, pale and soft. Blue eyes, so beautiful. She had a feminine shape that made him ache to touch her.

No earrings, though, he thought sourly. And she was a part of the rodeo. That would never do. She had shown up with Sinclair, and while they weren't side by side all the time, he had seen them together often enough to know that if Mary disappeared, Sinclair would miss her right away.

No, best to stick to his original plan. It had worked for the past four years, it would work this year.

But she distracted him, when he should be searching the crowd for another victim. He was very particular. He only allowed himself two kills per tour, and so the women he chose had to be perfect. The hair, that was most important. The earrings. No matter how shy and quiet a woman might pretend to be, when she wore a certain kind of earring she was shouting out to be noticed.

Once he saw the right kind of woman in the crowd, he had to make sure she was alone. Not only alone, but lonely. A few words, that's usually all he needed to ascertain that the woman suited him and his plans well. There was a desperation in the eyes of the right woman, a hunger.

No one would miss them when they didn't go home, and he needed them, so much.

If the new girl continued to be distracting, he'd have to get rid of her. One way or another.

* * *

"You have absolutely no common sense," Mary said for at least the fifth time since they'd climbed into the truck to head back to the hotel. She still wore her costume, he still wore his. There were a few other rodeo folks in the lobby, but when Clint and Mary stepped into the elevator they were alone. "For God's sake, Sinclair, why didn't you just kiss the bull! You were close enough."

"Yeah, but he smelled bad," Clint answered.

Mary gave him a censuring glare. "You were too close."

"I thought you knew very well what a bullfighter did," Clint said as the elevator began to ascend.

"On film and in person is *not* the same," she insisted. Unexpectedly, she smiled.

"I see by your happy grin that my lack of common sense pleases you," Clint said as the elevator doors opened and they stepped into the hallway.

"It proves that you're not perfect," she said. "I knew you had a flaw."

"Trust me, I have plenty."

She opened her door and he opened his. The connecting door between those two rooms was standing partially open, just as they'd left it.

Mary reached out to swing the door shut, but Clint's quick hand stopped her. "Leave it open," he insisted.

"Dammit, Sinclair," she muttered. "I like my privacy. Especially since I'll probably have to shower for an hour to remove the face paint, sweat and the *odor*. I smell like your barn, only worse." She lifted her sleeve to her nose. "I smell like a farm animal. I probably smell every bit as bad as that bull you slapped on the nose. Does this odor wash out?"

"Close the bathroom door," he said. "But leave this

one open.'' He didn't have to repeat his earlier threat to tell all to Brisco.

"Yeah, sure, why not,'' she muttered as she walked away.

Makeup removed and face freshly scrubbed, Mary stood at the sink, eyes pinned on her own reflection, and tried to make her heart stop pounding. In the privacy of her own room, she didn't have to put on a happy smile and pretend she hadn't been shaken tonight.

She didn't need this kind of aggravation. She couldn't take it. To watch Clint purposely put himself in danger tore her apart in a way she thought was impossible. No one made her weep or long for what she did not have. If she didn't care too much, she couldn't get hurt.

Logically, she knew she shouldn't care what happened to Clint. Emotionally, she knew she didn't dare get involved.

So why did she want nothing more than to walk through the connecting door and into his room, go to Clint and hold him? That's all she wanted. She wanted to hold him and tell him not to take foolish risks with his life…. Mary closed her eyes. Her hands shook, and her heart did not stop pounding.

Her reaction was extreme, considering what had happened in the arena tonight, and she knew that. But when she had seen Clint hit the bull her heart had nearly come through her chest.

Mary undressed slowly and turned on the water, hoping maybe the long shower she'd told Clint she wanted would help. Maybe she could wash away all the anxiety she didn't want to face head-on.

She prided herself on never being afraid, and here she stood, still trembling and worried over something that was an everyday part of Clint's job. He was a bullfighter. And he wasn't hers to worry about.

* * *

When Clint stepped out of the shower, he heard the water in the next room still running. Maybe Mary hadn't been kidding about showering for an hour.

He stepped into a clean pair of jeans and a navy-blue T-shirt, and turned on the television, the sound low so he could hear what was going on in Mary's room.

He was tempted to toss Mary over his shoulder and carry her...somewhere. Anywhere. Some safe place where there were no serial killers, no rapists who had a thing for pretty blondes. Why couldn't she be more agreeable? More reasonable? And she thought *he* had no common sense.

There was one chair in the room. Clint sat in it and pretended to watch television. The local news was over, and he was stuck with pretending to watch a late-night talk show, while out of the corner of his eye he watched the crack in the door between his room and Mary's.

The shower in her room stopped and was followed a moment later by the sound of her hair dryer. Every nerve in Clint's body was tense, wound so tight he felt as if he were about to explode. He was usually pretty wound up after a rodeo, but this was different. This was Mary, in his blood, in his mind all the time. How the hell was he going to get her out?

He was a little surprised when the door swung open and she stepped into his room. She was perfectly decent in her thick, shapeless robe. He could even see the hem of a plain nightgown beneath. This wasn't a woman dressed for seduction.

Her toenails were red, he noticed as she walked into the room.

"How do you sleep after a performance?" she asked. "All I did was make balloon animals and juggle and show kids how to use those trick ropes, and right now I can't imagine sleeping.''

"Give it a little while. You'll crash soon enough."

"I suppose." She sat on the edge of his made bed, and the bottom half of her robe parted, revealing a perfectly prim and proper nightgown. She crossed her ankles, teasing him with those red toenails. "I saw Boone and his wife, Jayne, tonight," she said.

"So did I."

"The two of them, they're so...so..."

"Perfect." Clint supplied the word Mary had been searching for. He couldn't stand to have her here like this, freshly scrubbed and ready for bed and smiling softly. "What do you want?" he asked gruffly.

Her smile faded. "I just wanted to thank you. Maybe talk about the rodeo while I wind down."

"Don't thank me," he said, turning his gaze to the television he hadn't been paying attention to. "And you'll wind down before you know it."

She stood slowly. "I don't think so," she whispered.

He wanted Mary close, he wanted that damned door to stay open so he could hear her, know she was only moments away...but unless she wanted to spend the night here in his bed, she needed to get out of his sight. Damned if he couldn't smell her.

And she smelled so good.

Instead of walking to her own door, Mary came straight to him. "Thank you," she said softly.

Clint looked up at her. How could a woman be tough as nails one minute and look at him this way the next? She tried to hide it, but he saw the vulnerability in her, he saw the scared girl inside the confident woman.

"About last night..." she said. She didn't turn or walk away, but stood right there before him.

"I don't think we should talk about last night."

"I just don't want you to think…it's been a very long time since I…" She blushed. "I don't sleep around," she said too quickly.

"Why not?" he asked, intent on driving her away before he did something they would both regret. "You're a grown woman, a decidedly modern woman who can do everything any man can do, and I suppose that includes sleeping around if the mood strikes you."

It should be enough to send her running, but it didn't work. She didn't budge. "I was married," she whispered.

Clint's heart sank, a little. They had never really talked about her personal life. Mary Paris was all about her job; nothing else seemed to matter to her. "Was," he repeated. "You got divorced?"

Mary shook her head, gently but very quick. "He died." She had a difficult time saying the words. Two little words, and they came out a hoarse whisper, as if they didn't want to pass through her throat without fighting all the way.

His heart broke for her. He felt it, as if something physically altered in his chest. To get dumped was one thing; it happened to just about everyone. But to lose someone that way… "I'm so sorry."

She didn't cry, but it seemed her eyes grew brighter. "His name was Rick, and he's been gone a little more than two years now. He was crossing the street to get coffee at this little shop, and a drunk driver ran him down." She shook her head. "Such a stupid way to die. So incredibly senseless."

From where he sat, he could reach out and touch her. Should he? Or would she fall apart if he were so bold as to try to comfort her?

"Since then, there hasn't been…anyone. And then I

met you, and now I feel like my life has been turned upside down. I know I come on too strong sometimes, and I've been...confused. Not about the case," she said quickly and assuredly. "But about us, I'm confused. If there is an us. Sometimes I think there is no us, and then I watch you doing something incredibly stupid like popping a bull on the nose, and I know that whether I like it or not, there's...something."

"There's most definitely something," he said, his voice lower and softer than it had been before.

Mary's time to run had come and gone. Clint reached up and snagged her wrist, and with a gentle tug he pulled her onto his lap. She landed on his thigh with a gentle thump. He expected her to jump up, indignant and blushing, but she didn't.

"Last night..." she began.

"It was a mistake," Clint interrupted tersely. "I guess it's a good thing I had an attack of honesty, or else—"

"It wasn't a mistake," Mary said. "I didn't lose control, I wasn't swept off my feet and out of my mind by the meteor shower or the kiss or anything else." She licked her lips. He had never seen Mary hesitant before, but she seemed almost timid as she reached out to touch his shirt with feathery fingers. "I don't know exactly what happened."

He knew exactly what had happened. They'd been spending a lot of time together, working, laughing, and all that time something had been building inside him. "I wanted you last night," he said. "I still want you." Maybe that would scare her into her own little room.

"I wanted you, too," she said. "It's that simple. The timing is wrong, you're not my type and I'm not yours, I should be concentrating on solving the murders and nothing else." She lifted her eyes to his. "I was so sure I would never feel this way again. Never. Tonight, when I watched you hit a bull on the nose and then play with him, I was so worried. I don't get worried, Sinclair,'' she said. ''Not about anybody. You drive me absolutely crazy.''

Clint could think of a hundred reasons why he should send Mary on her way. There were equally good reasons, however, why he should keep her right here.

He liked her, he felt this growing need to keep her near and safe, and he needed her more than he'd ever needed anything.

Clint grabbed one end of the belt of her robe and slowly pulled. It came undone and her robe fell open.

There was so much she hadn't told him, so many things she was afraid to say.

She was afraid of so much, and being close to him took those fears away. Far, far away. When he kissed her, nothing else mattered much. When he touched her, she forgot why she had been so determined to keep him at a distance.

She hadn't lied when she'd told Clint she didn't sleep around. Not before Rick or after had she ever seen sex as entertainment. A few of her father's old-fashioned teachings had taken too well. She didn't cook, she didn't clean unless she had no choice and she could do any job any man could do.

But sex without love was a sad thing, indeed.

She'd made a lot of bad decisions in her life, and there were times she would have done anything, paid any price, to go back in time and fix her mistakes. But she had never slept with a man she didn't love. She'd never thought of sex as sport or casual or meaningless. Two people coming together was important, it did mean something. But it had been a long time, and she was so scared. Deep down, dry-mouth scared.

She didn't fool herself into thinking that Clint loved her. And maybe what she felt for him was just gratitude and infatuation, not love at all. This was a kinship between two very different people. An unexpected friendship.

Call it love or not, the affection was there, dancing between them, teasing them with what might be and what might never be. It was more than passion, more than physical.

And she didn't want to be alone tonight.

Clint slipped his hand into her open robe, cupping her breast while he kissed her deep. Mary placed her hands on his face, touched him while they kissed, while he caressed her. She said she didn't lose control, that she didn't get swept away…but that's what was happening to her right now. The world went away, and there was just Clint and her and the way their bodies came together.

There was comfort in his kiss, as well as passion, and the way he held her made her feel as if she'd never be alone again. She wanted to hang on to him tight, tell him everything, open her heart as well as her body. She touched her fingers to his neck, caressed his warm skin, feathered her fingers over the stubble on his jaw.

She took her mouth from his, slowly, reluctantly. "Make love to me," she whispered.

He stood, arms around her, mouth returning to hers. With a gentle shove the robe fell off and pooled at her feet.

"Are you sure?" he asked as he led her to the bed.

"Yes." She reached out and began to unbutton his jeans. "You don't have any surprises for me tonight, do you?"

Clint smiled down at her. "No. Not tonight." He pulled her nightgown over her head, leaving her standing before him in nothing but her panties. She wished she had something enticing and sexy, but she hadn't been prepared for this—she hadn't been prepared for Clint Sinclair.

She pulled his T-shirt off, and it fell. Before it landed on the floor, she saw the scar on his side. Her fingers reached out to trace the old wound. Last night, in the dark, she hadn't seen the scar. "Oh, Clint," she whispered. "What happened?"

"My last bull ride."

Her heart turned over. "It gored you?"

"Yeah," he said, as if the old wound meant nothing.

"I should've been there," she said, tracing the scar with gentle fingers. "I would have taken care of you."

"It was four years ago, long before I met you."

At the moment, it was hard to believe that she hadn't known him forever.

He kissed her and lowered her to the bed, and while she was lying there, almost naked, with her heart pounding so hard she could feel it thudding against her chest, he walked across the room to the overstuffed bag that was sitting open on the dresser, and began to remove his neatly folded clothes and toss them onto the floor.

Mary rose up on her elbows and smiled. "What are you doing?"

"Looking for something I really didn't think I'd need on this trip."

"Oh." She drew back the covers and slipped between the sheets, laying her head against a pillow as she relaxed completely, while Clint removed almost everything from his bag. Finally, he came up with a condom.

He tossed the foil-wrapped condom onto the bedside table and turned off the light. They weren't lost in dark-

ness, though. The bathroom light shone, bathing the room
in a soft, warm glow. Mary was glad they weren't fum-
bling in the dark. She wanted to see Clint finish undressing, wanted to watch him touch her, lay his lips on her
skin, press his tanned, hard body against her pale, rounded
flesh.

He did finish undressing, there by the side of the bed.
Heavens, he was gorgeous, scars and all. The one in his
side was the worst, but there were others, smaller marks
along the length of his tightly muscled body. The sight of
the way he was aroused excited her.

Clint didn't slip beneath the covers with her, but tossed
them back so she was almost as exposed as he was, there
atop the crisp sheets. He lay down beside her and hooked
a finger beneath the waistband of her panties. Moving
slowly, deliberately, he slid the panties down and off.

Mary's heart pounded. Places deep inside her that had
been untouched for so long flared to life. She was afraid,
but the desire was stronger than the fear. Her need to be
held, to be loved, to love in return, was suddenly more
powerful than her fear of being hurt again.

Clint kissed her, so tenderly her heart thudded impossibly harder. He touched her, gentle fingers tracing the
swell of her breasts, teasing the taut nipples. She laid her
hand on his chest. Yes, his heart beat as fast and hard as
hers did.

And yet he didn't rush. He didn't fumble or move too
fast or push too hard. He made love to her, with his mouth
and his hands, as if they had forever.

Maybe they did have forever, she thought dreamily as
Clint laid his mouth on her throat. A lifetime of lying here
with their bodies entwined, with that warmth she had forgotten growing inside her.

Clint kissed her, he touched her, and that warmth grew,

steady and strong, until there was nothing else. The need had once been tingly and intriguing, but now it pounded inside her, it screamed. Hands on her breasts and her thighs, lips everywhere, gnawing heat growing inside her.

She reached out to touch Clint, to run her hands over his skin. He felt like a man should, hot and hard. She laid her lips on his neck, tasted his sweat, flicked her tongue there while she feathered her fingertips through his hair. She lifted her leg over his hip, his arm went around her and he lifted her mouth to his, and they were entwined. Close, but not close enough. Throbbing with a need so deep it made them shake.

He touched her intimately, those fingers remaining as gentle as ever, and she almost fell apart then and there. He was so near. A shift of her hips or his and he would be inside her.

"Touch me," he whispered.

She didn't hesitate, but wrapped her fingers around his erection and stroked up and down the length. There was trust in this bed, love and trust and passion. She trembled, knowing what would come to them soon, knowing that this night was meant to be in a way she had not expected.

Clint reached behind him, snagged the condom from the table and put it on. And then he was above her, and then he was inside her, long and hard and deep.

She closed her eyes and moaned at the sheer pleasure, as Clint held himself deep and still for a moment. He was a part of her, finally.

Her hips moved, and so did his. Eyes closed, there was nothing but the sensation of intimate touch, the smell of their bodies, the sound of their breathing.

Clint made love to her, and she opened her eyes to watch the man above her. His gaze met hers, in the half light, and something in her heart twisted. Her breath wouldn't come to her, her lips parted. Words she could not say teased her tongue.

She laid her hand on his chest, there above his heart, while he pushed deep inside her and held himself there. Her body reacted so strongly, so intensely, that she quivered and gasped.

Mary closed her eyes and simply let herself feel. Her body, left cold for so long, spiraled toward completion. Too soon. She wanted more. She wanted Clint to love her all night. But the needs of her body would not be denied. He surged, and she shattered. She cried out, and he came on the ebbing waves of her completion.

And then he drifted down, kissing her gently all over again.

She opened her eyes and did something she'd been longing to do for two weeks; she brushed the lock of hair at his forehead back, the way a lover might.

What could she say at a moment like this, when *I love you* was a confession she didn't dare make?

Chapter 10

"I think you should quit," Mary whispered.

Clint rolled up on one elbow and stared down at her. "Quit what?"

She scooted over and into him. He never would have suspected that Mary was a snuggler, but here they were, still naked, and she had nuzzled against him all night. "The rodeo," she said softly.

"Why?"

"It's too dangerous," she said, her voice muffled against his chest.

He placed his finger beneath Mary's chin and made her look up at him. "You're searching for a man who's already killed eight women, seriously considering using yourself as a decoy, and you think what *I* do is dangerous?"

"I told you, I'm not setting myself up as a decoy." Did she really look guilty? Just a little, perhaps. "You play with angry bulls," she said accusingly.

"You play with serial killers."

Her expression changed subtly. "I'm not playing," she whispered.

If he thought he could talk some sense into her, he would try, here and now. The thought of Mary in harm's way made him antsy as hell. "When's your backup going to get here?"

"I told you, I'm working solo for now."

"Tell me they didn't send you after this guy on your own." They wouldn't, he knew that. "Training on the ranch was one thing, but this…if you're right and he's out there…"

"All I have to do is make one phone call, and the rodeo will be crawling with agents."

"Mary…"

She fought dirty. This was an argument she couldn't win, fair and square, so she fought with her hands, and with her mouth on his neck, and with a subtle shift of her body. Her skin was so soft and warm, her fingers arousing. When she touched him this way, when she came to him so easily, he forgot everything else.

"You're changing the subject," she whispered while her fingers trailed across his belly.

"*I'm* changing the subject?"

For a brief moment, the tip of her tongue danced across his neck, beneath his ear. "We started out talking about you giving up chasing bulls for a living."

"It's more of a hobby these days," he argued, already impossibly distracted.

"Still, you're not a young whippersnapper like Sam," she teased. "You can't be a bullfighter forever."

"I'm not ready to give it up, not yet." He didn't want to think about the day when he couldn't do anything and everything he wanted to do. Maybe he and Mary had more in common than he'd first thought. "It's too big a part of who I am," he confessed.

Mary's hand settled over his scar. The bad one. "Tell me," she whispered.

"Not much to tell."

"Why do I think that's not so?" Mary very gently rolled Clint onto his back and leaned over him. "You have this expression on your face. I can't describe it exactly, but it's a little bit sad." She kissed his chest. "This is no time to be sad."

It wasn't sadness that made him shy away from any discussion about the scar. What was it? Denial, maybe. He didn't want to admit that he still hurt, a little. Not the scar, not the tough old wound. Memories. It was the memories that hurt.

"The accident happened a long time ago, and I'm sure it's nothing you want to know about."

"Tonight I want to know everything." She rested her cheek on his chest. Her hands fluttered at his sides. Oh, those fingers. Strong and soft, fearless and relentless. "Tomorrow things will change. Everything will change. People can't know about us. They can't know that I…that we're involved." Her head snapped up and she looked into his eyes. "Are we?" she asked, her voice soft and breathless.

"Involved?"

She nodded.

"Most definitely."

She returned her head to his chest and relaxed, letting out a long breath. "Tonight I want to know everything. For God's sake, Clint, why didn't you give up the rodeo after you were hurt?" She shuddered.

"I did quit for a while," he said. Why not tell her everything? She was here and she wanted to know. Like it or not, he had a difficult time denying Mary anything he could give her. "I gave up competing, but when I was properly healed and Oliver called and asked me to take a job as a bullfighter, I figured…why not? I didn't want to be afraid. I didn't want to walk away and never look back."

"Knowing Shea the way I do, I can't imagine why she didn't lock you up until you came to your senses."

"My family doesn't know much about the accident."

Her head popped up again. "What?"

"They know I was hurt, but they never knew how bad it was."

"Why not?" Mary shook her head. "Shea would be furious if she knew one of her brothers was seriously injured and he kept the news from her. She loves you all so much."

He stroked her cheek. "I called, to make sure everybody knew I was okay, and I told them not to come. I lied and told them I'd probably be out of the hospital the next day."

"You shouldn't have been alone."

"I wasn't alone. Wes was there." He took a deep breath. "And I was engaged to be married."

Mary wrinkled her nose. "I have found another flaw."

Clint smiled at the woman who continued to make herself a part of him. With every touch, with the way her body shifted and aligned against his…that's exactly what she was doing. How could she make this terrible old memory feel not quite so bad? With a smile and a stirring of her body against his, what had seemed so devastating at one time was now unimportant. "Definitely a very serious flaw. Her name was Tonya, and—"

"You can spare me the details," Mary interrupted. "At the moment I'd prefer to come up with my own description. Let's see…big hair, buck teeth, horsey laugh. Am I close?''

''Scary how accurate you are. Do you *know* her?''

Mary laughed at his joke, but the laughter died quickly. It faded away, like a whisper, as Mary placed her hand on his chest. ''What did she do to you?''

She wasn't going to leave this alone. Mary Paris didn't ever leave things alone, he imagined. ''She left,'' he said curtly. ''I got hurt, and it was bad. I decided that was it for me as far as the rodeo goes. I didn't want to ever get on a bull's back again.'' And he hadn't, not in four years. ''Tonya walked out.''

Mary looked genuinely surprised. ''I don't get it.''

''She wanted the cowboy, not the man, and the idea of a quiet life on a little horse ranch in Alabama didn't appeal to her at all.''

Mary snorted. ''What a moron. Did she think you were going to ride bulls until you were an old man? I saw what those guys did tonight. I'm surprised any one of them ever gets on a bull's back for the second time! They're all insane.''

''You think more than a day ahead. Tonya didn't.''

Mary snuggled, laid her head on his shoulder and ran her hands down his arms. ''That's why you have such a soft spot for Wes and Katie,'' she said softly.

''I do not have a soft spot…'' he began.

''Don't deny it,'' she interrupted. ''I saw it from my first day at your place.''

It was true, he supposed. In spite of everything, Wes and Katie had made it. They gave him hope. He looked at them and realized that there was good in the world. He ran his hands down Mary's back. Had anything ever felt so good as holding her? He didn't think so.

''It's okay, you know,'' she said. ''You should be angry, and you shouldn't forgive that horrible skank for what she did to you."

"Skank?" He couldn't help but smile.

"That's what she sounds like to me."

He didn't want to talk about Tonya. Not tonight. Not ever again. At the moment she seemed like such a trivial part of his past. She was nothing. Tonight...tonight was everything.

"What about you?" he said, running his hands down her sides to her hips, tracing her curves and loving every minute of it. "Where are your scars, Special Agent Paris?"

Her smile faded away. "They're all on the inside." It was a telling statement, as was the shift of her eyes.

"Your husband," he whispered.

She nodded gently.

He didn't want to talk about any man Mary had loved. And she had loved her husband; he could see it in her eyes, when she spoke of him. Mary Paris, who tried so hard to be tough and unfeeling, had a big heart. She loved well and deeply.

"Do you want to talk about it?"

She shook her head, much too quickly.

"Okay." He tucked a strand of pale hair behind her ear. "Another night, maybe over a glass or two of muscadine wine." Somehow he knew there would be other nights. Lots of them, if he had his way.

Mary was having trouble shaking it off. She was calm and in control when it came to talking about his past. A mention of her own past and she closed off. Everyone had a past. Mary was right; she was a woman, not a girl. He knew he wasn't the first man in her life. Right now, he just had an unexpected urge to be the last.

"We don't have to talk about anything you don't want

to,'' he said. ''Tonight we'll forget the past, and we'll pretend that tomorrow will never come. This bed is safe, Mary. Nothing will hurt you here.''

He spun Mary onto her back and parted her lips with his, for a proper kiss. He didn't want to talk about Mary's past, Wes and Katie, Tonya, the rodeo or serial killers. Not tonight. He wanted to be inside her again. He wanted to watch her come again. He wanted to feel every tremble, hear every sigh.

And he would.

She ached a little, but it was a good ache. Mary stood beneath the hot shower and closed her eyes. She even allowed herself to smile, but only for a moment. She'd been afraid of what getting involved with Clint might mean, and she couldn't deny that the timing was bad. No, not simply bad. It was terrible. The worst.

But what was she supposed to do? Waiting until this investigation was over should have been her course of action, but last night when she'd walked into Clint's room to look at him, it had ceased to be an option.

Until she'd met Rick, her luck with men had been dismal. A couple of charmers had broken her young heart, but it always healed. And then Rick came along and swept her off her feet, and proved to her that he wasn't like every other man. He wasn't like any other man.

His death had broken her heart all over again, and this time the healing had been much harder.

But she was healing, finally. If not, she wouldn't be falling for Clint Sinclair.

And she was definitely falling for Clint. To be honest, she'd been fighting it since that night at Shea's house. There was just something about him that got to her.

But the timing was bad. Very bad. Until she found the

man who'd killed Elaine, her own life and love didn't
matter. Once that was done, then maybe she could think
about whether or not there was a place in her life for Clint,
and whether or not there was a place in his life for her.

The shower curtain whipped back, and Mary spun
around to find Clint standing there, obviously annoyed
and wearing nothing but a towel.

"I woke up and you were gone," he said.

"I'm not gone, I'm right here." Mary smiled as Clint
dropped his towel and stepped into the shower.

"So I see."

He kissed her while the warm water from the shower
rained down on his back. She was heated from the shower,
and still his mouth was warm. Warm and passionate, his
body and his mouth fitting against hers as if he had been
made for her. Maybe that was true. Clint was hers, in
more ways than she could explain. He wrapped his arms
around her and raked his hands down her wet back.

"I want you to go back to the ranch and wait for me,"
he said when he took his mouth from hers.

"What?"

"You heard me," he said in a lowered voice. "I want
you to go there and wait until I find this guy you're looking for."

She shook her head. "No. Clint, this is my *job*." More
than a job, but she couldn't risk telling anyone how personal this quest was. Not even Clint.

"I don't care. I won't have you putting yourself out
there as bait for a murderer."

She didn't bother to tell him that she wouldn't do any
such thing. They'd had this discussion before; she had
never been completely honest with him.

"I'll be fine."

"What if you're not?" He traced her jawline with one

finger. "What if you're not?" he asked again. "How am I supposed to live with that?"

She had never thought she'd be so comfortable with a man that she could stand in the shower, completely naked, and carry on a conversation. But Clint was different. He was close to her in a way she could not explain, in a way she had never expected.

"I should be insulted that you're trying to take care of me as if it's the 1950s and I'm some helpless housewife."

"But you're not."

"No, I'm not." This was more than the sex, more than companionship or friendship or affection. "It's very sweet that you want to protect me."

He looked a little surprised by her comment. "I want you safe."

She rose up on her toes to kiss him again. "And I want you safe," she said as she took her mouth from his. "But sometimes life isn't that way. It's hard and dangerous and cold." And it was so nice to know there was a place to go at the end of the day that was gentle and safe and warm.

"Come on," she said when Clint didn't respond. "Let me wash your back." She took a soapy washcloth to his back. He had such a fine, muscled, lean body. She spent much more time washing than was necessary, her fingers tracing the muscles, caressing the scars. When that was done, he washed her back, his hand dipping low on her backside, his mouth occasionally resting on her shoulder.

When that was done she washed his chest, and he washed hers. He spent much longer than was necessary getting her soapy and slick and clean. They forgot about everything, laughing and touching in the shower.

Mary quit laughing when Clint bent his head and took one nipple deep into his mouth. She was already aroused, and so was he, but his warm mouth and flickering tongue almost sent her over the edge. How could she want him so much already, after last night and this morning?

Her body throbbed. She wanted him…she needed him. And she loved him. She couldn't tell him, not now. He already wanted to send her away, to keep her safe. If he knew she cared for him so much, he'd surely insist…

The last thing she wanted was to go to war with Clint. He was the only person in the world who had a chance at winning her over.

He knelt down before her, and with his hands on her wet thighs he gently urged her legs apart. His thumbs rocked against her inner thighs, rising higher. His tongue flicked against her intimately, and she grabbed onto the shower rod to keep her knees from buckling, the sensation was so intense. A quiver shot through her body.

Clint made love to her with his mouth, the touch gentle and yet so powerful. The shower rained down on them both, while he fluttered his tongue against her most sensitive flesh. Mary closed her eyes, lifted her head to the warm droplets of water, and climaxed so intensely that if Clint hadn't put his arms around her she would have fallen to the shower floor.

He kept his arms around her as he stood, and she wrapped her arms around his waist and rested her head against his chest.

How was she supposed to look at him all day and not glow and smile in a way that would tell everyone that they were lovers? She'd have to keep her distance, she imagined. She wouldn't be able to talk to him, spend time with him, stare at him. People would see, if she were so foolish, and her chance to draw out the serial killer she hunted would be gone.

"Clint," she said as they stepped out of the shower.

She needed to tell him to be careful, to keep what was happening between them a secret.

He picked her up and carried her from the bathroom, through the connecting door, and into his room. ''What?'' he asked with a half smile.

But not now. She didn't want to ruin this moment. ''How long before we have to leave for the arena?''

''An hour and a half.''

''Good.''

Clint grumbled as he climbed into his truck. He should be wearing a big grin on his face, he should be the happiest man in Birmingham. But no. Mary had hitched a ride with the Kirkland twins, instead of going with him to the arena. She hadn't even looked back, as the three of them had headed out of the parking lot.

He had a great speech planned, for this trip he'd be making alone. After last night and this morning, surely Mary would let him talk a little common sense into her. There were other, better ways to catch the man she was looking for. He could call in Boone and Dean and some of their cohorts, and Mary could wait safely at the ranch.

Who was he kidding? Mary wasn't the kind of woman who would ever be satisfied to wait safely anywhere. She wasn't going to go home and twiddle her thumbs while he did her job for her; that's not who she was.

He could still bring in Boone and Dean, if he could drag Boone away from his pregnant wife for a few days or weeks. There had to be an easier way to catch this guy than to put Mary in harm's way.

Things at the arena were no better than they'd been as he left the hotel. Mary ignored him. She'd told him before they left their hotel rooms that no one could know they were involved, that once they left their adjoining hotel rooms they would have to act as if nothing had happened last night. She had even made him leave by way of his own door, in case anyone was lurking in the hallway. Heaven forbid that anyone should know they were sleeping together.

How was he supposed to act as if nothing had happened? She was undercover, she was accustomed to pretending. He wasn't. Dean and Boone lived that way, and so did Shea, on occasion. Not him. He liked to lay all his cards on the table. No secrets. No faking it. Life was too short to waste it playing make-believe.

But if he blew Mary's cover, she'd never forgive him.

"Friday night," Brisco said as he came up behind Clint. "I love Friday night. We're going to have a full house tonight. The place is already almost sold out."

"Good." Clint looked long and hard at Oliver Brisco. Oliver had taken over for his old man, what, six years ago? For the first time Clint had to ask himself: how well did he really know the man who owned and operated the Brisco Rodeo? "Good crowd last night, too. If we keep this up you'll make a nice profit this summer."

Brisco shrugged. "I'm not in this for the money, but it would be nice to make a healthy profit one of these days." He looked past Clint to lay his dark eyes on Mary. She was busy blowing up those long, narrow balloons. "The girl," he said, nodding in her direction. "She's not bad."

"I guess not," Clint said casually.

"Attractive."

"Yep."

"I find it hard to believe that someone who looks like that doesn't have a husband or a serious boyfriend."

Clint's stomach knotted. He was so tempted to grab Oliver by the collar and warn him off. Unfortunately, he couldn't do that. "I know what you mean."

Brisco continued to stare at Mary. "I guess I might let her hang around for the summer. The kids seemed to like her last night, and the price is right."

"She'll be glad to hear that."

Oliver's assistant and cousin, Brett Brisco, joined them. Even in jeans and a western-style shirt, Brett looked more like an accountant than a cowboy. Clint suspected that Oliver kept his cousin on because he was family.

The younger Brisco was great at keeping things organized. He took the entry fees from cowboys, paid off the winners, handled a hundred details Oliver didn't want to be bothered with.

"We've had two bull riders cancel for tomorrow night," Brett said, making notations on a sheet of paper as he informed his cousin of the change.

"Round up a couple more," Oliver said, irritated.

"I'm trying, but there's a rodeo in Atlanta this weekend, and a lot of our usual boys are already riding there."

Oliver grinned at Clint. "What about you?"

"Ride?" Clint took his eyes off Mary.

"It's been a long time, but I have a feeling you could handle it."

"No, thanks."

"I could get Frank to take your place with Sam, for the last section of the bull riding. He's worked as a bullfighter in a few smaller rodeos."

Clint shook his head. He loved being a bullfighter, he truly did, but last time he'd been on a bull's back he'd almost died. He liked the adrenaline rush that came with his job, but he couldn't imagine himself ever riding again. "It's been too long."

"Think about it," Oliver said. "We can run short if

we have to, but I'd rather not. Hell, I'll even pay your entry fees if you decide to take me up on the offer.''

First Mary and now this. His life had been so simple for so long…and all of a sudden everything had been turned upside down.

Chapter 11

The Kirkland twins, who had been with the rodeo since they were twelve, when Oliver Brisco's father had been running the show, were a wealth of information. All Mary had to do was ask a simple question about one of her suspects, and within minutes she knew all the gossip.

Gossip wasn't foolproof, but Mary was a firm believer that where there was smoke, there was fire. The twins' observations might offer her an investigative direction she hadn't thought of.

She'd managed to eliminate a couple of her initial suspects. The lighting "guy," Mel Lawrence, was actually a forty-two-year-old woman. Mary's info on most of the suspects was sketchy, since she didn't have the full resources of the bureau at her fingertips. Still, she felt a little foolish as she mentally marked Mel off the list. Brisco's secretary Dennis Walker, who assisted Brett Brisco with the administrative details, only had full use of one arm. The left. The man who had killed Elaine and the others had struck often and forcefully with his right arm. So she marked Walker off her list, as well.

Even though she had eliminated a few potentials, she had an abundance of suspects.

Her money was still on the man who owned the rodeo. Oliver Brisco didn't have his father's easy charm, and was not a particular favorite with his employees or the athletes. He was too gruff and demanding to be popular. Physically, he had the strength to overpower his victims, and his divorce had left him pretty bitter where women were concerned. It was his ex-wife that nailed it for Mary. The former Mrs. Brisco looked very much like the eight victims. Mary couldn't dismiss that similarity as coincidence. Still, she had to admit there were a lot of pretty blondes in the world, and as for the earrings Mrs. Brisco liked to wear…it certainly wasn't concrete evidence.

Because all Mary had was gut instinct and coincidence, she had to continue to consider others as suspects. Brett Brisco didn't fit in at the rodeo, but he tried very hard to do just that. He dressed the part, he knew the slang, he knew every cowboy by name. But according to the twins, he just didn't have rodeo in his blood. Amber thought Brett was kinda cute, but Tiffany did not.

Eugene Hitt was a complicated man. A clown. The barrel man. He liked to drink and tell jokes, and while the jokes he told to the crowds were good family fun, the ones he told away from the microphone were almost always off color. He had a wife at home, Amber said, but they'd never seen her. According to Eugene his wife didn't care for the rodeo at all, and she hated telling her friends, when they asked, that her husband made his living as a clown.

Tony Colbert, the exuberant announcer, was an outrageous flirt. He smiled constantly, and he had a lame joke for every occasion. Tiffany was almost positive that even though he was in his early thirties, that thing on his head was a toupee. Something about him gave Amber the willies, even though she'd known him for years. She steered well clear of him.

If Sam was her man, he'd started killing very young. At twenty-one, by her calculations. That in itself would be unusual, but not impossible. Nothing was impossible. Was she subconsciously moving him to the bottom of her list because he was Clint's friend?

She couldn't allow that kind of influence to sway her. Allowing Clint's friendships to color her own opinion and slant the investigation was absolutely unthinkable.

Both twins openly adored Clint and Sam, with an innocently girlish infatuation. And what wasn't to like? Both of the rodeo clowns were in top physical condition, and they put on a display of that strength and agility every night the rodeo was in town. Not only that, they both had more than their share of charisma, and they were both handsome. Handsome and strong and charming. What impressionable girl wouldn't be besotted?

There was something about Clint that would drive any woman wild, Mary imagined. Had she let herself fall for a pretty face and a come-hither smile without knowing what was inside the man? The very thought made her shudder. Work was so much simpler than love!

Even after they arrived at the arena, the twins continued to talk and Mary listened. Listening was an art, one the twins had not yet discovered. That fact worked well to Mary's advantage.

Things were already bustling as the workers prepared for the night to come. Mary blew up a number of long, thin balloons she'd hang from her belt once she got into costume. Out of the corner of her eye, she saw Clint standing to the side, talking to the two Briscos. She was tempted to watch him more closely, to lay her eyes on his face and look her fill. He was natural and at home, in his jeans and cowboy boots, with that black hat that shaded his eyes so she couldn't be sure that he was actually looking at her. She suspected he was watching her like a hawk.

Since she'd arrived at the arena, she'd spotted him close by several times. If he wasn't careful, he was going to blow her cover!

No. She relaxed a little. His attention wouldn't reveal in any way that she was here undercover. But it would ruin any chances of the killer coming after her, if it came to that.

Somewhere deep inside, in a place she tried to deny, she wanted the pervert to come after her. Admitting as much to Josh or Lewis or Clint would send them into a tizzy, so she'd kept it to herself. She didn't want to find incriminating evidence, call in the squad and watch someone else take their murderer down. She wanted him to attack her so she could kill him. She wanted to teach him that not every woman was a victim, that not every woman was weak. And she wanted him to know that she'd come after him because he'd made the mistake of killing her friend.

Unlike the killer's victims, she was prepared. She was ready, and she could take the man who had raped and murdered Elaine down in a matter of seconds. He wouldn't know what hit him.

Like it or not, Clint saw that desire in her. He always had. From the beginning, he'd been able to look at her and know what she was thinking, what she wanted. All along, he had accused her of setting herself up as bait, of putting herself in danger.

She'd denied Clint's accusations more times than she

could remember, even to herself. But now that she was here and the serial killer was hers for the catching, she couldn't deny it any longer.

The man who'd killed Elaine was here. She felt it, sensed it in her bones. Before it was all over, she was going to bring him down.

This would never do. Mary kept drawing his attention away from his work and his well-laid plans. He could stare at her all day and all night, imagining so many exciting possibilities. Once she got into that ridiculous costume of hers, he'd be able to direct his attention to the crowd, where it belonged.

Why had Sinclair brought her here! He clenched and unclenched his fists. To vex him. To taunt him.

No. Sinclair knew nothing. No one knew anything about his activities. He was smarter than they were, so they would never discover who he was and what he had done. Not until he was ready to take due credit, and that time wouldn't come for years.

Mary shook her head and brushed back a pale, golden strand that had fallen across her face. His fingers ached to touch that hair, to grab the strands and pull her to him. He closed his eyes tight and then turned away.

By the time the show was over, Clint was more than ready to return to the hotel. Watching Mary was every bit as exhausting as chasing bulls! Doing both in one evening had drained him.

Again, Mary refused to go with him, preferring to hitch a ride with the Kirkland twins. On the drive back to the hotel his hands clenched the steering wheel, and his jaw was every bit as tight as his fists. He followed the twins' car, trying not to tailgate even though he really wanted to see inside the vehicle.

What was he going to do with Mary? This was her job, he knew that, and it was important to her. But to watch her put herself in harm's way…it was painful. Now she had *him* wondering if one of the men he'd worked with for the past three years could be a cold-blooded killer.

Clint parked several spaces down from the girls and watched them head into the hotel—the twins in their body-hugging tights, Mary in her clown costume. He sat in the truck until they disappeared into the hotel. If Mary saw him following her, she'd have his hide. In spite of his dilemma, a smile broke out on his face. She could have his hide anytime.

When he'd given them time to get to the elevator, he left his truck and followed their steps, his cleats making strange clacking noises on the pavement with each step. Once he was alone with Mary, he had to find a way to make her see that he just couldn't allow this. She wasn't going to like it.

Luckily he didn't run into anyone he knew on the way to the fourth floor, though he did get plenty of stares on the way. Yes, there was a trailer at the arena where they changed into their clothes before the show, and they could change there afterward. But the shower in that trailer was weak and sputtering, and the water was almost always cold. After an evening in the arena what he wanted and needed most was a strong blast of warm water.

He let himself into his room and breathed a sigh of relief when he saw that the connecting door still stood wide open. He listened for the sound of the shower from Mary's room, but heard only water running into the sink. He stepped through the doors and peeked beyond the open bathroom door to see her standing over the sink rubbing cold cream onto her painted face. She still wore the clown costume, minus the red wig.

"How did it go tonight?" he asked, as if he hadn't been watching her every possible minute.

"Fine," she answered. She glanced at him and smiled, with that cold cream all over her face. Why was she so tempting, even now? "Except for that one kid."

"What one kid?" he asked, already concerned. He hadn't seen anything noteworthy happen tonight.

"This little redheaded runt decided to lasso me with his trick rope. The rug rat ended up hitting me over the head with the damn thing about a dozen times."

"When was this?" And why hadn't he seen it?

"You were chasing a bull at the time," she said. She gave him a bright smile. "At least you didn't try to kiss that one."

"I really don't know him all that well," Clint dead-panned, his mind already searching for a solution. To-morrow night he'd ask Boone to watch Mary when he couldn't. That should work. And when they got to Hunts-ville next week...he'd think of something.

Mary rinsed off the cold cream, and the greasepaint with it. Fresh-faced and gorgeous, she was a temptation he had not expected.

He wasn't interested in a serious relationship, and mar-riage was out of the question. For all his talk about finding the right woman and settling down, he wasn't ready to settle down; the very idea scared him spitless. Women had certain expectations from a husband, and he wasn't sure he could ever fulfill any woman's hopes in that re-gard. There was just...this. The way Mary looked at him, the way he wanted her like no other woman. For now, that was enough.

She removed his hat and tossed it aside, then smeared

a little cold cream over his face. He didn't wear as much greasepaint as she did, just a smear here and there, but she very carefully raked her fingers and the cold cream over it all. Just that touch, her gentle fingers on his face, made him hard.

With a slightly damp washcloth, Mary wiped the cold cream and greasepaint from his cheeks, moving slowly. Gently. Her eyes didn't meet his but watched the progress of her own hands on his face. Did she realize how intimate this moment was? He did. He felt it, so deep there was no denying the sensation.

"Take a shower with me?" she asked with a smile that would do any man in.

He slipped her suspenders off her shoulders and began unbuttoning the huge buttons down the front of her polka-dot shirt, smiling as the costume came undone. "I've never undressed another clown before."

Mary slipped her fingers beneath his suspenders. "Neither have I."

Beneath the outrageous costume she was silky skin and enticing swells, all woman and flushed with desire. There was also a gun holstered to her right thigh and a knife in a leather sheath lower, strapped to her calf. He removed the weapons and set them aside without comment.

He loved the way she breathed, the way her lips parted as she undressed him, the way her eyes grew hooded and smoky as he touched her.

Their clothes ended up on the floor, tangled and half inside out.

Clint felt like the brightly colored shirts on the floor: tangled and half inside out. He'd come in here with every intention of laying down the law. He'd tell Mary how he felt, how he worried for her, and she'd let someone else hunt for the serial killer. After all, it was just a job. Any

FBI agent could take up where she left off. Simple—and still he knew she wouldn't like it. With her body wrapped around his, her mouth on his, her hands wandering, he forgot everything but the need to be inside her.

She tilted her head back and he devoured her mouth. He couldn't kiss her deep enough, hard enough. He wanted to inhale her. While they kissed, he cupped her breast and flicked his thumb over her nipple. She arched into him, she pressed her body against his and laid her hand on his hips, pulling him into her so his erection pressed against her belly.

He lifted Mary off the ground, swung her around and propped her against the sink. She wrapped her legs around his hips and drew his body closer to hers as she kissed him passionately.

"Now," she whispered.

Clint guided himself into her, slowly pushing deep. Her body was wrapped around his, tight and sure, from her arms to her thighs to her wet, hot center. He was conscious of nothing but the way they fit together; her softness and his driving need to possess her; Mary's mouth and Mary's hands and Mary's heat.

She wasn't still. Her eyes closed, and she rocked up and against him, then swung down to take him deeper. Harder. Almost instantly, she began to quiver. She tossed her head back and moaned, and he took a nipple into his mouth, suckling deep while her inner muscles tensed and relaxed, while she rode him and cried out with pleasure.

He climaxed while she was still spiraling around him, while her body trembled and she moaned low in her throat. Everything slowed gradually. Her movements, his thrusts; her breathing, his heartbeat.

Mary rested her head on his shoulder and sighed, then

laughed lightly. "Wow," she whispered on the tail end of the laugh.

"Definitely wow." Clint threaded his fingers through her hair. He felt as if he'd drunk too much muscadine wine, as if he'd fallen into something so deep and beautiful he would happily drown in it.

Mary lifted her head and looked him in the eye. "I'm not sure exactly what this is."

"It's…"

She laid a silencing finger over his mouth. "I can't even think about it right now." Her blue eyes went soft. Soft and serious. "I shouldn't be here with you. I shouldn't let this happen. Not now."

"Too late."

"I know." She traced his jaw with one finger; the finger she had used to silence him. "Clint, you're going to have to stop watching me all the time."

He could deny that he'd been following her around the arena, but why? He didn't want to lie to her. Besides, he was pretty sure fooling Mary was tough to do. "What if I can't?"

"Trust that I'm good at my job, that I know what I'm doing."

"Are you telling me to leave you alone?"

"Outside this room, yes."

He was still inside her, her body still quivered, and she was telling him he had no right to protect her.

Clint slept, but Mary couldn't. She stretched out beside him in his bed, her eyes on the ceiling.

Give her a gun and a bad guy, and she was in her element. For the past two years her life had been cut and dried, black and white. She knew who she was and what she wanted from life.

Clint turned everything around, and that terrified her. Earlier tonight, they had come together so fast and furiously she hadn't even thought of slowing down, much less stopping. Nothing else had mattered but the way he felt in her arms and the intensity of her need for him. They hadn't used protection. She had never, never made that mistake before. Mary Paris didn't make mistakes.

Nothing scared Mary more than losing control. Tonight, she had most definitely lost control.

She knew very well that Clint Sinclair liked living dangerously. She'd known that all along. He liked everything faster and higher, closer to the edge. He played with bulls, he knew no fear. But tonight, tonight had been truly dangerous. Did Clint get the same rush from her that he got from popping a bull on the nose? Was there anything else to this relationship, or was she kidding herself?

One thing for sure—she didn't have time for this now. Clint was distracting her, keeping her from doing her job. She didn't have a personal life, and now was no time to develop one! Maybe when this was over and Elaine's killer was dead or behind bars, she'd have time to figure out what this was…if it was anything at all.

She knew what she had to do, and while her brain had accepted she had no choice, her heart didn't like it at all.

Clint rolled over, finding too much empty space beside him. Mary was already up. He lifted his head and glanced around the room. His first thought was that she was in the bathroom, but everything was so quiet. Too quiet.

And then he noticed that the connecting door between their rooms was closed, and when he sat up he saw that the clothes he'd left in her bathroom last night had been tossed onto the floor on his side of that closed door.

He grabbed a pair of boxers and stepped into them, then

walked over his clothes to get to the closed connecting door. "Mary," he whispered as he knocked. Maybe she was filing a report or making a phone call. She did that now and then, making contact with her boss. But she'd never closed the door on him before. "Mary," he said again, a little bit louder this time. He heard nothing through the heavy door.

He was getting worried, then he glanced down and caught sight of a folded sheet of paper stuck into the pocket of the shirt he'd worn last night. He grabbed it and shook it open.

There was no *Dear Clint,* no *sorry, darling,* just two simple sentences that told him more than he wanted to know.

This is happening too fast for me. I need to step back.

Too fast? Maybe. Step back? No way. He crumpled the sheet of paper in his hand and tossed it into the garbage can by the desk.

She might be the one. He almost licked his lips at the sight of her. It was a Saturday night, and yet she came in alone. She had that look about her, the look he always recognized. The way her gaze flitted here and there, the way she stood apart from the others...she was shy, lonely.

Trusting.

He moved closer and took a quick peek at her left hand. Perfect. No wedding ring, but there was a tan line there, where a ring had once been. She was divorced, recently by the look of that tan line.

Best of all, when she walked the dangling earrings she wore swayed with her blond hair. They caught the light, as did the golden highlights in her hair, dancing enticingly. She wouldn't wear earrings like that if she didn't want him to notice her.

He noticed.

She wasn't flawless; she wasn't as pretty as Mary. That thought robbed him of a small portion of his excitement. Not all, but some. Damn Sinclair for bringing her here! He should wait another week or two before choosing his next victim, but Mary had his insides tied up in knots. She was the one he wanted, but he couldn't have her. She would be missed right away. He wouldn't be able to hide her body and slip out of town before anyone knew she was dead.

He followed the newly divorced woman, noted where her seat was and watched until he was certain she wasn't meeting anyone. He watched as long as he could, and then he had to go. He had a job to do, after all.

Chapter 12

Mary had never thought of herself as a coward, but tonight she definitely felt lily-livered. The way she'd left the bed this morning, the note, the way she'd avoided Clint all afternoon; she was definitely in need of a good dose of courage.

But she couldn't allow herself to be distracted by her own usually dull personal life. Not now. Later, after she'd done her job, she'd explain everything—if Clint would listen to her.

The place was packed once again. All night she'd worked the crowd, entertaining the kids and keeping an eye on the throng that filled the civic center. Some of the faces in the crowd were the same as on the previous two nights, but no one acted overly suspicious. And their eyes were on the arena floor, not on the women in the seats.

Since she'd never believed the killer hid himself in the audience, she wasn't surprised.

The evening's performance was almost done. Clint and

Sam chased a bull from the arena as a cowboy who'd been thrown three seconds into his ride hobbled to safety. From the mezzanine she couldn't see Clint's face nearly well enough, and that black hat of his shaded his features, in any case. It did seem that he moved differently tonight. There was a new tension in the way he moved, a tautness in the length of his body. His moves were not as fluid as they usually were, and he didn't seem to be having fun. If nothing else, Clint always had fun on the arena floor. Not tonight. Was he angry?

Of course he was angry. She'd slipped out of his bed and closed the door on him, figuratively and literally. A note. A short, precise, insufficient note was all she'd offered in way of explanation. She should have had the guts to tell Clint to his face that she didn't have time for this. For *him*. Not now.

If she were honest, she'd admit to him that she was scared of the way he made her feel again. So scared. Life was so much easier without messy emotions getting in the way. The last two years had proved that to her. Clint's life was a roller coaster; he readily admitted as much. Even with the excitement of her job, Mary's own life was much more ordered and sedate. Clint lived on a roller coaster; Mary was on a long, steady train ride to nowhere.

At the end of the night's performance, the crowd made its way toward the exits and Mary went downstairs to meet the twins. Maybe, if she was lucky, she could hook up with them and get out of here before she ran into Clint. She was still such a coward.

She found Amber, but Tiffany wasn't with her twin sister. That in itself was unusual. They were always together!

Amber gave Mary a big smile. "We're going out. Wanna come with us?"

Mary's heart sank. She was in no mood to party with two exuberant girls. But if she didn't stick with the twins, would she have to ask Clint for a ride back to the hotel? Talk about uncomfortable! "Thanks, but I'd better not."

Amber tsked. "Come on. You have to go! It's your first tour with the rodeo, and you've survived three nights. Time to celebrate. Everyone else will be there! It's Saturday night."

Everyone? Mary began to relent. This might be her chance to see her suspects in a more casual setting. Would they open up after a beer or two? Let something telling slip? "Okay." She glanced down at her costume. "But I can't go like this."

"We'll go back to the hotel for a quick change, then meet the others at a club down the road. You in?"

In the distance, she caught sight of Clint talking with Sam. You'd never know to look at him that anything had happened between them. He was so cool, so…normal. She had to consider that maybe he wasn't angry with her. Maybe he didn't care that much.

She'd tried to put her feelings for him aside, she'd done her best all day to forget Clint Sinclair. And still he was interfering with her investigation!

"I'm in," Mary said softly.

The blonde with the dangling earrings was alone, apart from the others. He kept a decent distance between himself and the woman as they exited the civic center arena, a horde around and between them. His blood was pumping hard, his skin felt as if it were on fire. He should wait before striking. He should plan more carefully and wait a few days or even a few weeks. But no, he couldn't wait.

"Hey!" a familiar voice called.

He tried to ignore that voice, but the call came again,

closer this time. He turned to face one of the twins. Tiffany, he thought. Her hair was a little different. It curled near her temple. Quickly, he glanced over his shoulder. The woman was not too far ahead. He could still catch up with her, outside.

Tiffany smiled at him. "I've been trying to run everyone down before they got out of here. We're going out to grab a drink or two, maybe dance a little bit. Wanna come?"

He shook his head. Why was she bothering him? They didn't socialize. He'd always had the distinct impression that the twins didn't even like him. He wished they'd leave him alone. Every second that passed, his victim got farther away. But he could not run, he could not escape without rousing suspicion. "I don't think so."

"We want everyone to be there!" Tiffany argued. "This is Mary's first rodeo. We have to show her a good time. Tonight will be a good chance for her to get to know everyone."

He forgot the lonely woman who was now almost out of his reach. "Mary?"

"You know, the new girl."

"Yes, of course," he said. Suddenly he knew it was Mary he wanted, not the flawed woman who had probably made her escape by now. Mary wouldn't be wearing her clown costume for a social evening. Her hair would be down, her luscious shape would be revealed. Would she laugh? Would she flirt?

He could not have her, but the idea of getting close was appealing. Maybe, if the circumstances allowed, he could lay his hands on her. Casually. Briefly. Maybe he could "accidentally" touch her hair.

He forgot the woman who was now gone. Out of the

arena, out of his head. "Of course," he said with a smile. "I'd love to join you."

The lights in the bar were low, the noise a dull roar. It was all Clint could do to keep from grabbing Mary by the arm and dragging her out of here.

A large group of rodeo employees and a few athletes had claimed a corner of the bar, pulled several tables together and ordered enough appetizers to feed an arena full of bull riders. Beer was the drink of choice. The twins were carded, and they happily showed their driver's licenses to the waitress. They were barely legal.

Mary ignored him. They sat on opposite sides of the tables that had been pressed together. He couldn't touch her from here, he couldn't even catch her eye.

She was on tonight. Smiling, laughing, nursing that one beer and munching on appetizers. Tony and Eugene flirted outrageously with her, Sam tried to make her feel like one of the gang and even Brett seemed smitten. A couple of the bull riders tried to get chummy, but she quickly put them in their place. She had a way of doing that with a look, a simple word or two.

When Oliver arrived, he pulled his chair up next to Mary's and shoved everyone else aside.

Clint seethed. He was tied up in knots for more reasons than he cared to ponder at the moment. Most of all, he was jealous. Jealous! Mary was his, and here she was putting herself on display for her suspects. Making herself a target as surely as if she'd painted a bull's-eye on her back.

Oliver said something that made all the girls around him laugh. Why was he being so entertaining tonight? He usually steered clear of these get-togethers.

Tony was no better. The rodeo announcer was single

and thought himself a ladies' man. For a ladies' man, he was alone an awful lot. Clint had never known the man to be involved in a serious relationship. There was something calculating about the way Tony smiled at Mary. Clint didn't like it.

When Clint couldn't take any more, he stood, walked around the jumble of chairs and leaned slightly toward Mary.

"Dance," he said.

She looked up at him and smiled, but it wasn't a real smile. There was tension in the set of her neck, in the hardness in her blue eyes. It was a look that should have sent him running, but did not.

"No, thanks," she said softly.

Clint didn't budge. "Dance," he said in an even lower voice. "Or I make a scene here and now."

Mary took a deep breath, excused herself with a smile and took his hand. She squeezed that hand too tightly as they walked away from the table.

A slow song was playing on the jukebox. Something twangy about broken hearts. He took her in his arms and pulled her closer than she wanted to be. Since the song had been playing for a minute or two, they didn't have much time. He knew better than to think he had Mary in his arms for more than this one half dance.

"What the hell are you doing?" she whispered.

"I was just about to ask you the exact same question."

Mary pursed her lips for a moment, then relaxed and smiled gently. She knew people were watching. "Blow this investigation for me, and I'll make you pay in ways you never imagined."

He gave her a tight smile. "Sounds interesting."

Even in the low light, he saw her blush. "You know what I mean!"

"Do I?"

"Clint..."

He lowered his head and placed his lips close to her hear. "Let me help you," he whispered.

"No."

"You shouldn't be doing this alone. At least have the FBI send in backup. I can get a couple more people into the rodeo if necessary. We always need people for concessions and taking care of the animals...."

"No!" she said, more stridently this time.

He held her so close, he could feel her heart beat faster. Harder. Her breathing changed subtly. Something about his suggestion frightened or alarmed her.

Why? It didn't make any sense. "Mary..."

The song ended, and she broke away with a sigh of relief.

When had she begun to rely on Clint? Mary lay in the dark, in her own bed. Alone. Clint was on the other side of the wall, and damned if she couldn't feel him anyway. A wall between them, a confession she could not make, a relationship that had come together too quickly and much too strongly...and she felt him to her bones.

Was he sleeping? Tossing and turning? Pacing?

Rick had been a good guy, like Clint, but he hadn't been such a stubborn ass, and he certainly hadn't been such an overprotective, macho, interfering man.

Was it possible that she could find two truly good men in one lifetime? It seemed too much to ask, too much to even hope for. When Rick had died she'd been so certain that was it for her. She'd found love, she'd embraced it, it hadn't lasted nearly long enough. Maybe love wasn't meant to last.

Clint was going to ruin everything, with his talk about

bringing in more agents. If he found out that she wasn't here officially…

Work usually soothed her, took her mind off the messiness of real life. Mary turned her mind away from Clint and went over her list of suspects once again. They had all been very nice to her tonight, but no one had paid what she'd call unnatural interest. Once Clint had asked her to dance, they'd all taken a turn.

Eugene was…enthusiastic. There was no other word for it. When that dance was finished, she had a good idea of what a bull rider felt like after he'd been thrown. Tony had wandering hands, but responded properly to a cutting glance. Brett had been a perfect gentleman, and a better dancer than she'd expected. Sam was a cutup, with a smile that surely broke hearts and a body that was almost as good as Clint's. He'd told her, as they danced, that if Clint hadn't already laid claim to her he'd ask her out himself. When she'd told him no one had a claim on her, he'd only smiled wider. How much did he know?

Oliver Brisco, who remained at the top of her suspect list, had held her a little bit too close when they'd danced, and she could swear that once, just once, he'd taken a long whiff of her hair. She couldn't be sure. But he never crossed the line into inappropriate territory. When he held her tight, was he offering her a subtle reminder that he was stronger than she was? Maybe. The man had eyes that told her nothing. Deep, dark eyes that looked more like those of an animal than of a human being.

How was she supposed to sleep, with those faces running through her mind? One of them had killed Elaine. Who? Even if she could dismiss her investigation, how was she supposed to forget that Clint was sleeping just beyond the wall?

There were a few relaxation exercises she called upon

when she couldn't sleep. Lying in the dark, she tried them now. Deep breaths, a clear mind, a pleasant picture. Roses. Sometimes she thought of roses. She didn't have time to grow flowers of any kind, and there certainly hadn't been any men sending her roses, but still…the mental picture of something so simple and beautiful soothed her.

Right before she drifted off to sleep, another image entered her mind. Clint. Instead of disturbing and rousing her and making her angry all over again, that image soothed her as much as any rose.

Clint paced, staring at the solidly closed connecting door. He could pound on that door until Mary was forced to answer. He could make a lot of noise if he had to; he could see that everyone on this floor came running.

He didn't.

Something was wrong. Mary was hiding something from him, and he didn't like it. Tonight when they'd been dancing and he'd mentioned backup, she'd reacted more strongly than she should have.

He knew her better than he'd ever known anyone, and in the depths of his soul he was certain something was wrong.

Clint sat on the edge of the bed and lifted the phone from the nightstand. He dialed the number from memory.

Dean answered on the second ring. "Sinclair," he said gruffly.

"I woke you," Clint said.

"It's almost three-thirty in the morning. Of course you woke me."

Clint glanced at the clock by the phone. Two-thirty here, three-thirty in Atlanta. Either one was too late an hour to be calling anyone. "Sorry. I'll call back in the morning."

"No," Dean said quickly, his voice no longer quite so gruff. "I'm already awake. What's up?"

"Special Agent Mary Paris." Clint took a deep breath. This was a huge risk. It was the kind of interference Mary might never forgive. But what choice did he have? "You know people in the FBI."

"Sure."

"Think you could call around and see what you can find out about her?"

There was a moment of silence. "What's going on?"

"Nothing," Clint said quickly. "Okay, almost nothing. I just have this really bad feeling that she's not telling me everything."

"I have a couple of good friends over that way. I'll see what I can find out."

"Thanks," Clint said, feeling a rush of relief. If there was anything to find out, Dean could do it.

"It might be Monday morning before I get in touch with anyone," Dean added.

"That's fine." Clint shifted his weight on the bed. "Do me a favor and keep it low key. I don't want you stirring up a hornet's nest and causing problems for Mary. I just need to know what's going on."

"Clint," Dean said, lowering his voice. "Is this thing with Agent Paris getting personal?"

He could deny it, but why? If he had his way, before long everyone would know that things between him and Mary had gotten very personal. "Yeah."

Dean let loose with his big brother sigh. "Are you sure that's a good idea?"

"Nope."

There was a short pause. Was Dean trying to come up

with an argument that might sway his youngest brother? In the end all he said was "Be careful. I'll call you next week."

"Call me on the cell," Clint said. "We head out of here early Monday morning."

"Good enough. Just remember to leave it on, will you?" Clint was notorious for tossing his cell phone in the glove compartment and forgetting about it for days at a time, something his eldest brother did not understand. "Where are you headed next?"

"Huntsville. I might take a day or two off and go home before the rodeo gets started, but I'm not sure that Mary will go for it." Time to make a confession. "And I'm not leaving her behind."

They ended the phone call, and Clint fell back onto the bed. He wanted Mary here, he wanted her wrapped around him. He couldn't be certain she was safe unless he could see her, touch her. He wouldn't sleep well unless she was in the same bed, sharing a pillow and hogging the covers.

If he blew this for her, she might never lie with him again. Never.

He lay in his bed, eyes wide open, heart pounding furiously.

Mary. He'd touched her, danced with her, and she'd smiled at him. She was more beautiful up close than from a distance, more delicate and feminine. More fragile.

The other woman, the one in the crowd, was almost completely forgotten. It would have been wrong to waste one of his precious kills on her. He had been hasty in selecting her, and it was good that fate had prevented him from following her to her car. She wasn't special.

Mary was special.

It was true he would have to break his pattern to take

her, but perhaps it was time for a challenge. Time to test his intelligence, time to take another step. The others had been easy. Mary would not be easy.

She would fight him. He'd felt the muscles beneath her baggy blouse as they'd danced. Yes, she was strong for a woman, but she was too small, too weak to fight him efficiently. He would win; he always did.

He closed his eyes and imagined what it would be like. Mary. He hadn't been this excited about any woman since Kristin had been a part of his life. He had loved Kristin, he had craved her, he had been deliciously obsessed with her. Every waking moment had been filled with Kristin. In every dream, she was there. He had made her his whole world.

In the end, she had discarded him, laughing at his inadequacies. Belittling him. Making him feel insignificant.

He never should have told her how much he loved her. That had been the beginning of the end for them.

No matter how much he wanted to, he couldn't kill Kristin. He could never murder someone who had been so close to him. Suspicions would turn his way if he did.

But Mary…Mary might be the next best thing.

Chapter 13

She had planned to make the trip from Birmingham to Huntsville, a two-hour trek, with the twins. Clint wouldn't hear of it. Again, he threatened to make a scene if she didn't do as he commanded.

This was going to have to stop. She couldn't allow him to hold what he knew over her head indefinitely! He had the power to blow her cover, to send her quarry under so deep she'd never find him.

"We can go back to the ranch for a couple of days," he said, his eyes on the highway before him. "Some of the rodeo workers will be in Huntsville and setting up by tomorrow morning, but most take a day or two off between shows."

"I can't take any time off," she said. "You know that."

"Everybody needs a little downtime now and then," he argued in a sensible voice. "Even you."

She wasn't a big believer in vacations or days off. Her

job helped her to forget. Working was her crutch, her place to hide.

"We need to talk," she said tersely.

"Go right ahead," Clint responded casually, as if everything between them was perfectly normal. What was he thinking? Nothing between them had ever been normal.

In her mind, she had this speech well rehearsed. Would anything she said make a difference? She had to try. "You have got to stop this."

"Stop what?"

His casual response made her angry. "Getting in the way, for one thing! Every time I turn around, you're there. Watching. Staring at me. Following me around as if I need a bodyguard."

Again, he remained calm. "You do need a bodyguard."

She turned her head to gaze out the window. Trees, tall and green, lined the interstate. It was summer, the trees were in full leaf, and it seemed as if there was nothing else anywhere near but the cars Clint passed. On a Monday morning, traffic was sparse. What kind of argument could she offer, besides threatening to have Clint arrested?

It had been right to bring things between them to a halt. Even though she missed being with him, she knew ending it had been the right thing to do. Clint distracted her. He made her think that she was missing something… something like a life beyond her job. It would be too easy to fall into his arms every night, hide in his bed, let him hide in her body… It would just be too easy….

The cell phone he'd placed on the seat between them rang, and he answered quickly. Mary's first thought was of Katie and Wes, her second of the very pregnant Jayne Sinclair. Since Clint didn't chat casually on his cell phone, she figured that whatever this call was about, it was important.

All she could hear, of course, was Clint's side of the conversation.

"Hello…what?" His eyes cut her way, his jaw tensed. "No. Not yet. I'll call you back."

He turned off the cell phone, glared at her and without warning pulled the truck sharply off the road. She grabbed onto the door handle to keep from being tossed around, his change of direction was so fierce.

"Out," he said curtly as the truck came to a jerking halt.

For a moment, Mary thought he actually intended to leave her stranded on the side of the road…then he turned off the engine, exited from the driver's side and rounded the front of the truck to stalk into the tall grass on the shoulder of the road, pushing his fingers through his hair in obvious exasperation.

Mary threw open her door and stepped down. "What's wrong?" Again, she thought of Jayne and Katie and their babies.

When Clint turned to face her, she knew the pregnant women had nothing to do with him pulling the truck off the road.

He stared at her, hard, for a long moment. "I understand you're on an extended leave of absence from the FBI."

She felt the blood drain from her face. All along, she had known that Clint wouldn't help her if he knew she was pursuing this case on her own. "I can explain."

"You can explain," he repeated, taking a long step toward her. "You're risking your life hunting down a sick serial killer *on your own.* You've put your life on the line for a man who rapes and then carves up or strangles his victims, a butcher you called him, and you stand here and tell me you can *explain?*"

Her only way out of this was to reason with him, rationally and calmly. "I had a theory about the killings, but no one would believe me. I didn't have enough for the authorities to admit that they'd put two innocent men in prison. So yes, I'm on a leave of absence. I'm spending my vacation time trying to find a serial killer. It doesn't change the fact that I'm right, or that if I don't find this guy, he's going to kill again."

She could see that Clint was not moved. "It's over. I'll see Oliver as soon as we get to Huntsville and I'm going to tell him everything. You're out," he said, leaning down toward her.

Her heart began to kick. She wanted to argue rationally, she wanted to remain cool and detached. But inside, she was anything but detached. "Don't do this to me," she whispered. "Please."

"I fell for that sweet *please* once, darlin', but it won't happen again."

"Why are you doing this to me?" Panic welled up inside her. She was so close. She'd never be this close again. This was her chance, her only chance.

"Why?" Clint repeated, growing angrier as the moments ticked past. "You want to know why it's important to me that you keep yourself safe? Because I think I love you!" he shouted.

She flinched.

"Not what you expected me to say, I'm guessing," he muttered in a calmer voice.

"It's just…not a good time."

"Not a good time." He laughed hoarsely and ran his fingers through his hair again. "Is there ever a good time to have your life turned upside down and inside out?"

"I guess not."

He laid one hand on her face and made her look him

in the eye. "I can't let you do this. I can't." His other hand reached out to touch her stomach, very lightly. His fingertips brushed against her blouse and the skin beneath. "A couple of nights ago, I was inside you. No protection, nothing between us. Just you and me. What if we made a baby?"

Mary shook her head. "That's unlikely," she said quickly. "It was just that once."

"Unlikely, maybe, but not impossible," Clint argued. "What if I let you continue and something happens, and it's not only you I lose but our baby, too?"

Another wave of panic swelled inside her. "There is no baby!"

"You don't know that," he whispered. "Maybe I've been spending too much time around Katie and Jayne. I've never given much thought to babies before."

She shook her head. "We can't talk about babies, Clint. And you can't start shouting orders at me. Back off and let me do my job."

"No," he said in a firmer voice. "I can't stand back and let you put yourself in danger!"

"It's my life!"

"It's mine, too."

Her world was falling apart, one piece at a time. Everything she wanted was so close, and Clint was going to ruin it. "You can't do this to me," she whispered.

"I can." He turned his back on her and started to walk away.

"No!" She ran for Clint, threw herself at him and knocked him flat on the ground. Since she had the element of surprise on her side, she managed to knock the air out of him. They struggled, briefly, and he ended up on his back, on the ground, and she straddled him. Her every breath was deep as she tried to push her panic down. A semi flew past, and a rush of warm wind washed over them both.

"You don't understand." Her words were caught on the wind that died as quickly as it had come.

Clint didn't try to push her off, he didn't tell her that he didn't care to understand. He wrapped one hand around her wrist, manacled her with gentle, firm fingers, and said, "Explain it to me."

She'd never said the words out loud. They'd been in her mind, in her heart, but she'd never spoken about this to anyone. Mary stared down, looking into Clint's green eyes. They were nice eyes, kind eyes. Was there any truth in what he said? *Love.* Was it a word he'd use to control her? Or was there a touch of the truth in his angry words? She wasn't ready to say the words out loud, might never be ready…but there was a very good chance she was falling in love with him, too.

As she began to speak tears filled her eyes. "Elaine was the seventh victim. She was murdered last year."

"You knew her," Clint said gently.

Mary nodded, and tears ran down her face. "We went to college together. Over the years we talked on the phone and e-mailed and exchanged Christmas cards. She was…" Her heart lurched as she began to sob quietly. "Sweet. Elaine was always quiet and shy and sweet."

"I'm sorry."

"That's not enough!" Now that the tears had started, they wouldn't stop. "Sorry. Everybody's sorry!" It was her own failing that made her so angry she couldn't focus properly on Clint's face. "I should've known. I should've been able to save her."

"You couldn't know…"

She slapped Clint on the chest. "He picked Elaine because she was expendable! No one missed her for days!

I should have been there for her, I should have stopped him!'' Again, she hit Clint on the chest. Her eyes were so filled with tears the man beneath her was a blur. She wanted to be strong, to be solid and emotionless, but she had started to sob and she couldn't stop. ''She was my *friend,* and I wasn't there for her. No one was there for her. She was *expendable.* Someone should have been there for her. Someone should have known she was gone.'' Inside, she felt as if she were literally falling apart. ''It's just not fair,'' she whispered hoarsely. ''I couldn't save Rick, and I couldn't save Elaine, and…and…''

Clint slowly sat up, wrapping his arms around her, and pulled her face to his shoulder. For a moment or two she fought him. She wasn't a little girl, she didn't want any man to take care of her. But he stroked her back and she gave in. She wept hard, she sobbed until she ached all over.

She clutched Clint's shirt in her hands, held on tight while she cried. She hadn't cried in so long, she hated to cry! But she couldn't stop. She wept until she didn't have any tears left, and all the while Clint cradled her against his body and whispered soothing nonsense into her ear.

When the tears stopped and the sobbing ended, Mary lifted her head to look Clint in the eye. She knew she was a mess, red-eyed and puffy. Her nose was running, her breath kept hitching.

''Don't take this away from me,'' she whispered.

''Do you know how hard it is for me to watch you do this?'' He brushed back a strand of hair that had fallen across her cheek. ''Do you know how much it hurts to watch you put yourself in danger? And if…''

''No ifs,'' she interrupted. She couldn't deal with the idea of a baby right now. No matter how unlikely the concept, no matter how frightening…it was a possibility she could not even consider.

Clint didn't answer for a while. He touched her, he frowned. He muttered beneath his breath. "All right," he finally said. "I won't blow your cover. I won't yank the rug out from under you."

She nodded, relieved and near tears all over again.

"But darlin', you have to let me help."

Mary glared at him when they checked into the hotel near the Von Braun Center in Huntsville. Yes, he had requested connecting rooms again. If she didn't like it that was too bad. There was no way he could let her out of his sight—especially not now.

She was working alone. The very idea gave him the shivers. If she was right about her serial killer being with the rodeo, she had exposed herself in the worst way. Without backup. Without authority. She insisted she was only gathering information, searching for evidence, but he didn't believe her. When she'd broken down in his arms, she'd revealed too much. This case was much too personal to her. She was way too close.

Once they'd gotten back on the interstate, after he'd confronted Mary with the truth, her tears had dried and she'd spent the next hour staring out the passenger side window. Was she angry that he knew her secret? Or embarrassed that she'd broken down in front of him? He had a feeling Mary made damn sure she only cried when she was alone.

They'd ignored his unplanned confession once they were back on the highway. Love? No way. He cared about Mary, he truly did, and there were moments he was certain she was an important part of his life and would be for some time to come. But love? No. He'd fallen into that trap too quickly once before and he'd been burned. Maybe the "I think" had saved him. Maybe Mary was going to be just as anxious to forget the moment as he was.

He was surprised that she knocked on the connecting door before he had a chance to.

When he opened the door, she walked into his room. "Not bad," she said, glancing around his room with a critical eye and refusing to look directly at him.

"You're sure you don't want to go back to the ranch for a couple of days?" he said to her back as she walked toward the windows and pulled back the drapes to look down on the parking lot.

"I need to be here to see who's around and who's not, just in case…" She faltered. "Just in case he took someone in Birmingham." She trembled gently and then tried to hide her telling reaction. Clint knew that if another woman died before Mary found her man she would blame herself for not finding him in time. She didn't need that horror, on top of so many others.

He nodded. "All right. You're calling the shots here."

Mary turned to face him, allowing the drapes to fall shut. She wasn't the cool, sexy woman he'd met in Shea's living room. He knew her too well to be fooled by the facade she'd built for herself. She was still sexy, in her jeans and white buttoned-up shirt, she still had a figure that would stop traffic. But inside she was anything but cool. The emotion she tried to hide simmered, warm and real, close to boiling over. That emotion made her vulnerable, and Special Agent Mary Paris did not want to be vulnerable. She didn't want anyone to know that she could be hurt.

"I can call Boone and Dean," he said.

"No," she insisted quickly. "No one else. Just you and

me, Clint. I can't afford to stir things up, and if those brothers of yours are hanging around…''

''I got it,'' he said. ''You don't want to scare off your suspect. But I have to tell Dean something. If I don't, he might mention your presence here to someone who shouldn't know, and that would make a mess for you, I imagine.''

Mary remained stoic. Stubborn. ''My supervisor knows that I'm here to gather information. I can do whatever I want to on my own time.''

''You're not just gathering information,'' he accused. He'd seen her reaction this morning, knew how very personal this was to her. She was the kind of woman who would do anything to get what she wanted, or to catch the man she hunted.

''I am,'' she said softly. ''All I need is something new to take to the bureau. Something solid. I just need to find something that will force them to take a good hard look at Brisco.''

''You really think it's Oliver, don't you.'' He couldn't imagine anyone he knew doing the things Mary's killer had done. Oliver was brusque at times, but he wasn't the kind of man who would do something so cruel, so violent.

Mary nodded. ''He's still my primary suspect. Did you know his ex-wife?''

''No. They were divorced before I joined the rodeo. I never met her.''

There was a new twinkle in Mary's eyes, a light that was almost mischievous. ''It was a very ugly divorce.''

''Lots of men go through ugly divorces and they don't turn into psychos.''

''I know that.'' Mary claimed a chair by the window and stretched out her blue-jeaned legs. He wanted to join her, pull her to her feet and drag her into this bed. He didn't want to talk about killers, evidence and danger. He wanted to make her forget.

"Four years ago, the ex Mrs. Brisco showed up at the beginning of the tour," Mary said in a businesslike voice. "She raised some kind of a stink. I've asked around, but no one seems to remember exactly what she did. They only remember that Brisco was furious that she was hanging around."

"Did you ask him about it?"

She looked horrified. "Of course not!"

Clint sighed and sat on the edge of the bed. "That's really not much in the way of evidence, Mary. Even I know that."

"Kristin Brisco is blond, pretty and given to wearing fancy, dangling earrings."

"Like the victims," Clint said.

"Like the victims."

"That seems pretty flimsy to me."

"It is," Mary said. "But it's all I've got."

No, that wasn't *all* she had. She had him, well and good. She had him wrapped around her little finger.

That didn't mean he had to play her way. "All right. I'll watch your back. I'll see what I can find out as far as old gossip goes. But Mary, one thing has changed."

She looked very suspicious. "What's that?"

"You will no longer make yourself appear to be expendable."

She pursed her lips but said nothing.

"By nightfall, everyone will know that we're sleeping together."

"Clint!"

"We're involved, we're serious and if you went missing I would most definitely notice."

"I could tell everyone you're imagining things."

Clint grinned at her. "You could. Think anyone would buy it?" He expected a heated argument, but Mary accepted his edict with surprising grace.

Maybe she was afraid he'd pull out the possibility of a baby as ammunition if she didn't back down gracefully.

He knew she was right; it was a definite long shot. But they had been together without protection that one time, and it was a possibility.

One that should have terrified him, but did not.

He smiled at the jeweler. "Yes, that's exactly what I'm looking for."

The thin little jeweler, a man in his sixties, boxed the gold earrings.

With a continuing smile, he counted out the bills. A small gift for Mary, that wouldn't be too far out of bounds. And she would love the earrings. They'd be beautiful on her, gold swinging from her delicate earlobes and catching the light as she walked. There was something so erotic about pale hair and gold earrings lying across his pillow. At the moment, he could very well imagine Mary's blond hair and these earrings on his pillow.

When he left the store, he removed his purchase from the jewelry store box, dropped the earrings into his pocket without touching them and discarded the box in a nearby garbage can. Sitting inside his car, he pulled on a pair of rubber gloves before removing the earrings from his pocket. One could not be too careful.

Hands properly covered, he carefully placed the earrings in a small, unmarked box. With his gloved hands, he dropped the new box into a plain brown paper bag, folded down the ends as if he were packing a lunch for himself, and then took his pen and wrote *Mary* on the side of the bag.

She would be so pleased with the gift, and she would look so pretty in the new earrings.

This week he would dance with her again. Perhaps on Friday, perhaps Saturday. He would wait for the proper opportunity to arise. And when the week was done and the rodeo packed up and left town, he'd take her away for a few days. He never had a problem taking a couple of days between shows if he needed the time. Mary would wear his gift, and he'd seduce her. He had a special place planned for her. A secluded place. Everything was arranged. They'd be alone.

And when their long weekend was through, if she didn't love him as madly as he had come to love her…he'd kill her.

Chapter 14

Mary sat before the mirror in Sam's trailer, putting on her makeup. She was getting good at this; even Lewis wouldn't know her under all this greasepaint.

Clint paced behind her while she got ready for Huntsville's opening night of the rodeo. True to his word, he'd stuck close to her since he'd discovered that she was working on her own. At the hotel, they slept in their own rooms, in their own beds, and they rarely discussed anything but the case. It was easier that way. That's what she tried to tell herself anyway.

When they were at the rodeo site, Clint remained with her almost constantly. The only time he left her alone was when he had to be in the arena. He didn't kiss her, he didn't touch her and still she felt sure that everyone knew there was more to their relationship than met the eye.

Why wasn't she angry? If any other man had dared to step in and play the white knight, she'd set him straight in a heartbeat. Mary Paris needed no one to take care of her, she didn't need or want a protector.

But Clint wasn't any man. Wasn't that the truth! There was no one in the world quite like him.

The trailer door opened and Eugene walked in. He was always the last to arrive, always the first to leave when the rodeo was over. "Hey, Mary," he called, swinging a small brown paper bag before him. "I think you have an admirer." He sniffed suspiciously at the bag, which she now saw had her name written crudely on one side. "Someone left this on the trailer steps for you. I hope it's from an admirer." He sniffed again. "And I really hope there's no manure in here. I swear, I can't smell a thing anymore."

Eugene offered the bag to Mary, but Clint snatched it before she could.

"Don't…" she said, too late. Clint whipped the bag open and glanced inside.

He lifted his head and looked her in the eye. "No manure."

She could call in the crime lab, have them study the contents of the bag and check for fingerprints other than Clint's and Eugene's. But she had nothing to indicate that the bag had been sent by the killer, and even if it had been—he'd been careful up until now. If he didn't leave prints and clues at the crime scene, he wasn't going to leave the lab anything to find on or in the bag.

"Is your name Mary?" she asked, for Sam and Eugene's benefit, offering her hand, palm up.

Clint reached into the bag and withdrew a small white cardboard box, which was less than two inches square and about half an inch high. Mary's heart crawled into her throat. She knew what was in that box, long before she took it from Clint and removed the lid.

A pair of gold earrings sparkled on a square of cushioning cotton. For a second, she couldn't breathe. She'd believed all along that she was right, that the killer was here, hiding among the innocent rodeo personnel. This was her proof. Not only was he here, he'd noticed her. He'd targeted her.

Was this a new twist? Or had he given gifts to his victims before?

"Give me those," Clint said brusquely, snatching the box out of her hand.

"Oh, my," Sam said with a wicked smile. "I'm guessing they're not from you."

Clint glared momentarily at his friend, and Sam backed off. He was a smart man who knew how far to push and when to step back. Clint stuffed the small box deep in the pocket of his jeans.

"They look expensive," Mary said as she finished with her makeup and studied the results in the mirror.

"What difference does it make?" Clint snapped. "You're not going to wear them."

Mary stood and grabbed her red wig, pulled it on as she glared up at Clint. "I might want to try them on this weekend, if we go out like we did last week."

"No way," he said softly.

"Clint Sinclair, the jealous type," Eugene said with a grin. "I never would've thought it."

His friends didn't know why he was so damned and determined to keep her from wearing those earrings. No one could know.

"We'll talk about it later," Mary said as she turned her back on them all. Usually she got ready and then left the trailer while the three men changed into their work clothes. Clint and Sam wore bright suspenders, baggy pants and cleats. Eugene wore one of three outrageous Elvis-like costumes.

Her hand was on the doorknob when Clint stopped her with a clipped, ''Wait.''

She turned her head. Sam and Eugene thought Clint was jealous, that this thing with them was some sort of innocent flirtation that would burn out before the summer tour was over. But in his eyes, Mary saw the truth. Clint was worried, he was scared. And this thing between them wasn't innocent and it wasn't a flirtation. She suspected it might never burn out.

''Wait for me in the back while I change,'' he said softly. There was so much he couldn't say, with Sam and Eugene here. ''We need to talk. Please,'' he added in a lowered voice.

Mary was willing to do almost anything to catch the man who had killed Elaine. *Almost* anything. Clint made her realize that, standing there looking at her this way. She wanted the killer caught, she wanted him dead.

But she was no longer willing to put her life on the line in order to catch him.

''Okay,'' she said, giving in too easily. She never gave in! She never let any man tell her what to do.

But Clint had a good point. She'd gotten what she wanted with the delivery of those earrings. Proof. The killer was here, he was watching her.

And she was next on his list.

''Just get here!'' Clint snapped into the cell phone when his brother expressed dismay and reluctance at the initial request.

''Tell me why,'' Boone said sensibly.

Of course Boone was reluctant to leave Jayne. She was very pregnant, and Boone adored his wife and the little girl who would join them in a few weeks. Clint reminded himself of that as he said more calmly, "I can't. Not over the phone. I need you and I need Dean."

"When?"

"Now." From here, behind the chutes, he could see Mary as she worked the crowd on the mezzanine. He'd told her to stay in plain sight. Would she listen to him? What would he do if she didn't?

"Okay," Boone said. "Jayne's mother has been wanting to come stay awhile and help us get ready for the baby. I'll tell her to come on. That'll free me up for a few days."

Clint breathed a sigh of pure relief. "Thanks. You'll call Dean?" He only had a few minutes.

"Sure."

Clint ended the phone call and turned around. Oliver Brisco stood just a few feet away, watching. Listening? He'd been so sure, once upon a time, that Oliver couldn't possibly be guilty of rape and murder. Now, looking at the man, he wondered.

"Sinclair," Brisco said, stepping forward.

Almost automatically, Clint looked up to the mezzanine where Mary worked. She was presently talking to a little kid who was probably no more than four. No one who watched would know that she was an FBI agent searching for a serial killer, that she was capable of more than just about any other woman, and most men.

Clint was afraid it didn't really matter how capable she was, not this time.

"Looks like a decent crowd, and there's still forty-five minutes until showtime," he said. "Not bad for a Thursday."

Oliver ignored the business chitchat. His eyes were

trained on Mary, just as Clint's were. "I thought you said she wasn't your girlfriend."

"She wasn't," Clint said succinctly. "Things change, though."

"That they do," Oliver said thoughtfully. "Care for a little advice from someone who's older and wiser?"

"Sure." Clint's heart started to pound.

"What's on the outside isn't always a good indication of what's on the inside," Oliver said in a lowered voice, "especially where women are concerned. I was taken in by a pretty face and a come-hither smile once. It got ugly in the end. Be careful."

Was that a warning or a friendly word of caution? "I'll be careful."

Oliver nodded.

Brett Brisco, dressed in jeans that appeared to be brand new and shiny boots that looked like they had to hurt his feet, rushed up with a notepad in hand. "We have a problem."

"What?" Oliver turned his full attention to his cousin.

"We've lost two bull riders for tomorrow night. One has a broken collarbone, and the other one has a family funeral."

"Dammit, I hate to run short again." Oliver looked at Clint and grinned. "What about you, Sinclair? Ride one more time. Impress the new girlfriend. Maybe make a little money. The pot will be good tomorrow night."

"No, thanks," Clint said.

"Why not?"

"When I'm an old man, I'd like to be able to get out of bed on my own when morning rolls around."

Oliver laughed. "If you change your mind, let me know."

"Will do."

The two Briscos walked away, heads together, and Clint looked up at Mary again. How was he going to watch her twenty-four/seven?

She was here. The bitch was actually *here!*

He stared at the audience members who sat directly on the rail, near the chutes. He wasn't surprised that she had a good seat. She'd always demanded the best. Was she alone tonight? Or was that man next to Kristin her *date?*

His insides churned, his vision blurred. It had always been this way. He looked at her and he saw nothing else. No one else. She became his whole world, in a flash. She was so beautiful still. It was as if she had a sheen about her, a glow that no other woman had.

He still loved her. The last time he'd seen her, she'd laughed at him. Right in his face, she'd laughed at him. His world had come crashing down then, as she'd stood there and laughed in his face and told him things he didn't want to know. How was it possible to love someone and hate them at the same time?

Kristin Brisco was here in Huntsville, right under his nose and watching the rodeo as if she had a right to be here. As if she wasn't here to stir up trouble.

None of the others had ever compared to her, though he'd tried to pretend they did. They had been substitutes. Poor, pale substitutes. A bull rider was thrown and ran for the fence. Sam and Clint danced with the bull and led it to the gate. And Kristin laughed. The man next to her glanced her way and laughed. Yes, they were together. He was sure of it now.

She turned her head, and dangling gold earrings sparkled in the light.

Freshly showered and dressed for bed in demure pajamas, Mary felt a little better than she had earlier tonight.

Her heart still pounded too hard, her brain would not be still. But deep inside she felt the beginning seeds of calm. She was close, he was here. She'd been right all along.

"Hi." She stopped in the open doorway between the connecting rooms. Clint reclined on top of the covers of his king-size bed wearing nothing but a pair of boxers. He was showered and clean and unusually pensive.

"Hi." Clint didn't look at her but kept his eyes on the television, on a late-night show he wasn't paying any attention to.

"What did you do with the earrings?" she asked as she stepped into his room.

He turned his head to glare at her. "Why? Planning on wearing them anytime soon?"

"No."

He turned his eyes to the television again. Perhaps he relaxed, a little. "Good."

She crossed the small room and sat on the side of the bed. Confessions never came easily to her, and this closeness, this need to be with Clint…it scared her a little. No, it scared her a lot.

"You were right," she said softly.

Clint turned his head more slowly this time, snagged the remote and turned off the TV. "Say that again. I don't think I heard you correctly."

She smiled. "I said you were right."

Some of the hardness in his eyes softened, the length of his body seemed to relax a little more. "Right about what, exactly?"

Mary lay down beside him, close but not too close. Comfortably near, but not as near as she really wanted to be. "When I came here, I was ready and willing to put myself out there with a bull's-eye painted on my back. I wanted this guy so bad, I was willing to do anything to get him. Anything,'' she whispered. "A month ago, I would have snatched those earrings back from you and worn them all night, clown costume and all. I would have worn them day and night until this guy showed himself.''

"And now?''

"I still want him,'' she said. "I want the man who killed Elaine and those other women, I want him so very badly.'' She scooted a little closer. "But I'm not willing to die to catch him. I don't want that bull's-eye on my back anymore, Clint.''

"What changed your mind?''

"You,'' she whispered.

She didn't mention Clint's argument that she might be carrying his child. It was too unlikely, too far-fetched. And yet, that possibility lurked in the back of her mind. Not what could be at this very moment, but what might be later. A month from now, a year from now. She saw her future again, in a way she hadn't since Rick had died.

They hadn't slept together in days; her argument that he distracted her still stood. Unfortunately, not sleeping with Clint had done nothing to get him off her mind or out of her heart.

He pulled her into his arms, and she rested her head on his shoulder. "I almost have enough to contact my boss and get the squad in here.''

"Almost?'' Clint asked, incredulous. "Those damned earrings scare the crap out of me.''

"It's not enough,'' she said calmly. "We still don't know who he is, only that he's here. If I bring the squad in they might scare him off. We'll never get this chance again.''

Clint held her, but he didn't say a word for a while. She was content to lie still, to know that she was safe here. To believe, for the first time, that she had a life beyond today.

"Do you know how much I hate this?" he finally whispered.

"I believe so."

"I don't think you do," he said sharply. "It's one thing to put yourself in danger, but it's another entirely when you have to watch someone you care about basically step in the path of a bullet. I'm glad you've decided to be more careful, but it strikes me that it might be too late for that. He knows you're here, he's noticed you. That alone is enough to give me nightmares for the rest of my life."

Mary lifted her head so she could look down on Clint's face. Was this love she felt inside her? Warm, heady, hopeful. Love. She'd loved Rick, and when he'd died she'd been so sure she would never feel this way again. There was only one shot at love in a lifetime, right? One man, one chance…and hers had died with Rick.

But now she thought…maybe not. Maybe she had been given a second chance.

She didn't know how they would make it work. She loved her job; Clint was a rodeo clown. She loved the city; he was a country boy through and through. But deep in her heart, she believed that they could make it work somehow.

Mary leaned down and gave Clint a kiss, something short and sweet. It was so hard to be in his arms and not kiss him! She let her lips linger on his a moment too long, soft and moving ever so gently.

"I thought we were keeping it cool until this was all over and done," he said in a husky whisper.

"We are," she said. "It was just one kiss."

"Just one. Right." He placed his hand on the back of

her head and pulled her down to kiss her again. Deeper, this time, his tongue dancing with hers.

The kiss was such a bad idea. What she wanted was such a bad idea. Until Elaine's killer was caught, she didn't have time to think about her future, and when she kissed Clint this way that's what happened.

She saw forever. She saw nights under the stars and peach cobbler and racing horses and the kind of laughter that bubbled up from so deep inside it felt like pure happiness rising to the surface. One kiss—two—and she saw all that, and more.

She settled back down beside him and closed her eyes, thinking that she could very easily sleep right here all night, when a sharp rap sounded through the room. Clint jumped up and she was right behind him as he walked silently to the door. He peeked out the security viewer and then sighed long and deep as he opened the door.

"Do you know what time it is?" he asked.

The two remaining Sinclair brothers walked into the room, Boone in his leather jacket and jeans, Dean properly dressed in a suit and tie even at this time of night. They each looked at her briefly, without surprise or brotherly glee, and then returned their attention to Clint.

"You said 'now,'" Boone said as he closed the door behind him. "Not tomorrow morning, not at a decent hour. *Now.*"

Mary glared at Clint, ignoring the others. "What is this?"

He didn't look ashamed or contrite, and he wasn't at all apologetic. "Reinforcements."

Chapter 15

Mary had been initially resistant. Okay, she conceded silently, she'd been much more than resistant. She'd been furious. Clint hadn't checked with her before calling Boone, he hadn't asked her if she minded that he was asking others to help.

But now that they were working together, she was less annoyed. The four of them had had breakfast in this room, and she'd told Dean and Boone everything about the case. They already knew more than she'd anticipated; they didn't walk into this unprepared. She'd been ready to do battle if they came at her with the same rationalizations she'd gotten from Josh. They hadn't. They took her and her ideas very seriously.

The two elder Sinclair brothers sat at the table where they'd had breakfast. The dishes had been cleared away; only coffee cups remained. Mary was unable to sit. She stood beside the table. Clint alternately paced and sat on the side of the bed.

"Did you check in the areas where your suspects live, to see if there were other murders?" Dean asked. "It seems unlikely that he would only kill during the summer."

Mary glanced over his shoulder. He had been going through the files on the most recent murder, apparently finding a few new details. "I didn't have time to check thoroughly in every hometown, though I did check on the areas surrounding Oliver Brisco's ranch."

"Nothing?" Boone asked.

Mary shook her head.

"He might've traveled," Dean suggested. "This killer is very careful. Very controlled. He goes to the trouble to occasionally change his MO, in order to keep the authorities from tying these murders together, and he's consistently killed two women for each of the past four summers. No more than two, and always with a great deal of caution. I can't see him murdering in his own backyard."

"He probably plans his crimes all through the year," Boone said softly as he sifted through one of Mary's files. "That's what keeps him from striking near home, that's what keeps him going. He dreams about his plans for the next summer and his past attacks, fantasizes, plays with those damn earrings."

Dean looked up at Mary. "He doesn't make many mistakes."

Clint tossed the earrings onto the table. "What about this? Isn't this a mistake?"

Neither of Clint's brothers touched the jewelry. "I don't think so," Dean answered. "They're not distinctive, and I have a feeling they're moderately expensive but not outrageously so. You could probably get these same earrings at a dozen places in Huntsville alone, and we have no idea if he bought them here or not. I'll check around town to see if anyone remembers selling them, just in case.''

"Good idea," Mary said.

Clint continued to pace. ''He must've made a mistake somewhere along the line. In the beginning, maybe, with one of the first murders.''

"I'll look into it," Dean said, closing the folder before him.

Clint stood beside the table where Dean and Boone continued to study the case files. "If you can find something in these files, fine," he said. ''If you can hunt down the jeweler who sold those earrings, great. But that's not why you're here.''

They looked up at him. ''Why are we here, then?'' Dean asked.

''I want you to watch Mary when I can't. There are too many blind spots in the arena, and when I'm working I can't always see her. Whoever this guy is, he knows we're involved, and I have a feeling that's when he'll make his move. While I'm chasing a bull, he's going to be stalking Mary. I want you two watching her.''

They both nodded.

"I don't need..." Mary began.

"Yes, you do," Clint insisted.

She didn't argue with him. Not because she thought she needed a trio of bodyguards, but because if someone else wasn't watching her while Clint was in the arena, he was going to be distracted. That would never do. The last thing she wanted was for Clint to get hurt because he was watching her instead of an angry bull.

Clint felt better knowing Dean and Boone were in the building. They might not be able to catch the killer, but they could keep Mary safe. That was fine with him.

Mary's job was finding the killer. His was keeping her alive and unhurt.

Mary was working the crowd. Fifteen minutes until time for the show to begin. The usual rush he felt before a performance was muted. He didn't want his brothers watching Mary, he wanted to do it himself. Still, if he had to trust someone else with the job...

"Sinclair," Oliver snapped.

Brisco was in a bad mood, worse than usual. His eyes were on the crowd, and he cursed beneath his breath as he studied a section in the reserved seats. At the moment, he did look like a man who could commit murder.

"What's wrong?" Clint asked.

Oliver glared at him. "I need a bull rider for the second round. You up for it?"

Clint shook his head. "No, thanks." He'd already given Oliver his arguments. It had been too long. He didn't need to ride anymore.

"One time, Sinclair," Oliver snapped. "Give me a break. I need someone in the second round. You were great. You were the best. What the hell happened? You get gored once and just give it up forever?"

"Makes sense to me," Clint said gently.

Oliver shoved his hands in his pockets. He took a long, deep breath. "Ride for me tonight or you're fired," he said, his eyes on the crowd again.

"What?" Surely he hadn't heard right.

"Ride tonight or you're fired," Oliver said again, more slowly. "How much plainer can I make it for you, Sinclair? I need a rider, you're capable and if you're not willing to do as I tell you I don't need you at all."

"Fine," Clint snapped. "I'll get Mary and we'll—"

"No," Oliver interrupted. "You go. She stays."

"I don't think so."

"We'll just have to ask her what she wants to do. You're not exactly a team." Oliver rocked back on his heels. "I think she'd like to continue on as Mary Mary Quite Contrary. She seems to like it very well."

Given the choice, Mary would stay. Clint knew that. She was being more careful these days, thank God, but she wasn't one to give up. There would be too many hours when he couldn't be close to her if Oliver fired him.

"The second round," Clint said softly.

Oliver grinned. "I knew you'd come through for me. Who knows, you might even decide to take riding up again full time. You were the best, Sinclair. The best should go out on top, not from a hospital bed."

He hadn't ridden in four years. Clint knew too well that he wasn't going to go out on top; he was going to eat dirt, one way or another.

Every now and then she caught a glimpse of one of the Sinclair brothers. She saw Clint a couple of times after the first round of bull riding was done. Boone and Dean she saw all night long. They weren't obvious, not to anyone but her. But they were there, and she had never been more confident of her backup.

It was almost time for the second round of bull riding, so Clint was gone. He was down behind the chutes, waiting for the bull riders to be introduced. The lights went down, and Tony began to introduce the riders. Mary recognized a couple of the names; the cowboys had been in Birmingham the week before. Fools all, in her opinion.

She half listened to Tony's introductions. Next he'd introduce the bullfighters, Clint and Sam, and the event would get under way.

"A special treat tonight," Tony said. "Clint Sinclair,

one of our bullfighters, is coming out of retirement for us tonight and will ride Red Thunder!''

Mary was certain she'd heard wrong. She stepped to the mezzanine railing and looked down into the arena. Clint stepped up to join the riders who had already been introduced, lifting his hat and waving to acknowledge the hearty applause. He had gotten rid of his clown attire and greasepaint and wore a black shirt, black chaps and beat-up boots.

''No,'' she whispered. ''He can't do this to me.'' She turned and ran smack dab into Oliver Brisco.

''You should watch from here,'' he said with a smile. ''This is where you really get the best view.''

''Why is he doing this?'' she asked.

Brisco shrugged. ''Maybe he wanted to impress you. After all, what woman can really get excited about a clown.''

''He wouldn't do that.''

''Maybe he's doing me a favor, since I came up a couple of cowboys short tonight.''

''You did this,'' she whispered.

His answer was a shrug. ''Clint works for me, and I needed him to ride tonight. He'll be fine, most likely.''

The lights came up, and Mary forced her way past Brisco. She didn't worry that he might try to stop her. If she couldn't get past him on her own, Boone or Dean would take care of him. She didn't see them, but she knew they were close by.

She ran down the stairs, but a child standing at the foot of the stairs stepped into her path.

''Hi!'' the little girl said brightly. ''Can you show me how to use this?'' She held up her trick rope.

Mary leaned down and placed her hands on the child's shoulders. ''I'll be right back.'' She weaved around the little girl. The footsteps on the stairway were Boone's, she guessed. They were heavy, booted and as quick as hers had been.

She didn't wait for him, but looped her way around to the reserved seats and down the steps to the railing around the arena. Her heart leaped into her throat, her mouth went dry. She was too late. Clint was already sitting on a bull's back. Sam was there, sitting on a fence top and assisting Clint with the rope. Clint's head was down, so he didn't see Mary as she waved frantically at him. A few people behind her laughed; they thought her frantic behavior was all part of the show.

Last time Clint had been on a bull's back, he'd been hurt. Badly, deeply hurt, in more ways than one. Hurt by the bull, hurt by the girl. One scar she saw on his flesh, the other she sometimes sensed.

Mary's hands gripped the top of the fence. She held her breath as Clint raised his hand and nodded his head, and the chute gate opened.

Eight seconds was a long damn time when someone you loved was up there getting tossed and bucked and jerked about violently. Usually she watched from up top, and even from there a bull ride was a frightening sight. To be so close, to see Clint riding that bull…it was too much.

She'd never told him that she loved him. She'd never even told him that she *might* be falling in love with him, that she cared whether or not he got his fool head busted, that he had given her hope where she'd been so sure there was none.

The buzzer sounded and Clint remained on the bull's back. Mary almost breathed a sigh of relief. Just a few more seconds and he'd be out of there. Just a few more, very long seconds.

He dismounted, but Red Thunder turned on him and knocked him flat. Sam and the bullfighter who was filling in for Clint rushed forward. Clint was trapped on the ground, under the bull's thrashing hooves. Dirt swirled, and an angry head was lowered. The animal wasn't going to be easily distracted.

She didn't remember going over the fence, but there she was, standing in the arena. There was nothing to do but run. She ran to the bull, not away.

"Hey!" she shouted as she ran toward the melee in the center of the arena. "Pick on someone who's standing up, you big bully." Once Clint was on his feet he'd be fine. Lying on the ground, he had no chance.

The bull turned his head and glared at her. A chill ran up and down Mary's spine. Yeah, Red Thunder was definitely glaring at her. Clint was still tangled up beneath the bull. Mary ran for the beast, distracting it, and Clint rolled away.

Just before she reached the bull, it turned its head toward Clint again. Mary did the only thing she knew might save him; she threw herself on top of Clint and covered her head with her arms.

Mary waited for the bull to trample them both, but nothing happened. People began to laugh, then they began to applaud. She lifted her arms to peek to the side, just in time to watch Sam guide the bull out of the arena.

Eugene's voice boomed through his microphone. "Ladies and gentlemen, one of our clowns has just saved the other by tackling him in the arena. A first for this rodeo."

"You didn't remember anything I taught you," Clint said gruffly.

Mary rose up slightly. Clint was covered with dust and

dirt, but he appeared to be unhurt. "I did, too. You should have seen me hop over that fence."

It was clear by the laughter and applause that the crowd thought this was part of the show. Mary stood, and Clint was right behind her. He favored his left leg, but there was no blood. Nothing was torn or smashed. He might be a little battered…but she could tell that he'd be fine. Just fine.

"Don't you ever do that again," she said as they climbed over the fence.

"I don't know," he said. "It was kind of fun."

They were straddling the fence, facing each other. Mary went very still. "What do you mean, it was kinda *fun*. I almost had a heart attack."

The next rider was getting ready to go. Clint smiled at her.

"Don't grin at me like that," she snapped. "I've seen too many people I care about hurt. I can't…it's just too…"

While she struggled to find the words, Clint leaned forward and kissed her. It was quick, sweet and over too soon. The crowd howled. Eugene pretended to faint in the barrel.

Kristin hung back, waiting while the crowd cleared away. Tonight she had come to the rodeo alone. The man who had accompanied her last night had not come with her to tonight's performance. His heart caught in his throat. Was she here to see him? After all this time?

He bravely made his way toward her seat. There was no one left sitting in her section. She looked thoughtful and beautiful, sitting there. She looked lonely. He was lonely. No matter how he tried not to be…he was always lonely.

"I'm surprised to see you here," he said.

She smiled widely. "Are you? At the last minute I decided to come down and have a look at the rodeo again. It was a whim."

"You don't get seats like this at the last minute," he said.

"With enough money you do."

"Where's Annie?" he asked. His daughter? Perhaps. Perhaps not. "Did she make the trip with you?"

"No," Kristin said. "She's staying with my mother for the week."

There were still people around, people who might notice him talking to Kristin even though they seemed to pay him no mind. Some audience members were asking for autographs. A few young women were flirting with the cowboys who remained in the arena.

It was dangerous, but he didn't care. "Can I buy you a drink?"

She smiled widely. "I don't think so."

"Can we talk...privately?"

Kristin glanced around. "Sure. Why not?"

She followed him to the trailer, her eyes taking in everything. She'd always considered herself too high and mighty for the family's rodeo. Nose in the air, sarcastic grin and cutting remarks, she'd made fun of the Brisco lifestyle. She'd never really been a part of it. Never.

He knew where everyone should be at this moment. He went over a mental list as he opened the trailer door for her. Everyone was accounted for; he and Kristin would be alone here, at least for a while. In his dreams, and in his frequent nightmares, he was alone with Kristin again.

With his body shielding the door from her, he locked it behind them.

"Why are you really here?" he asked sharply.

She leaned against the desk and smiled at him. "I'm bored."

He knew what happened when Kristin got bored. She made things happen. She entertained herself.

"You said some very ugly things to me last time we spoke," he said, trying to remain calm. She was so beautiful, so vexing.

"I wish I could say they were all lies," she said. "They weren't."

"Do you still think your time with me was a mistake?"

"The biggest of my life," she answered.

He swallowed hard. "We were good together."

She shook her head. "No, we weren't. We were a disaster together."

His hands balled into fists. Something crawled into his throat. All the others had been substitutes for Kristin. Poor, insufficient substitutes. And now here she was, right before him, taunting him as she always had.

"I loved you," he whispered.

She laughed at him. "No, you didn't. You don't even know what love is." She shook her head, and her hair shone, her earrings sparkled.

"But you…"

"It was a mistake," she said sharply. "When will you get that through your thick skull? You know why I came to you, you know why it lasted as long as it did. I never loved you. Some days I didn't even like you." She shrugged her finely shaped shoulders.

"Don't say that." Everything inside him went still.

"It's the truth. Face it. Move on with your life. Please don't tell me there haven't been other women since me."

"There have been other women," he confessed.

"I hope you never got all weepy on them, the way you

did with me. It's very off-putting, you know, to see a grown man whine and sniffle.''

He took a step forward. "No. You were the only woman who ever made me cry.''

She didn't move away from him as he walked to her. Her smile didn't fade, her eyes didn't darken. Poor Kristin, she didn't know she had reason to fear him. She didn't know she was about to die.

Chapter 16

As they walked through the hotel lobby, Mary turned on Boone; she was fierce even in her clown costume. "If you don't stop laughing at me I'm going to hurt you."

Her threat only made him laugh harder.

Clint placed himself between Mary and his extremely amused brother. "Now, now. Play nice." He didn't want to see Mary go after Boone in a rage. One of them would get hurt; he just wasn't sure which one it would be.

They had the elevator to themselves. Thankfully, Dean turned the subject away from Mary's daring rescue and to the case. "I have people checking into unsolved murders in the hometowns of all the men on your list, just in case. I don't think they'll find anything, but it can't hurt to do a little digging."

Mary nodded. She looked less than daunting in her clown costume, and with that smeared makeup on her face...why was she still beautiful? Why did he still see the curve of her cheek and the sparkle in her eyes and the elegance in her body, no matter what she was wearing?

Boone and Dean got off at the third floor. Clint and Mary were on the fifth. Once his brothers exited the elevators, Mary got very quiet. It was unnatural. She was usually so wound up after a show. Of course, she didn't usually fling herself in front of a bull.

She didn't even bother with her own key. Clint opened the door to his room and Mary walked in.

"You're limping," she said softly as he slid the dead bolt on the door.

"Just a little." He put his arm around her. "You really shouldn't have jumped into the arena that way. It was dangerous."

"Not as dangerous as what you did." She plopped herself on the side of the bed and sat there, staring up at him. "My knees are still shaking. I think I sprouted a few white hairs. Clint, I can feel my heart beating!"

You wouldn't know it, to look at her. "You shouldn't have—"

"Don't tell me I shouldn't have!" she snapped. "What am I supposed to do? Just sit back and watch the people I love die and do *nothing?*"

He didn't know what was more startling: that Mary had actually thought he might die out there, or that she'd just admitted that she loved him.

He grabbed Mary's hand and gently hauled her to her feet. "Come on," he said as he pulled her against him. "Let's get cleaned up and ready for bed."

"A shower does sound good." She wrapped her arms around him and leaned in, resting her face against his chest. For a long moment they just stood there, and it was nice. Comfortable. And right. More right than anything he could remember.

Finally she asked, "Will you scrub my back?"

He grinned. "You got it."

"I really need a long, hot shower."

"Me, too." Still, they didn't move. They held on. They breathed. At the moment, they didn't really need anything else.

"Maybe a shower will help me shake off the memory of seeing you lying in the dirt with a bull named Red Thunder trying to stomp you into the ground. Why would anyone in their right mind decide to ride an animal that's ten times their weight and has *Thunder* in its name?"

"Come on," Clint said as he gently released Mary and then guided her toward the bathroom. "I want you. I need you." He pulled her close. "But I am not making love to you while you've got that clown face on. It's just not right."

She hadn't known, when she'd decided to take a leave of absence and find Elaine's killer come hell or high water, that her life would change so drastically. It had. And the change was so extreme, she didn't even feel like the same person who had stood before Clint a month ago and all but demanded that he help her.

"You're hurt," she said, reaching out to touch the discolored flesh on his side as he walked with her to the bed. They were both clean, damp and naked.

"It's just a bruise."

"It's a huge bruise," she argued. "There's another one here," she said, gently laying her hand over the large bruise on his thigh.

He pulled back the covers, and they slipped between the sheets. This was where she'd wanted to be, all these nights when she'd been trying to get Clint out of her head and her heart. She rested her head on his chest and wrapped her arms around him.

"I'm such a coward," she whispered.

Clint laughed lightly. "You?"

"It's true." She rose up and kissed his jaw. It was dusted with a day's beard growth, stubbly and scratchy against her lips. Physical danger she could bear. But when it came to her heart… "I didn't want to fall in love with you," she said quickly. "I really, really didn't."

"And yet here we are." He held her close and stroked a strong hand up and down her back.

Clint didn't say he loved her, too, but her confession didn't seem to frighten him either. Maybe he was holding back because he knew, as she did, that love might not be enough, not this time.

Once she'd finally told Clint how she felt, they didn't talk. They touched, remembering and relearning everything they'd forgotten in the days they'd slept apart. They kissed, they tasted, and they held on to each other as if there was no tomorrow.

Tonight there was no forgetting protection. They didn't know what tomorrow would bring, so they couldn't forget. Not again.

Clint started to spin Mary onto her back, but she stopped him in midroll and reversed the process so that he was on his back and she straddled him. He smiled up at her, giving her a completely wicked grin that grabbed her heart.

When they were together, truly and completely together, nothing else mattered. There was only this bed, her body and his, love and need. Pleasure and yearning. She closed her eyes and rode Clint, allowing herself to get lost. Truly, wonderfully lost, in sensation and emotion. She moved slowly, taking him deep and rising up, plunging down so that he was completely inside her. Lost. No, not lost. *Found.* She was found here, with Clint.

She climaxed with a shudder and a cry, ribbons of release and intense pleasure sparking through her. Clint came with her, pushed deep and held himself there.

Mary drifted down and placed her head on Clint's chest. This was the scary part. She loved the way Clint loved her, the way she loved him back, but what came after was so much more important.

"I meant what I said," she whispered.

"What are we going to do about it?"

"I don't know."

He threaded his fingers through her hair. "You could always give up the FBI and come live with me. It's a big house. It's going to be lonely if I have to go home without you."

"I could learn to make peach cobbler and ride a horse and…" And what? Sit around and cook dinner and learn to sew and…oh, this would never work.

"Maybe I could come stay with you for a while."

"In D.C.?"

"Why not?"

"I'm gone a lot," she said softly. "More than I'm home, actually. Maybe I could ask for a…desk job, or something. I'd be home more that way." In truth, the thought of a desk job gave her the heebie-jeebies.

"Maybe," Clint said softly.

He said maybe, but she heard the no in his voice. He wasn't going to move to D.C. and become a house husband who waited around for her to come home between assignments, and she wasn't going to give up a job she loved to settle in at his ranch and take up gardening and knitting as a hobby.

She loved him, and maybe he loved her. He hadn't said

as much, not tonight, but in a fit of anger on the side of the highway, he'd shouted out his true feelings, hadn't he? It didn't matter tonight, not tonight. In Clint's arms she felt like she'd found her true self again. But they had nowhere to go from here, and they both knew it.

Clint felt as if he'd hit a brick wall, in every sense, as he walked through the arena. Two hours until show time. Mary was in costume and was making balloon animals. He could see her from here. Dean and Boone would be among the first to enter, once the gates were open, and maybe then he could relax. Until they arrived, he was keeping a close eye on her.

He hurt all over, he ached in a way he hadn't in four years. There was nothing like being whipped around by a bull to let you know where every muscle you'd ignored was located.

And then there was Mary, his other brick wall. She was driving him crazy, in more ways than he'd ever expected. When this was over, what would they have?

"Sinclair."

Brisco approached with a half smile on his face. Clint did not return the smile. "What do you want?"

"I thought you might want this." Oliver waved a check in the air. "Your winnings from last night."

"I won?" He and Mary had left before the end of the competition. "It wasn't that good a ride."

"Maybe not," Brisco said as he reached Clint and slapped the check into his hand. "But last night it was better than the others, and that's all it takes to win."

He glanced down at the check. Not bad, as far as money goes, but nothing to get excited about either. There had been a time when a win had been everything. No matter how ugly, no matter how large or small the purse, no matter if he felt he deserved it or not. There was a rush that came with winning, but he couldn't enjoy it now. He had too many other things on his mind.

Oliver's smile died. "Listen, about yesterday...I got carried away. I wouldn't fire you, Sinclair. You have a job here as long as you want one."

Clint folded the check and slipped it into his pocket.

"My ex-wife has reared her ugly head," Oliver said quietly. "She came by to see me before the show last night, and...well, I took my anger out on you. I'm sorry about that."

"No harm done," Clint said. He wouldn't tell Brisco, or Mary, but he was glad he'd ridden one last time. His last ride should be a better memory than the one he carried from four years ago. And painful or not—it had been a rush to ride again.

Oliver spread his arms wide. "If you want to compete tonight or tomorrow afternoon or any time, you just let me know. You've still got what it takes. And the bit with Mary was great. The crowd went nuts when she jumped over the fence." His smile came back. "A little more advice from an old man who probably gives advice more than he should—if you find a woman who'll run in front of an angry bull for you, you might want to keep her."

Brisco walked away before Clint could respond.

When he disappeared around the chute, Mary walked to Clint, twisting a balloon animal as she walked, very casually, toward him. "What did he want?"

Clint removed the check from his breast pocket and waved it at her. "I won last night."

She looked surprised. "You did?"

"It wasn't that bad a ride," he protested.

"Oh, I know, it's just that..." She wrinkled her red nose. "If you start to win, you might decide maybe you should get back into bull riding, and I just couldn't take it. I swear, Clint, if you take up riding again it will make an old woman of me in a matter of weeks.''

"If you weren't already made up, I'd kiss you," he said.

"Turned on by greasepaint?"

"Apparently so."

"You're just trying to change the subject. Why aren't you dressed?" She took in his jeans, perfectly ordinary shirt, cowboy boots. "You're not planning on riding again tonight, are you?"

"No. I'll go back to the trailer and change once Dean and Boone arrive." He tugged at a red pigtail. "If I could've found a way to get them in early without people asking questions I would have, but this will do."

"So you're not riding a bull tonight."

He shook his head. "You manage to supply me with plenty of adrenaline, darlin'. For the rest of my days, you'll be the only wild ride I'll need or want."

She looked unsure, but then Mary Paris had always been very suspicious. Of him. Of everything.

Amber interrupted, dressed in her blue tights and obviously excited. She grabbed Clint's arm. "Oh, my God! This is awful. It's terrible! They found a body in the park across the street. The cops are all over the place! Somebody said..."

Clint and Mary both ran for the exit, before Amber could say more.

"It's another one," Mary said as they jogged side by side. "I should have gotten him in Birmingham." She shook her head. "Dammit."

"We don't even know whether or not it's a victim of the man you're looking for," he said calmly.

"It is," Mary insisted. "I feel it." She cursed beneath

her breath as they ran across the street. Dean and Boone stood with the small crowd that had gathered around the crime-scene tape that cordoned off a section of the park, watching two officers scan the area for clues and make notes. The body had been covered by a sheet.

On the opposite side of the protected area, a man in a dark suit walked under the yellow tape and flashed his badge at the officer who was keeping the crowd back.

"Is that who I think it is?" Dean asked.

"Yep," Boone said. "Let's go." Without looking back, he lifted the crime-scene tape and stepped under. Dean did the same, and so did Clint. Mary stood back for a moment.

Did she not want to see the body? Or was she afraid that someone would see her talking to the police and suspect that she was more than a pretty clown?

Dean flashed his badge when a uniformed officer tried to stop him. Long before they reached the body, Detective Luther Malone turned around to face them. He did not look pleased to see them as he studied them each in turn.

Luther Malone and the Sinclair brothers had not met under the best circumstances. Shea had been missing at the time, kidnapped at gunpoint by an escaped convicted murderer. The man she was now married to. Ever since Malone had worked with the Sinclairs to prove Shea's kidnapper's innocence, he'd been more interested in *not* seeing the trouble-prone family again.

"Great," Malone said in a low voice. "You three."

"Nice to see you, too," Boone responded.

"I wish I could say the same, but I get the feeling the three of you together always means trouble." He gestured to the body behind him. "I have a murder investigation going on here and you three are trampling my crime scene. What do you want?"

"Can you tell us anything about the victim?" Clint asked.

"Not yet," Malone said. "I just arrived."

Behind him, Clint heard the officer shout, "Get back here!"

Mary was too quick for him. She sidled up beside Clint. Dean looked back at the uniformed officer and said, "She's with us."

Malone looked Mary up and down, taking in the baggy pants, the striped suspenders, the face paint. "Why am I not surprised?"

"Special Agent Mary Paris." Mary offered her hand. "FBI."

Malone stared at her hand a moment before shaking it and then quickly stepping back. "I see the bureau has relaxed its dress code."

"I'm undercover," Mary said softly.

Clint wanted to keep Malone fully informed and tell him that Mary was unofficially undercover, but he didn't.

"If the victim is blond, between the ages of twenty-six and thirty-four and has been raped and either stabbed or strangled, then I can help you."

Malone's expression changed subtly. "Have I caught a serial killer case?"

"I think so," Mary said in a lowered voice.

The detective nodded, then looked Mary in the eye. "Eleven o'clock tonight, Cleo's. We can swap info then."

Cleo's was an out-of-the-way club, but it was busy enough for a Saturday night. The place was packed. Mary glanced around the dimly lit club and finally found the homicide detective sitting in the back of the room, his back to the wall like a gunslinger.

The four of them, all three Sinclair brothers and Mary,

weaved their way through packed tables to reach Malone.
They sat, a waitress appeared quickly and a few minutes
later four beers and a cup of coffee for Mary were sitting
on the large round table. When Clint tried to pay, the
waitress waved him off with a laugh and a quiet "On the
house, sugar."

Mary didn't quite bristle.

She sat between Clint and Malone, and as soon as the
waitress was gone, the detective leaned in close. "I don't
know if this is your guy or not. The victim matches the
profile, but not all the details are consistent. There was
semen, so DNA won't be a problem. There was also skin
and a little bit of blood under her fingernails. She fought
the guy, and she made him bleed."

Mary's heart kicked. Was this another killer's work?
Or had her guy made a mistake at last? "Have you ID'd
the victim?"

"Not yet. I have the lab working on it now, and they
promised to call me the minute they have anything."

Mary nodded. Was this another woman who would not
be missed for a while? How long would it take to get an
ID?

"Can we be sure this is the same guy?" Clint asked.

"A blonde killed a few feet from the rodeo," Boone
said. "What are the odds?"

"I have to agree," Dean said. "There are too many
similarities to dismiss this one. You might have lucked
out, Mary. Looks like you'll have something substantial
to work with this time."

Clint knew how important this was to her. Maybe that's
why he took her hand, under the table where no one else
could see, and squeezed it. She didn't let go, but instead
threaded her fingers through his and continued to hold on.

It was so hard for her to admit that she needed anyone

or anything, but she needed Clint. She needed to know he was beside her, that he would be here for her, always...and she wanted to be here for him. She'd always been so insistent that she didn't need a man to protect her. It had never occurred to her that in a perfect relationship the partners would protect each other, no matter what.

"Detective Malone," Mary began, but he silenced her with a raised hand. "Not now." His eyes went to the stage. Well, they went to the woman who was presently climbing onto the stage. Slinky black dress, cleavage that would make any woman jealous and any man sit up and take notice, and a come-hither smile that was definitely turned this way.

Mary glanced at Malone's hand and noted the wedding ring. She barely contained a disgusted snort. He seemed like a nice guy, but *really*. She couldn't help herself. As the woman took a mike and a stool she leaned toward the detective. "What does your wife think about you hanging out in clubs for business meetings late on Saturday night and making eyes at half-dressed floozies."

Malone glanced at her and winked. "That half-dressed floozy *is* my wife."

"Oh." She sat back in her chair. Boone, who had heard the entire exchange, grinned wickedly. After a moment, he winked at her, too.

Malone's wife sang a few numbers. She was good. Openly sexy, talented, glowing with apparent happiness. Because of Malone? Or because she loved to sing?

When the set was over, she left the stage to hearty applause and walked to their table. Everyone scooted over and Malone pulled up a sixth chair. Beside him, of course. Quick introductions were made, though Cleo Malone obviously knew Boone. Before she sat down, she gave him a quick kiss on the cheek.

"I hear you got married," she said to Boone as she sat between him and her husband.

Clint laughed. "Everybody heard when Boone got married. That's what happens when you marry a senator's daughter."

Boone didn't say anything, but his smile said it all. "You're still singing in the club, I see."

"Every now and then. Maybe twice a month I get my friend Syd to sit with the baby and I come in and do a set or two." She shrugged, then leaned against her husband ever so slightly and smiled. Their shoulders touched. "Gets us out of the house."

They seemed perfectly suited, horribly content, and Mary felt a moment of jealousy. Just a moment.

They didn't discuss the case, not with Cleo sitting there. They talked about babies—the Malones' son Lucas and Boone's daughter on the way. There was talk about sleepless nights and teething, diapers and doctor's checkups.

Malone's cell phone rang, and he checked the number on the caller ID before answering. The conversation was brief and to the point, and as he disconnected the call he looked at Mary. Again, he was all business.

"We have an ID. The victim was arrested a couple of years ago for DUI, so her prints were on file."

Mary waited. All eyes were turned to Malone.

"Her name was Kristin Brisco."

Chapter 17

Messy. Messy, messy, messy. He placed his head in his hands and tried to disappear. He had always been so careful, and until now he'd been clean. Precise. There had been no mistakes, no clues for the police to study.

Kristin had made him lose control, with a word, with a tilt of her head, and his usual caution had gone out the window. In the end he'd killed her in a blind rage. He hadn't even realized what he was doing until it was too late. He'd been forced to dump her body in the park and cover it with bushes and a fallen limb while he prepared another place for her. He was lucky her body had remained there for a few hours before it had been discovered.

They would search here now. He had cleaned for hours, but if the police looked long and hard enough they would find the evidence of violence in the trailer. It wouldn't take them long to find the scratches on his chest and his neck, and then they would *know*.

His first instinct had been to pack a bag and disappear. He could do it. He had money, and even though Kristin had goaded him into foolishness, he was still smarter than the police. He could pull it off. No one would ever find him.

But if he disappeared now, they would know without a doubt. Maybe they wouldn't look at *him* for the murder. He needed to wait. A few days, at least. Maybe a few weeks. Then he could disappear quietly.

He held Kristin's earrings in his hand, clutching them tight. They were all he had left.

It seemed like a travesty, to hold the rodeo on Sunday afternoon when Kristin Brisco's body was barely cold. Her ex-husband didn't seem to mind. He didn't even try to hide the fact that he didn't care.

There was still the matter of the daughter. Tony, who knew the family well, said that Annie was staying with Kristin's mother. Would the girl continue to live with her grandmother, or would the father she barely knew become an important part of her life?

Clint saw beyond Brisco's cool indifference. Oliver did care, he just didn't want anyone to know.

Brett was more openly upset. Once Clint was almost sure the man had been crying. Made sense, he supposed. She had been family at one time, and she'd died a violent death. Anyone might be shaken.

Tony seemed distant, distracted. There was no wide smile today. No smarmy flirtation.

Eugene was in a foul mood himself. There hadn't been a single dirty joke told all day, and the usually jovial man scowled more than he smiled. Everyone who had once known Kristin Brisco was affected in some way by her sudden death.

The police were all over the place, in the hours before the civic center would open to the public. Uniforms and detectives in suits, they asked questions of everyone.

Oliver Brisco had been asked for a DNA sample, and he'd given it without hesitation. What else could he do? To refuse the request would only make him look guilty.

Forty minutes before the doors were set to open, two new men arrived. They were dressed in nondescript dark suits, but something about them both screamed *cop*. The men walked straight for Mary.

Clint headed in that direction. Mary didn't need anyone giving her grief. Why were they questioning her anyway?

He knew, moments before he joined them, why they were here.

"Nice look, Special Agent Paris," one of them said. The man tried very hard to hold his smile back, but he wasn't completely successful.

Mary responded with a succinct "Bite me, Lewis." When Clint arrived on the scene, she made introductions. Her boss. Her partner. Clint's heart sank as he shook hands with the men. They were a part of Mary's job, her life. Something he was not now and would never be a part of. And she was so damned good at it.

He couldn't ask her to give it up.

Now they believed her. The place was crawling not only with local cops, but with FBI agents. Mary felt that old familiar and very comfortable rush she always experienced when a job was about to come to a head.

The rodeo proceeded smoothly. Sunday afternoon was a time for families. There were more kids in attendance than usual, and she stayed busy the entire time. At least Clint didn't do anything incredibly stupid today, like kiss a bull. Or ride one.

When the afternoon's events were over, the place emp-tied quickly.

This was it, she imagined as she walked back to the trailer. There wasn't any reason for her to remain here. They had hard evidence now. DNA. Blood and skin sam-ples. He'd finally made a mistake.

She no longer felt the need to be the one to arrest the man who'd killed Elaine. As long as he was caught and punished, that was enough. She couldn't bring her friend or any of those other women back.

She couldn't bring Rick back either, no matter how long she punished herself for living after he was gone.

"Mary."

She turned and found Brett Brisco staring at her. Were those tears in his eyes?

"Are you okay?"

He shook his head but said nothing.

She was supposed to meet Clint here by the trailer. Where was he? He didn't like having her out of his sight for more than a few minutes, though since they had a victim this weekend it wasn't likely there would be an-other. If they could catch the guy, there wouldn't be any more victims for him, ever.

"I saw you talking to those policemen," Brett said in a soft voice. "Do you know them?"

Why lie now? She had performed at her last rodeo, most likely. "Yeah," she said simply. "I do."

"I thought so, when I saw you talking to them and laughing…" He shook his head. "They arrested Oliver," he said softly, as if to say the words aloud were offensive. "He had…sex with her, Friday before the rodeo. They found…evidence. I shouldn't be surprised. Kristin crooks her little finger, and Oliver comes running, no matter what he says about hating her. It was always that way."

"They arrested Brisco?"

Brett nodded.

Mary pursed her lips. Well, they could have waited until after the rodeo and let her in on the arrest! After all, it was her case, her baby, her pet project. So much for not caring who made the arrest.

"You seem annoyed," Brett said softly.

"I am, a little."

"Did you like Oliver in a special way, is that why you're upset?"

Since Oliver had been arrested, it didn't matter what Brett knew. Mary pulled off her wig and ruffled the strands of her hair. "I'm with the FBI," she explained. "I've been here undercover. I really wanted to be there when they arrested him!"

He paled. "You're…a cop?"

Mary smiled. "Yeah." Through and through, in her heart and soul, she was a cop.

Brett turned away, dipped his head, and she saw it. An ugly red scratch ran down the side of his neck. She couldn't see the scratch when his head was held high, but when he bent his head the tail end of the scratch peeked out slightly from under his collar. He began to walk away.

"Brett, wait up," she called, chasing after him. "I can see you're upset about Oliver's arrest. Will you run the rodeo while he's in jail? I mean, you are family."

"What difference does it make?"

"Just curious. I've really come to care about the people here."

He stopped and turned slowly, pinned his eyes on her face. "Curious," he said in a lowered voice. "A curious cop."

Mary's right hand traveled casually toward the large pocket in her costume, but before she could reach inside

Brett's hand snapped out and manacled hers. He snatched the wig from her left hand and tossed it aside.

"What gave me away?" he whispered.

Clint glanced back. "I told Mary I'd meet her five minutes ago. I don't like to leave her alone."

Mary's boss, Josh Hayes, shook his head. "We have the guy, Sinclair. He's in custody. We have a DNA match to the semen. Oliver Brisco's the guy, Mary was right all along. And even if he wasn't, she's an FBI agent and can take care of herself. I promise you that. Now, I just have a few more questions for my report."

"Later," Clint said as he turned around. Boone and Dean and even Mary were always talking about gut instinct, an itch in the middle of the back, a certain *something* that told you when things weren't right. He had that now.

Mary wasn't waiting by the trailer, where she should have been. She wouldn't have given up and left on her own, not after waiting five minutes. Maybe she was late, maybe someone was questioning her.

Who? And where?

He searched the area quickly, his eye landing on the red that stood out so starkly against the dirt. Mary's pigtailed wig, bright and tangled, lay there on the ground.

Mary allowed Brett to think he had complete control, that the knife he threatened her with was truly keeping her cowed and silent. Once he relaxed, once he truly believed he was in charge of this deteriorating situation, she'd have him.

No one was near as he yanked her up against the wall of a trailer at the edge of the crowded parking lot. "You were luring me,'' he whispered. ''All this time. It was a trick. You're no better than she was.''

The knife Brett had pulled from his pocket and flipped open with such ease as he'd dragged her away was grasped in his hand so tightly his knuckles were white.

''What did she do to you?'' Mary asked calmly.

Brett moved in too close. His eyes were dark and without any evidence of real emotion. His lips were pursed tight. ''She used me to make Oliver jealous. Then she turned around and used him to make me jealous. She was never satisfied. Never! No matter what I did, no matter what I said…it was never good enough. When she left the last time, when she told me it was over, she laughed at me.'' His lower lip quivered. ''She said I was a poor substitute for Oliver, that I would never be a truly adequate lover, that I was…never good enough for her.''

''Women are like that sometimes,'' Mary said. ''They don't appreciate what's right in front of them.'' If only she could get her right hand free. She'd fitted the bottom of the pocket with Velcro, so all she had to do was rip it open to get to the gun that was strapped to her thigh. Unfortunately, Brett had her right hand in a very tight grip.

''And they're liars,'' he said. ''Like you.''

''I'm just doing my job.''

The hand at her wrist tightened. ''I knew one day someone would come after me. I never expected it to be a woman. How insulting. I expected a better adversary when the time came. I expected a champion of justice, not a girl.''

''I'm not a *girl*,'' Mary said, leaning forward slightly to get in his face.

''Of course you are.'' He leaned in too close. ''You're a small, weak, inferior girl. You're a child, Mary. You're not a worthy opponent for someone like me. You never had a chance.''

''So what now?'' Mary asked. ''Are you going to do to me what you did to those other women?''

He raised the knife to her throat. The tip pressed against her skin, but didn't break it. ''Eventually.'' He looked her up and down. ''Not like this. You look ridiculous, with all that makeup on your face. I have a place chosen especially for us. A cabin, just an hour or so north, in Tennessee. You can wash your face there, fix your hair, put on the earrings I gave you.''

''They're kinda ugly,'' Mary said.

The pressure of the knife at her throat increased slightly.

''Gaudy,'' she continued. ''Tacky.''

''Then again, maybe I'll just kill you right here,'' he said angrily. Brett took a couple of deep breaths. ''No, no, not again. I can't lose my temper again. Kristin made me lose my temper, and look where it got me. I shouldn't have killed her so quickly, right here where others might hear. No.'' He calmed himself visibly. ''You can't do that to me.''

Mary heard Clint before he came around the corner. His step was heavy, his voice just short of frantic as he called her name.

Brett heard, too. He turned his head, and that was all Mary needed. She whipped her head to one side, away from the threat of the knife at her throat, and dipped down. The man who held her was unprepared for the move, and for the fact that Mary could move very quickly when she had to. One leg swiped out, and Brett fell to the ground, onto his back.

''Here!'' Mary called, and Clint came running. Brett tried to roll away, and she very quickly kicked at the hand that grasped the knife. He howled in pain, and the knife skittered away as Clint ran around the corner of the trailer that had shielded them from view.

Brett scrambled to his feet and tried to run, but he couldn't get past Clint. His victims had always been smaller, weaker and taken by surprise; he was no match for Clint and Mary, and in a matter of seconds Clint had Brett captured, hands tightly pinned behind his back. Brett struggled, but he wasn't going anywhere.

Mary drew her weapon, and when Brett saw the gun he stopped struggling. His eyes went wide as she aimed it at him. She tightened her finger on the trigger, ever so slightly.

"Mary," Clint said in a low voice. "What are you doing?"

"What I came here to do," she said calmly. "Tell me he doesn't deserve to die. Give me one good reason why I shouldn't pull this trigger."

"He's not going to hurt anyone else," Clint said. "I understand your thinking here, I really do, but—"

"You don't understand!" she said. "You couldn't possibly." She'd been willing to sit back, to let someone else tend to justice. But to have the man she'd been searching for right here in front of her…

"Think of your career," Clint said. "I've got him. He's not going anywhere but to jail. Mary, honey, you can't shoot a man who's restrained."

She looked Clint in the eye. "Let him go."

Brett actually backed up against Clint, as if he were looking for protection. "Don't let me go," he pleaded hoarsely. "She's crazy! She wants to shoot me!"

Mary took a step toward Clint and his prisoner. She aimed the weapon in her hand at Brett's head. "Run, Brett. Run. Try to get away. Think you can make it?"

She was so close, she could touch the muzzle to his forehead if she wanted to.

"Did you ever give any of your victims a chance to run? I think I'm being very magnanimous. Run. Maybe I'll give you a five-second head start." She shrugged. "Then again, maybe I won't."

"Mary," Clint said in a low, soothing voice. "You did it. You caught him. It's over."

"Not yet." It couldn't be over. She hadn't made Brett pay, she hadn't taken vengeance for what he'd done to Elaine and all those other women. The anger was still inside her, the need to exact justice still ate at her heart.

"Come on, honey," Clint said softly. "It's time to go home."

Home. Heaven help her, she'd forgotten what home was. She'd gotten so caught up in her quest for vengeance she'd almost lost a part of herself in the process. If not for Clint, she would've turned her back on the concept of *home,* and she likely never would've found her way back.

She drew her leg back and kicked Brett Brisco between the legs so hard he howled at the top of his lungs and buckled. He would have fallen to his knees if Clint hadn't been holding him up. "Now it's over."

Alarmed by Brett's howl, others came running. Josh and Lewis arrived first. Luther Malone and Clint's brothers were next on the scene. Uniformed officers were right behind them.

Mary holstered her weapon. "Great work," she said sarcastically, turning her attentions to Malone. "Did you even bother to check the blood and skin under Kristin Brisco's fingernails?" She yanked at Brett's collar to show them all the scratches on his neck.

"We don't have the lab reports back yet," Malone explained. "We considered the other DNA evidence we already had sufficient for arrest."

"What a bunch of clowns," she said beneath her breath but loud enough for everyone to hear. Her eyes snapped to Clint as Malone took custody of Brett. "Oh, sorry honey. No offense intended."

He looked her up and down; she had almost forgotten that she was in full regalia herself. "None taken."

"Oliver Brisco might've slept with his ex-wife," Mary explained, "but it was Brett who killed her. He killed eight other women, too, women he considered to be pale substitutes for the woman he hated."

"Get me away from her," Brett pleaded. "She tried to kill me!"

"Paris?" Josh asked, his eyes on her.

"He tried to kill me first," she explained. A new and unexpected serenity came over her. Clint was right. Her job, her obsession here, was over. "If I'd wanted to kill him, he'd be dead now."

"I want a full report," Josh snapped as Malone led Brett Brisco away.

"Give me five minutes," Mary said, her eyes on Clint.

"Now!" her boss snapped.

"Five minutes. Please."

He shook his head and left, and she was alone with Clint. Well, not really and truly *alone*. His brothers stood a few feet away, there were cops everywhere. But when he walked to her and she met him, and they put their heads together…they were alone.

"You did it," he whispered.

"Yeah. Thanks for showing up when you did."

He lifted a hand to her face. "I have a feeling you didn't need me to save you. You do a pretty good job of taking care of yourself."

''Sometimes,'' she conceded. ''Still, it's always nice to have backup.''

Would she have shot Brisco, given the chance? Would she have broken every rule if Clint hadn't been there to stop her? She didn't think so. The urge had been there, but it had been tempered. She wasn't about to become one of the bad guys by crossing that line. Still, it was nice to have someone close by to nudge that temperance along, when necessary.

Clint leaned in close. ''Remember when I said I think I love you?'' he added softly.

''Yeah,'' she whispered.

''We're going to have to do away with the *I think*. This is the real thing. I love you, Mary.''

Mary closed her eyes and smiled. ''I love you, too.''

The real thing.

Clint took a deep breath. ''So, what happens now?''

''I have to go back to D.C. Paperwork awaits. Lots and lots of paperwork.'' Her heart sank, and it had nothing to do with the dreaded reports she'd have to file. ''What about you?''

''There's a month left on the tour. If Oliver wants to continue…''

''A month.'' She rested her head against his chest, in a way so subtle no one would be able to see. Maybe. She didn't care if anyone saw or not. ''I have a little more vacation time coming. Maybe in a month I can…unless you'd rather not…''

He rested his hand in her hair. ''D.C. or Alabama?''

''Alabama,'' she said quickly. She wanted to go back to the ranch, see Wes and Katie, drink muscadine wine and make love under the stars and…

''Paris!'' Josh shouted.

She backed away slowly. "Stay off the bulls," she ordered.

"Yes, ma'am. You be careful yourself."

"I will."

She and Clint had been together almost constantly for a month. She'd come to depend on him, to need him...to love him. Saying goodbye was harder than she'd imagined it would be. After today, nothing would be the same. Nothing.

"Paris!"

She couldn't make herself say goodbye, so she spun around to answer Josh's call.

Chapter 18

"What on earth are you going to do in Washington, D.C.?" Wes asked, shaking his head as he poured himself another cup of coffee.

"I don't have any idea," Clint answered. "But what choice do I have? Mary can't come here, not indefinitely."

While she'd been back in D.C. and he'd been on the tour, they'd burned up a lot of cell phone time. She'd been here at the ranch once, to pick up her car, but he'd been in Mississippi at the time and had missed her.

He could have bailed out on the tour and let Frank fill in, and he almost did just that. But in the end he hadn't been able to leave Oliver in the lurch that way. The man's life had been turned upside down. An ex-wife he'd loved and hated was dead, his cousin was a serial killer who was now readily confessing to all his crimes, and he now had a daughter he barely knew to raise. Oliver might not be what anyone would call a nice guy, but his employees had decided to stand by him until the end of the tour; Clint included. No one knew what next year would bring.

It was surprising to learn that Oliver had known all along about Kristin's affair with Brett. He'd kept his cousin on all this time, blaming Kristin and her manipulative nature for the family affair, believing that his cousin had been used by her, just as he had. Never imagining for a minute what Brett was capable of.

Someone had asked about a paternity test to determine which Brisco had fathered Kristin's daughter. Oliver had declared that there would be no test. Annie was his, and no one was allowed to question that fact. Maybe he wasn't so hard-hearted after all.

Jayne had given birth to the latest Sinclair, a beautiful little girl she and Boone had named Miranda. Clint had already been to Birmingham twice to see his new niece.

It had been three days since Clint returned home from the rodeo. Wes hadn't changed, but Katie was getting bigger every day. Still, she was basically the same. The house had changed. No, he had changed. This place wasn't the same without Mary. There had been more phone time with Mary, since his return home.

It wasn't good enough. No matter how long they talked, it didn't come close to filling the void he lived in when Mary wasn't near. She was due in this afternoon, for a two-week vacation. While she was here he was going to ask her to marry him, and if she said yes he'd pack his bags and move to D.C. without a single second thought.

Well, maybe a fleeting second thought or two. What the hell would he do there? It didn't really matter. He loved his home, his ranch, the country life, but he was not old enough to be set in his ways. Learning something new might actually be interesting. He was due for a

change. This roller coaster of his was getting a little pre-
dictable.

"Car in the driveway!" Katie called from the living
room.

Clint set his coffee cup on the counter and hurried to
the front of the house, walking onto the porch just as
Mary's car came to a stop.

He held his breath as she stepped from the car. Damn,
she was beautiful. Of course, the last time he'd seen her
she'd had a painted face and had been wearing a baggy
clown costume. This…this was the real Mary. The smile
that spread across her face took his breath away.

He ran down the steps and into the yard to greet her,
but she didn't run to him. She stopped to reach into the
car to grab something. A lot of something, he saw as she
came up with her hands full.

"What's all this?" he asked.

"Kiss first," she said as she tilted her face up. He did,
and when his lips touched hers he knew it didn't matter
where they were, what he did, what she did. They had to
be together.

"Yum," she said dreamily as he took his mouth from
hers. "I have been fantasizing about that kiss for the past
three hours, as I drove down the road." She grinned. "I
almost got myself a speeding ticket. Twice."

"Let me take this," Clint said, reaching for the bags
in her hands. He'd been fantasizing about much more than
a kiss, and the sooner he asked her to marry him, the
sooner those fantasies would start to come true.

"No." Mary took a step back. "I have gifts for you,
and I want to present them in the proper order."

Clint took a step back and crossed his arms over his
chest. "All right."

Mary laid her things on the hood of her car, and reached

for one bulky bag. "Peach cobbler," she said, reaching into the bag and drawing out a frosty box. "It's frozen, but I promise to heat and serve it all by myself."

Clint grinned as she reached for the next bag. She delved into the brown bag and came out with a book. "Okay, technically this is for me. It's all about planting a garden." She reached into the bag again and came out with a few packets of seeds.

Clint's smile dimmed. "Mary…"

She held up a finger to silence him. "One more thing." She reached into a small canvas bag and came out with, of all things, a badge she flashed at him.

"What's this? Are you making me an honorary special agent?"

"Look more closely."

He did. The badge Mary held read Jackson County Investigator. "What have you done?" He knew. He saw the truth on her face, as much as in that badge. "I would never ask you…"

"You didn't ask, did you?" She came to him and wrapped her arms around his waist. "Malone did some checking around for me, and there was this job available in the area, and I can't be on the flying squad forever, so…howdy, neighbor."

He kissed her again, deeper this time. Longer.

"I have something for you, too," he said, reaching into the pocket of his jeans and drawing out a small velvet box. He hadn't been this nervous in…hell, he'd never been this nervous! "I love you" was one thing, but marriage? So quick?

Yeah. It was time, and it was so very right.

He opened the box and showed Mary the diamond he'd chosen for her. It was simple, not too small and not too

big. It suited her. The minute he'd seen this ring he'd
known it was the one. "What do you say?"

"Yes," she said. "I say yes."

He slipped the ring onto her finger, and she admired it
with a smile and the glint of a tear in her eye. "It's so
beautiful. And you're so sneaky! I bring you frozen peach
cobbler, and a book and a badge for myself, and you whip
out something like this. Are you trying to one-up me?"

"Never."

"Good," she said smugly. "Because trust me, I've got
you beat."

"Yep. I love frozen peach cobbler."

She draped her arms around his neck and grinned. It
was a devious, happy, contented Mary smile that grabbed
him down deep.

"Actually," she said in a lowered voice, "I do have
one more surprise for you. One more very small, very
important surprise. It's for us, really, not just for you."

"What is it?"

Mary rose up on her toes and whispered into his ear,
"Hang on to your hat, Daddy, things around here are
about to get very interesting."

* * * * *

There's one more Sinclair bachelor!
Will some lucky woman get to see
Dean out of his suit and undercover?
You'll find out in

ON DEAN'S WATCH,

available in July!

Don't miss the latest miniseries from award-winning author Marie Ferrarella:

The MOM SQUAD

Meet...

Sherry Campbell—ambitious newswoman who makes headlines when a handsome billionaire arrives to sweep her off her feet...and shepherd her new son into the world!
A BILLIONAIRE AND A BABY, SE#1528, available March 2003

Joanna Prescott—Nine months after her visit to the sperm bank, her old love rescues her from a burning house—then delivers her baby....
A BACHELOR AND A BABY, SD#1503, available April 2003

Chris "C.J." Jones—FBI agent, expectant mother and always on the case. When the baby comes, will her irresistible partner be by her side?
THE BABY MISSION, IM#1220, available May 2003

Lori O'Neill—A forbidden attraction blows down this pregnant Lamaze teacher's tough-woman facade and makes her consider the love of a lifetime!
BEAUTY AND THE BABY, SR#1668, available June 2003

The Mom Squad—these single mothers-to-be are ready for labor...and true love!

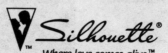

eHARLEQUIN.com

Becoming an eHarlequin.com member is easy, fun and **FREE!** Join today to enjoy great benefits:

- **Super savings** on all our books, including members-only discounts and offers!

- Enjoy **exclusive online reads**—FREE!

- Info, tips and **expert advice** on writing your own romance novel.

- FREE romance **newsletters,** customized by you!

- Find out the latest on your **favorite authors.**

- Enter to win exciting **contests and promotions!**

- Chat with other members in our **community message boards!**

Plus, we'll send you 2 FREE Internet-exclusive eHarlequin.com books (no strings!) just to say thanks for joining us online.

To become a member,
visit www.eHarlequin.com today!

Coming in April 2003

baby and all

Three brand-new stories about the trials and triumphs of motherhood.

"Somebody Else's Baby"
by *USA TODAY* bestselling author Candace Camp

Widow Cassie Weeks had turned away from the world—until her stepdaughter's baby turned up on her doorstep. This tiny new life—and her gorgeous new neighbor—would teach Cassie she had a lot more living…and loving to do….

"The Baby Bombshell" by Victoria Pade

Robin Maguire knew nothing about babies or romance. But lucky for her, when she suddenly inherited an infant, the sexy single father across the hall was more than happy to teach her about both.

"Lights, Camera…Baby!" by Myrna Mackenzie

When Eve Carpenter and her sexy boss were entrusted with caring for their CEO's toddler, the formerly baby-wary executive found herself wanting to be a real-life mother—and her boss's real-life wife.

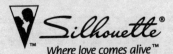

COMING NEXT MONTH

#1219 GABRIEL WEST: STILL THE ONE—Fiona Brand
Gabriel West would do anything to win back his wife,
Dr. Tyler Laine—even quit his high-risk career with the SAS.
Then he discovered that *she* was the one in danger. A stalker had
framed her for a priceless jewel theft, and now he wanted her dead.
Gabriel had lost Tyler once before, and no matter what, he wouldn't
let anyone take her away again.

#1220 THE BABY MISSION—Marie Ferrarella
The Mom Squad
Alone and eight months pregnant, FBI agent C. J. Jones
should have been taking it easy, but when an elusive serial
killer resurfaced, she couldn't ignore the case. Nor could she
ignore the feelings growing between her and her longtime partner,
Byron Warrick—a relationship that was strictly forbidden. But when
C.J.'s life was threatened, Warrick would break *any* rule to save her.

#1221 ENTRAPMENT—Kylie Brant
The Tremaine Tradition
For two years, CIA agent Sam Tremaine had followed
a criminal mastermind across the globe. Now, to finally apprehend
him, Sam needed help from an unlikely source: Juliette Morrow, an
international thief with a hunger for revenge and a weakness for sexy
special agents. Could Sam stick to his plan, or would the beautiful
thief steal his heart?

#1222 AT CLOSE RANGE—Marilyn Tracy
Corrie Stratton opened her heart to the many orphans she took in at
Rancho Milagro, but she had never been able to open herself to love.
Until she encountered Mack Dorsey, the ranch's intense new teacher.
She needed his help to solve an ancient mystery that threatened her
kids, but could he also discover the passion Corrie kept hidden
inside?

#1223 THE LAST HONORABLE MAN—Vickie Taylor
An innocent man was dead, his pregnant fiancée, Elisa Reyes, was
alone and Texas Ranger Del Cooper blamed himself. Due to Elisa's
dangerous past, the government wanted to deport her—an act that
would equal a death sentence. To save her, Del proposed, risking his
hard-earned career. But when she was kidnapped, he realized he was
willing to lose anything—except her.

#1224 McIVER'S MISSION—Brenda Harlen
Despite her undeniable attraction to attorney Shaun McIver,
Arden Doherty refused to let him into her life. But when a madman
targeted her, Shaun rushed to her rescue. As he investigated her
case, he uncovered painful secrets from Arden's past. But could he
convince her that she could count on him? And could he find her
killer before the killer found her?

SIMCNM0403